Tex Murphy
and the
Poisoned Pawn

Aaron Conners

ISBN-9798598878071

CreateSpace Independent Publishing Platform, North Charleston, SC

Cover Design by Bjorn Ottesen

For all the loyal, long-suffering, lovable Tex Murphy fans.

PROLOGUE

It's November 2050 and, once again, we are under siege from the Four Horsemen of the Holidacalypse: Premature Christmas, Crowds, Flu and Pumpkin Spice.

Halloween was a couple weeks ago—perfect timing for the case I was working, which featured decapitated heads, mad scientists, brain implants and undead zombies. I wore my usual costume: Maltese Falcon-inspired private detective, with a suit and tie, wingtips, trench coat and a soft felt fedora. Not very original, but I couldn't find a Spiderman suit in 48 Tall.

Trick-or-treating was a mixed bag. The biggest trick was a Rip Van Winkle special. One minute, I'm having dinner with the girl of my dreams; the next, I'm waking up and it's seven years later. All my memories in between erased…and my dream girl long gone.

The how and why of my amnesia is a whole other story. Bottom line is, life goes on. You play the cards you're dealt. My only consolation is that I may have an ace up my sleeve.

My Halloween case gave me one big treat: a flash drive containing information of significant value to certain people. One of the interested parties is a curious gent named Count St. Germain, who said he would pay—and I quote—'a king's ransom' for a particular piece of information I'm pretty sure is on my little flash drive.

They say money can't buy happiness. I wouldn't know, but I'd sure like to find out. Maybe, for once, I'll have something to be thankful for this Thanksgiving. It's time for me and St. Germain to talk turkey.

1

Sunset is torching the New San Francisco skyline—the last blast of radioactive napalm before night settles in like a dose of morphine.

Daylight is the new asbestos, which is why they enacted the Time Reversal back in '42. It's 5 p.m.—what used to be 5 *a.m.*—and I'm not usually up this early, but my body clock is out of whack. I got back in town three days ago and spent most of that time blissfully unconscious. Now I need to get out. I'm wide awake, starving, and my apartment/office is like a sauna. Clint, my landlord, must have fired up the ancient boiler down in the bowels of the Ritz Hotel. It is that time of year.

I open one of the large windows that overlook Chandler Avenue, take a seat on the wide sill and light a cigarette. A breeze is blowing in off the bay, cool and salty, dampening the voices of early risers on their way to Louie's diner down on the corner.

The city's just starting to stir. In the distance, toward downtown, air traffic is picking up. Directly across the street, the neon Open sign at Rook's Pawnshop turns on.

My eyes drift to where Chelsee's newsstand used to be. Most every day for years, I'd stop by to say hi, flirt a little bit, get gently turned down and then go out about my business. The ritual of unrequited love. Now, you'd never know her newsstand was ever there. I still can't quite get my head around the fact that she's gone.

But that's all in the past. It's 2050, not 2043. Life goes on, I keep telling myself. I let a little ripple of grief wash over me, then stub out my cigarette and turn away.

I walk to the bedroom and get dressed. One of the perks of 2050 is that I now have an extensive, expensive wardrobe I have no memory of buying. But as I stand at the mirror, tying a three-hundred-dollar silk tie into a classic four-in-hand knot, I see one of the downsides of 2050: some old guy staring back at me. It must have been a rough seven years. Good thing I never relied on my looks to make a living.

I lace up a pair of black Florsheim wingtips, tuck a tiny flash drive into one of my socks, and then slip on a tailored suit jacket. I grab my overcoat and fedora and head out to the fire escape stairs, bound for the Brew & Stew.

* * * * *

The world's finest diner is already half-full at the break of night. This used to be a happy little hole in the wall with a small and mostly mutant clientele. Now, at least on the weekends, there's a line out the door, starting around 7 p.m. People come from all over the city—mutants, norms and, worst of all, hipsters.

Which is another good thing about living in 2050: all that Mutant/Norm nonsense is mostly behind us now. Between the fall of the Law & Order Party and the Moon Child 'tragedy', no one was left to rally the bigots. So, while part of me longs for the old days when there was always a seat available at the Brew & Stew, I'm happy for Louie and all my other mutant friends. Even Rook.

Fortunately, it's early enough that my usual spot—the last barstool at the end of the counter—is unoccupied. The air is thick with the smells of strong coffee, bacon and just a hint of cigarette smoke. Underneath the voices and clinking of plates and silverware, I hear Dave Brubeck playing on the old jukebox in the corner. I cross the room through the heavenly haze, take my seat and grab a menu. Seven years ago, I had the menu memorized. I'm curious to see what's new.

"Hey, Moiph!"

I look up from the menu, but he's too fast for me. Louie LaMintz is already bustling back into the kitchen. And now there's a mug full of steaming Armageddon Blend in front of me. I take a sip and feel it sizzle into my blood stream like molten lava. If I wasn't fully awake before, I am now.

The entire menu looks amazing. I'm tempted to order one of

everything, but realistically, I could only eat half of it. And I shouldn't overdo it. I'm hoping to conduct some business later tonight and don't want to be in a carb-fueled funk, so that rules out pancakes or waffles. A grilled cheese sandwich always sounds good, but my heart's set on breakfast. Eggs, for sure, and meat. Lots of meat.

I decide on a new addition to the menu: a breakfast souffle filled with ham, bacon and sausage, served with straw potatoes, toast sticks and baked in a brick oven. The Big Bad Wolf. Perfect.

I pick up my mug and swivel around on the barstool. No familiar faces. Not surprising, I suppose. I have to remind myself it's been a long time since I was a regular here. The front door swings open with a tinkle and four more customers walk in.

From outside, I hear the sound of a distant siren.

A plump lady in a pink server's outfit swoops past the foursome, telling them to sit anywhere they like. Louie has two women working with him, also new to me, and the three of them are performing a breakfast-rush ballet all around the tiny diner, behind the counter and back and forth through the swinging kitchen doors.

The siren is louder now.

I sip my coffee and wonder if Taylor, Louie's niece, will make an appearance. That's a whole other story. More chapters to come, I expect, but there are other, more pressing things on my plate.

I hear two sirens now. Getting closer every second.

Customers seated in the booths by the large front windows have stopped eating and are looking outside. A moment later, an ambulance flies past. People are turning in their seats to see where it's headed. A man gets up and hurries outside; as he opens the door, a blast of sirens echoes through the diner.

I despise lookie-loos and usually make a point of not staring when everyone else is. But something big is going on. I take one more hit of the Armageddon Blend and then join the crowd of people heading out to the street.

Chandler Avenue is lit up in red and blue. The ambulance that just flew by has parked in front of the Ritz and two others are in the process of landing. There's a clanging fire engine getting closer each second, though I can't see any sign of a fire.

I start walking toward the Ritz. A police cruiser swoops down and a voice on loudspeaker says: "Stay back!"

The speeder descends quickly to street level, blocking me. I step back, into the assembled crowd, as the fire engine rolls past.

It's total chaos. Between the sirens and a dozen voices all talking at the same time, I barely hear the voice:

"Mr. Murphy!"

I glance around. Back near the entrance to the Brew & Stew, a cream-colored Rolls Royce is on the street, parked askew. The rear door is open and someone is waving at me from inside.

It's St. Germain.

"Hurry! Get in!" he says, as I get closer.

"What are you doing here?" I ask.

"I'll explain. Just come with me."

I'd planned to meet St. Germain, but not like this. I take a look back at the Ritz. I can't tell what's going on—and I'd really like to find out—but they won't be letting me in anytime soon. Might as well get down to business.

St. Germain wiggles his ample girth away from me, freeing up nearly half of the wide bench seat, and I slide in. The door closes automatically behind me and we lift off effortlessly. I assume there's a driver, but I can't see past a barrier of smoky glass. The engine growls as we accelerate and shoot up high above the city.

"Are you carrying any electronic devices?" St. Germain asks. "A cell phone, perhaps?"

I remember there's a Smart Alex in the pocket of my overcoat. Another new item I have no memory of buying. And I'm not sure what would have possessed me to buy it. I haven't owned a smart phone in years, for a variety of reasons. And this one is the worst kind. Anytime it's turned on, it won't shut up; it's like a pocket-size Jar Jar Binks.

I pull the device from my pocket and hold it up.

"Just this."

He plucks it from my fingers and examines it.

"It's not turned on," I say.

St. Germain cracks his window and tosses the phone out.

'Hey," I say.

"Nothing else?" he asks.

"Like I'm going to tell you."

"It's for your own safety."

"What's that supposed to mean?"

"I will explain everything," he says. "Do you have anything else on your person that could be used to track you?"

Track me?

I shake my head. "No."

"I apologize for my abruptness, but it was necessary, given the circumstances. You're in danger, Mr. Murphy. You very nearly died this evening."

2

As far as I know, I first met Count St. Germain about two weeks ago, though I can't say for certain, given that I have no memory of the seven years prior to that. Something tells me we may have crossed paths before, but he hasn't copped to it and I haven't asked.

Not that it matters. From what little I know of him, he's a good person to know. He drinks expensive liquor, smokes excellent cigars and, most importantly, likes to share. A week ago, I asked if he would post a million dollars bail for a total stranger. He barely blinked. These are the kinds of things that matter to destitute private investigators.

His role in my just-completed case is a bit of a mystery. There was probably more to it than met the eye, but the relevant thing is that he was searching for something…and I happen to have that little something tucked in my sock.

According to St. Germain, it's worth a fortune, which he seemed eager to pay. My plan had been to contact him today and figure out what a 'king's ransom' comes out to in 2050 dollars. Me 'very nearly dying' and having him show up unexpectedly to spirit me away hadn't been part of the plan.

"Are you usually up and about this early?" my prospective client asks.

"Almost never."

"What was different today?"

"I got hungry," I say. "Still am, as a matter of fact. What does that have to do with anything?"

St. Germain nods, like I'd answered correctly.

"Of course, you must be famished. I don't know how you do it. I've never in my life gone three days without eating. At least not in a row."

As I'm wondering how he would possibly know I've gone three days without eating, he smiles and pats his prodigious belly, then gives me a sidelong look.

"I hope you'll forgive me," he says. "Obviously I've been kept appraised of your movements—or lack thereof—since you returned from your recent adventures. For good reason, as it turns out. Do you know what was happening at the Ritz Hotel?"

"No, but you do, obviously."

"I have suspicions, but I'll wait to share them. I've made inquiries and should have more concrete answers after we reach our destination."

"Our destination? And where's that?"

The Count studies me for a moment, lips pursed.

"Your past."

My past?

"Interesting," I say. "Don't we need a DeLorean for that?"

St. Germain doesn't smile. Maybe he doesn't get the joke. I'm about to explain it when he fixes his eyes on me.

"Who are you working for?" he asks, his tone suddenly aggressive.

Not what I was expecting. Especially since I'm not working for anyone. Even on my last case, I wasn't working *for* anyone. And, as far as I know, I wasn't working on any other cases before that.

"No one," I say.

"Are you being blackmailed? Forced to do anything against your will?"

I can't help but laugh.

"Are you kidding me? Blackmailed? For what?"

The Count is dead serious.

"No and no," I say.

I try to match his dead seriousness and steely gaze as a brief game of chicken ensues. I'm pretty good at not blinking. Eventually, St. Germain concedes and takes a calming breath.

"Before we go any further," he says, "I need to be assured that you are absolutely trustworthy and transparent."

I hear this kind of thing all the time. Lots of people hire private investigators because of problems in their private lives. Often related to their private *parts*. And here's what I always tell them:

"As a former scout, I live by the 12 Points of the Boy Scout Law, which I'd be happy to recite for you. That being said, I can't prove that I'm trustworthy and transparent. All I can say is I've done my best for every client who's ever hired me. It hasn't always worked out. My clients haven't always been trustworthy and transparent with *me*. In fact, I'm not sure any of them have. But that's how I do business. Scout's honor."

St. Germain has watched me intently throughout my little speech. After a moment, he nods.

"I'm going to believe you."

I return his nod and say: "Good. Now, a little over a week ago, we talked about something that would be of great interest to you. Making a living is of great interest to me. As you once said to me: *quid pro quo*. So, if you've got the quids, I've got the quo."

The Count gives me the kind of look I've seen all too often when the subject of my getting paid comes up.

"Rest assured," he says, "I've been as eager as you to discuss what you found. But, perhaps, I wasn't clear as to why I wanted it. What I'd hoped to discover within it is only a stepping stone on a path to something of much more importance. I have learned things since we last spoke that have altered my priorities."

"So you're no longer interested in buying it?"

"Money is not the issue. This is, very literally, a matter of life and death. And not just yours. But I would think it might concern you to know your life is in danger. You appear quite nonplussed, all things considered."

"My life was in danger last week," I say, nonplussedly. "More than once. It comes with the job, at least the jobs I usually end up with. And, for once, I'd like a job to pay out."

The fat man chuckles, despite himself, and shakes his head.

"You are persistent, Mr. Murphy, I'll give you that. I will gladly pay you…when we're finished."

"Finished? Doing what?"

"Talking."

"About?"

St. Germain raises an eyebrow.

"Do you recall when we last spoke? We talked about Paradise Lost."

"Yeah, the story of my love life."

He gives me a reprimanding look, like an old school marm.

"Uh, sure," I say. "War in Heaven, Angels, Demons, Hell on Earth, etc."

"You don't believe in these things?"

"To be honest, I haven't given it much thought."

"What about evil? Do you believe evil exists?"

"Sure. But that's different. And I think blaming it on a devil is a copout."

St. Germain leans forward.

"There are devils, Mr. Murphy. I've had the misfortune of meeting several. They've existed from the beginning. And their only desire is to watch the world burn. Fortunately, we have resisted them each time. But there is a new devil at work now and I honestly do not know if this one can be stopped."

"I'm confused. Are you hiring me to find a devil?"

"In a manner of speaking. I believe you may have already crossed paths with him."

St. Germain waits for me to respond. I don't know what to say. Mostly because it sounds batshit crazy. But it's looking like I'll have to play along if I want to get paid.

"OK," I say. "Let's talk."

The fat man takes a deep breath, relieved, and eases back in his seat.

"Thank you. Now, in exchange for providing me with details about your past, I will pay you the price you would have asked for the Tesla Cache. But it won't matter if it's a million dollars or ten. If you are unable to provide the answers I'm seeking, all the money in the world may not save us."

3

St. Germain's speeder slows and dives into a cluster of dark, featureless commercial buildings. I recognize this part of town. It's been a while, but you never forget your first.

First *office*, in this case.

Thirteen years ago. Hard to believe. I guess this is what St. Germain meant when he said our destination was my past. He's watching me as the Rolls touches down. Waiting for a reaction, I guess. I don't give him one.

"I'll catch up to you," St. Germain says, as my door opens.

I climb out and walk to the lobby entrance, backlit in the glow of the Rolls' halogen headlights. The lobby doors are locked and the interior is dark. I glance back. St. Germain hasn't left the speeder. The glare of the headlights prevents me from seeing who, if anyone, is at the wheel.

Time for a cigarette.

I can't imagine why St. Germain brought me here. Maybe it's just his way of saying he knows things about me. Not that he had to prove it. In all my dealings with him, he's been impossibly well-informed and a step or two ahead of me. I don't like feeling a step or two behind, but the thought of making a million dollars—or ten—takes the sting out of it.

A minute later, the big man gets out of the speeder and waddles over. I start to ask what the holdup was; he lifts a finger to his lips. I'm not sure why he's shushing me, but whatever.

He has a key. We step inside and he relocks the doors. The place feels empty, though it's hard to imagine any building in New San Francisco being left vacant. Maybe he bought the place, just to give us some privacy.

We cross the lobby to the elevator and I press the up button. St. Germain is a few paces behind and digs for his handkerchief as we get into the lift.

I point to the 13 button and raise an eyebrow. The Count nods and I press it. A lot of buildings don't have a 13th floor, which I always thought was just plain silly. In retrospect, I may have been wrong about that. I'd had nothing but bad luck here. Maybe tonight will make up for it.

The 13th floor hallway looks pretty much the way I remember it. A bit darker and seedier. There's a biometric scanner on my old office door. That's new. St. Germain presses his manicured thumb on it and, after a click, opens the door. I follow him in.

The room is dark, the only light coming from a massive window with a spectacular view of the city. This window was the big selling point when I rented the space, which looks like it may not have been rented since. There are piles of boxes and loads of office furniture, all with a coating of dust. One of the desks and a couple chairs might actually be ones I leased and never got around to returning.

It appears St. Germain (or his helper elves, more likely) have done a little prepping. A table and two chairs have been cleared off and dusted. On the table is a large metal briefcase, a lamp, an ashtray, several bottles of water, two chunky tumblers and a $200 bottle of Lagavulin—the scotchiest of all scotches.

"Oh, good. Refreshments," I say.

The Count half-shushes me and pulls something small and black from his pocket. He peers at it closely, then presses a button on it. I expect something interesting to happen—music to start playing, maybe some nice mood lighting—but nothing does.

"Now we can talk," St. Germain says. "I've had equipment installed that creates a virtual Faraday cage. As long as we're here, we're invisible, untraceable."

"That's nice," I say.

"You think I'm being paranoid," my host says, turning on the lamp. "I assure you; I am not. I just received word that someone died in the Ritz Hotel."

Died?

"Three others are in critical condition," he adds, casually removing his cashmere overcoat and hanging it on a coatrack.

"How…?" I finally manage to mumble.

"Carbon monoxide."

My mind is reeling. I know two people who live at the Ritz: Clint, the landlord, and a very large, very friendly person named Sapphire. I don't know who else was staying there, but there were usually a handful of guests that rented rooms by the day or longer.

St. Germain uncorks the bottle of scotch and fills half a tumbler, then hands it to me.

"Do you know who died?" I ask.

"I didn't get a name."

I take a long drink and slump down into a chair. *Carbon monoxide.* From the boiler, most likely. But enough to kill someone?

"It could have been a freak thing," I say. "An accident."

St. Germain settles into the chair across the table from me.

"I'm sure that's what it will appear to be."

I look up.

"So *not* an accident."

He shakes his head.

"And you think the intention was to kill *me*."

He nods.

My shock turns to anger.

"If it was me they wanted, why do it that way?" I ask. "I wasn't hiding. There are a hundred other ways to take me out. Other people didn't have to die!"

"The other victims may have been intentional. If the police decided the circumstances were suspicious, no one could know you were the target. And, as you said, on almost any other night you might be dead, too."

I finish off the scotch and reach for the bottle. St. Germain beats me to it and pulls it away.

"We both want to find out who is responsible," he says.

I bite my tongue and nod.

"I believe we can," he continues, "but I'll need you to be relatively coherent."

After a pause, I nod again. St. Germain keeps his eyes locked on mine as he slowly slides the bottle back toward me.

"Food will help," he says. "I'll give you some time alone while we get you something to eat. I'd suggest switching to water until I get back. In the meantime, you can start by trying to think of who might want you dead."

4

An hour later, I'm feeling better…more or less. St. Germain had managed to verify that Clint and Sapphire were not among the victims. I didn't want to feel so relieved that it was a stranger who'd died, but I did. And I probably should have been more rattled about the thought of someone trying to kill me but, like I'd said, the novelty of that had worn off years ago.

The food St. Germain brought also helped. And I wasn't at all surprised when he showed up with exactly the kind of thing I would have ordered: Mongolian beef, steamed dumplings, fried rice and egg rolls. I wonder if it's from the Golden Pagoda. Wouldn't surprise me.

My host nibbles. I'm a little more aggressive. He seems to enjoy watching me eat and gives me a few minutes, uninterrupted, before getting back to business.

"Before I left," he says, "I asked you to think of who might want you dead."

I shrug and finish off a pot sticker before answering: "There's only one, off the top of my head, but he's doing a million-year sentence in Pelican Bay."

"Surely you've made other enemies."

"Oh, yeah. Plenty. But everyone I can think of who's ever wanted me dead already beat me to it."

St. Germain nods thoughtfully.

"You really are a mystery, Mr. Murphy."

"So I hear."

St. Germain gives me a quizzical look.

"From women, usually," I explain. "Right before they dump me."

"Baffled by the depths of your simplicity, I would expect. But I'm referring to your…history."

I reach for an egg roll.

"What about my history?"

He points his chopsticks in my direction.

"I told you before that I had a sense about you, that you may have an important role to play. So, over the past week, I've put considerable resources into investigating your background. There was surprisingly little to find. Your digital footprint, as they say, is…petite."

"Good," I say, dipping the egg roll into plum sauce. "I've made a point of keeping it that way."

"That being said," St. Germain says with a smile, "what did turn up was quite astonishing. I believe I've seriously underestimated you."

"How's that?"

"No need for false modesty, Mr. Murphy. In the course of your career, three different…events…have taken place, each of which was potentially catastrophic on a global scale. And, somehow, you—of all people—found yourself in the middle of all three."

"Actually, depending on how you define 'catastrophic', it's definitely been four, maybe five or six."

"Exactly my point. But would you agree that the odds of this are… improbable?"

I shrug, my mouth full.

St. Germain continues: "Let's be frank. It's beyond coincidence that a—shall we say—'low profile' P.I.—no offense intended—would find himself involved in all these pivotal events."

"No offense taken. I can't explain it, either. I just have a gift for getting in over my head. It happens with women, too, by the way."

"The question is why."

"Well, it's not mommy issues," I say. "My mom was a wonderf—"

"—The Moon Child…Roswell…the business with the Immortal Coil. I've gathered bits and pieces of information about your involvement in these events, as well as your time in the Martian Colony…enough to know that you played a crucial role every time."

St. Germain leans forward and clasps his hands on the table.

"What I *don't* know is how it all started," he says. "And that's why I've brought you here. It took some deductive work on my part, but I'm reasonably certain that thirteen years ago, in this very room, you began an investigation into the apparent suicide of a man named Carl Linsky. Your very first case after going into private practice, if I'm not mistaken. But I've found nothing on record that ties you to it. Can you tell me why that is?"

"Discretion is my middle name," I say, dabbing the corner of my mouth with a napkin. "I'm also a very poor self-promoter."

St. Germain fixes his eyes on me.

"What *is* on record is an unusual number of mysterious deaths and disappearances around the time of Linsky's supposed suicide. Not to mention everything that happened with the Law & Order Party."

"It was a nutty few days."

The Count watches me shake out a cigarette and light it.

"Imagine my surprise," he says, "when I dug a little deeper and learned that Carl Linsky had possible ties to members of the Law & Order Party, at least one murder victim and one of the disappearances. And, strangest of all, most of those crimes were never solved."

I take a drag. "Not that you know of."

"My thinking exactly."

A long exhale of smoke.

"You want to know what really happened," I say. "Why? Just curious?"

"Curious, yes. Always. But not just that. As I've learned about your past, it appears to me that you've been on a path…a path that led you to Mars, then to the Moon Child, to Roswell and beyond. That path had to start somewhere and I suspect it was during your first case. I realize it's been thirteen years, but I'd like you to tell me as much as you can remember about those events."

"You might be surprised at how much I remember," I say, flicking the ash off the tip of my cigarette. "For me, it's only been *six* years."

"True," St. Germain says with a smile. "I forgot. Ironically."

"And you'll never guess what I did right before I hit the seven-year wormhole. Or maybe you already know."

"Do tell."

"I went to dinner with…a friend. She also had questions about my past, so I ended up telling her the whole story of the Linsky case."

The Count raises an eyebrow.

"So, it's still fresh in your mind. How serendipitous."

"Actually, I shouldn't say I told her the *whole* story. I had ulterior motives with this woman, so I may have left a few things out, maybe taken some dramatic license."

St. Germain nods appreciatively, then turns serious—almost stern.

"It's crucial that you be as factual and detailed as possible. As you know, conscious memory is a tricky business. We forget important details, remember events incorrectly, even mix in other memories. The beauty of the *sub*conscious is that it records what *really* happened. Our senses are aware of virtually everything around us at all times and that information is stored, like data on a hard drive. If needed, I may be able to help you tap into your subconscious. This could allow you to recall conversations as if you were actually there, re-experience events, see them in a new light…perhaps even discover new insights that were meaningless back then but are relevant to what's happening now."

"And how can you help me tap into my subconscious, exactly?"

"There are techniques to calm and clear the mind. Hypnosis can be useful. Regression is a more intensive method to unlock the subconscious."

I take a long drag, then an even longer look at my host. His interest in my memories is a little unsettling. And I'm not exactly sure what 'regression' means, but I don't like the sound of it. Also, there's no way I'm getting hypnotized. I've seen it make people walk around like chickens.

St. Germain seems to sense my discomfort.

"Nothing to be concerned about," he says with a gentle smile. "And the techniques may be completely unnecessary. For now, just sit back, relax and start from the beginning. And remember: as much detail as possible."

I snuff out my cigarette in the ashtray.

"And you need me to be sober?"

"Not at all. Being relaxed facilitates the process." He smiles. "Up to a point, of course."

I reach for the scotch.

"Good."

Part I:

Queens & Bishops

5

I don't recall the exact date Sylvia Linsky walked into my office, but I remember everything else.

This was before the Time Reversal, when people still did business during the day, and the early afternoon light was radiating through the large window, bathing my office in burnt orange.

I'd rented the place a month earlier and Ms. Linsky was the first person—other than me and the property manager—to walk through the door. She led with her chin, head back, chips on both shoulders. Platinum blonde hair, bobbed, framing a porcelain face with wide brown eyes and full red lips. A tight white dress with black polka dots. Shiny black pumps. It was one hell of a first impression.

She knocked but didn't wait for an invitation. I was halfway out of my chair when she stepped into the room and asked: "Are you the private investigator?"

"That's what someone painted on the door," I said.

I hadn't had an actual conversation in over a week. I was a little rusty, apparently.

"I'll take that as a 'yes'", she said, a hint of a smile tugging at the corner of her mouth. She stayed by the door.

"What can I do for you, Ms.—?"

"Do you know Carl Linsky?" she asked abruptly.

"Sorry. I don't."

She paused, took a look around the office, then seemed to make a decision.

"I'm Sylvia. Sylvia Linsky."

She approached and extended her hand in a formal way, like I should kiss the back of it while bending slightly at the waist. I just took it and shook it.

"Nice to meet you, Ms. Linsky. Have a seat."

She'd interrupted a fierce game of solitaire Parcheesi. As she sat down, I picked up the game board, slid the tokens into a desk drawer and then flipped the board over and back onto the desk. *Voila!* Instant blotter.

"Sorry if I disturbed your game," Sylvia said.

"That's all right. I was losing anyway."

My first-ever prospective client took her time getting situated, crossing her legs and smoothing her dress. She was controlled, confident and deliberate. I wasn't. Between being desperate for work and a mere mortal in the presence of a goddess, I was trying not to mouth-breathe.

"Do you mind if I smoke?" she asked.

I shook my head, reluctantly. I didn't smoke, but I was willing to let clients do almost anything if it meant getting a job. That's why I kept an ashtray on my desk, but filled it with candy to discourage smoking. On this day, it was tootsie pops with their delightful chewy centers.

She opened a black and silver cigarette case and selected one of the death sticks. Pressing a button on the side of the case triggered a tiny flame, which she held gently to the tip of a long brown cigarette.

"Would you like one?" she asked, straightening up.

"Uh, no, thanks. I hear those things are bad for you."

She picked up my ashtray and dumped the tootsie pops onto the desk, then leaned back, holding the ashtray, and tapped the end of her cigarette delicately.

"Lots of things are bad for you," she said. "That doesn't stop me from enjoying them."

I swallowed and cleared my throat.

"So…you're in the market for a P.I.?" I asked.

"I don't know. I might be." She took a deep breath. "My father, Carl Linsky, died a week ago."

"I'm sorry."

"The police say he committed suicide. I think they're wrong."

Butterflies fluttered in my stomach. This sounded good. My very first solo case—and maybe it was an honest-to-goodness murder investigation. I grabbed a notepad and pen and jotted down Carl Linsky's name.

"Well, if it wasn't suicide, it has to be one of three other things:" I said, trying to sound like an expert, "natural causes, an accident…or murder."

Sylvia looked down at her cigarette. "He jumped off the Golden Gate Bridge."

I paused, feeling the butterflies scatter.

With an air of annoyance, Sylvia added: "The cops say they have witnesses."

My butterflies hit a bug zapper.

Sylvia glanced at me, then inspected the end of her cigarette before ashing unnecessarily.

"He wasn't depressed," she said, emphatically. "He was in great shape. He was dating. He was excited about the future. I don't know what made him do what he did, but I know it wasn't suicide."

I looked at my prospective client, wondering why she was here. It's hard to lose a loved one, but especially to suicide, I would imagine. The people left behind might look for reasons…excuses…someone to blame.

An ethically-challenged P.I.—the usual type—might take advantage, humor her and pocket her money, but ethics were about the only thing I had going for me. I probably couldn't help her, but if I wasn't willing to try, she'd just find someone else. It wasn't like I had anything better to do. And she was really nice to look at.

For the next few minutes, I got as much information as I could from Sylvia. Her father had died a week earlier. He was sixty-seven years old, single and lived alone in Pacific Heights. He was 'semi-retired' after a long, distinguished career as chief neurologist at the North Hill Clinic.

Sylvia, his only child, couldn't—or wouldn't—give many details about his recent activities, which led me to believe they weren't as close as she wanted me to think. It also made me wonder how she could be so sure that he hadn't been suicidal. But I didn't ask about that.

For now, I was happy to have a legitimate reason to leave the office. I could pay a visit to police headquarters, get the official story and, hopefully, some inside info from the coroner's report. Maybe they found a brain tumor or stage-four cancer—something that would provide an understandable motive for a sudden decision to jump off a bridge. If I could come up something, I'd feel ok about letting her hire me.

Speaking of which…

"If you want me to look into this," I said, almost apologetically, "we need to talk about payment."

"I'm afraid I don't have much money."

Sylvia flashed a regretful smile.

"But I know you're the right person for this," she said. "And I expect to have more money soon. I hope we can work something out."

It felt like I was back in junior high, with the cute girl asking me to do her homework. It would be easy to rationalize, tell myself that she'd actually pay me at some point. Or that it didn't matter because I had nothing else going on. But would I have done the same thing for a big smelly man?

Maybe. Maybe not. But it probably helped that Sylvia was the exact opposite of a big smelly man. And, to drive the point home, she rose from her chair and leaned over my desk, offering a breathtaking view of the majestic Linsky Peaks. I tried valiantly to avert my eyes as Sylvia picked up my pen and wrote on the legal pad.

"Come see me when you're done talking to the cops," she said as she wrote. "I'm staying at my father's house. This is the address. And my phone number."

She held my eyes as she slowly straightened up. Her smile was a little crooked, which just made it sexier.

"I don't know how I can thank you enough for doing this," she said. "I had nowhere else to go. Now I know everything's going to be ok."

I stood and handed her a business card. The very first one I'd ever given out.

"I'll do my best, Ms. Linsky."

"Call me Sylvia."

6

A little backstory: Nine years earlier, I'd been hired by the Dobbs Detective Agency, the largest private investigation firm in California. A detective was all I'd ever wanted to be since I was kid, so I worked my way up—slowly, from the very bottom—taking whatever lousy, warm-body job I could scrounge, until I finally got a chance to prove myself. Eventually, the head of the D.D.A., Colonel Roy Dobbs, saw my potential and became my mentor. For a year or so, I was living my dream.

But Dobbs and I didn't see eye to eye on some things. For him, the ends always justified the means, while I was a straight-arrow boy scout. In the end, my idealism got me fired.

The Colonel had introduced me to the 'P.I. Rules', a collection of guidelines designed to keep his protégés productive, employed and, most importantly, alive. He always said Rule #1 was 'Never Betray Your Friends'. When I reported him for ethics violations, I thought I was doing the right thing; he saw it as the ultimate betrayal.

Not only did he fire me, he made sure I got blackballed. No one in town was ever going to hire me. And even if I looked for work somewhere beyond his sphere of influence, he'd never give me a reference. After a while, I realized my only option was to go into business for myself.

Maybe I should have hung my shingle somewhere far away, but San Francisco is my city, the place I love and know like the back of my hand. Plus, moving away would have been admitting defeat. Knowing when to cut my losses has never been my strong suit.

So now I was on my very first case as a *private* private investigator and headed to the N.S.F.P.D. headquarters, where every cop knew Colonel Dobbs, and at least some of whom might have heard he'd fired me and why.

But screw it.

* * * * *

Sylvia said she'd spoken to a detective named Eve Clements. I'd met Clements before, but never worked with her. I had to hope she didn't remember me or, at the very least, hadn't heard about my spat with Dobbs.

I knew my way around the N.S.F.P.D., so I walked in like I owned the place and avoided direct eye contact all the way to Clements' office. As I got closer, I could hear her reaming someone out all the way down the hall. The whipping boy turned out to be Mac Malden, a lumpy, middle-aged cop who somehow kept a job despite a total lack of any discernible skills. I didn't know what he'd done, but I'm sure he deserved it. We passed each other outside her office. He looked like a beaten dog. I, on the other hand, bounded through her office door like a happy little puppy.

"You busy?"

Clements rolled her eyes and then waved toward a chair.

"If it isn't Tex Murphy. Sold out any fellow P.I.'s lately?"

So much for avoiding the subject.

"I guess you heard about me and the Colonel," I said, pleasantly, still in puppy mode.

"We had a drink together a while back. He said if I saw you to tell you to go to hell."

She said it with a sneer.

"OK, so—"

"—The last thing I need," she said, cutting me off, "is some pansy, unemployed wannabe P.I. wasting my time. Go play boy scout somewhere else."

Her comment included at least three things I took exception to. But I needed help, so it wasn't in my best interest to point out that I *was*, actually, employed—albeit without pay—*and* had a valid P.I. license…*and* that being trustworthy, loyal, helpful, friendly, courteous, kind, obedient, cheerful, thrifty, brave, clean and reverent does not, in fact, make one a 'pansy'.

"You know, Detective Clements, we could sit here all day and trade friendly insults—and that might be fun—but I'm here on behalf of a client.

This is my first case on my own."

"Maybe you shouldn't have gotten yourself fired."

"Maybe not. But I'm gonna give this a go and try to do it with some integrity. If you could just throw me a bone, I would be eternally grateful. And, for what it's worth, I'll be in your debt."

The cop tilted her head slightly, sizing me up. Maybe I wasn't what she was expecting. Or maybe she was deciding what kind of favor I could do for her. Scary.

Eventually, she pursed her lips, then smiled. "You're lucky you caught me right before a long weekend. I'm in a charitable mood. Just be quick about it."

I did feel lucky, so I was extra quick about it.

"Carl Linsky?"

"*That's* your first case?" The detective rolled her eyes. "There's nothing to investigate. A dozen witnesses saw him take the dive. Unassisted and hell-bent. And no question it was him. He had a distinctive look. Really thin. Huge nose. Balding in the front with lots of curly white hair everywhere else. Kind of clownish, actually."

"Positive ID on the body?"

"Yup."

"DNA?"

"Unnecessary. He was ID'd by his fiancée."

Fiancée?

Sylvia hadn't said anything about her father being engaged.

"His fiancée?" I asked. "Why not his daughter?"

"We couldn't track her down. She didn't show up until yesterday. And he had no other immediate family."

"Who's the fiancée?"

Clements shook her head. "No can do."

"Autopsy?"

"Nothing out of the ordinary. No alcohol or drugs. In great shape for his age. And it looked like he'd had a little work done recently."

"A little work?"

Clements pulled her cheeks back, stretching the skin tight across her face.

A facelift?

"Doesn't that seem odd to you?" I asked. "Getting a facelift and then committing suicide?"

"Maybe he didn't like how it turned out."

"Any personal effects?"

"Usual stuff. Wallet, keys, an ID badge...and a suicide note, neatly sealed in a Ziploc bag. And, before you ask, we compared the handwriting and it was a one-hundred percent match."

"Any chance I could see the note?"

"A one-hundred percent chance of 'no'."

"Could his daughter see it?"

"Sure. She can come in and sign for everything. How's she holding up, by the way?"

I shrugged.

"Hard to tell. I think she's in denial about it. Insists her father wasn't suicidal."

"A lot of people say that."

I leaned back in my seat and took a long, slow breath. Clements saw this as a cut-and-dried suicide and I couldn't see any compelling reason to disagree with her. As much as I wanted this to be a big case, it was looking more and more like a figurative—and literal—dead end.

7

"So you're saying you're not going to take my case."

Sylvia was standing by a window, her back to me, holding a glass of something and looking out at the napalm sky. I was sitting on a couch and surveying the front room of Carl Linsky's home. At first glance, it was neat, clean and expensive, but lacking personality.

"I don't want to take your money if I can't do anything for you," I said.

"Fine," she said flatly. "Leave."

"I'm just trying to be straight up with you."

She took a drink, then said: "If you won't help me, I'll find someone else or do what I can on my own. It certainly won't be the first time."

I felt bad for her. Maybe my recent exile from the Dobbs Detective Agency made me especially empathetic. I knew how it felt when no one had your back. And even if I couldn't do what she wanted, maybe she just needed someone to believe her. There's value in that. And I could put a price on it.

"I charge four-hundred dollars a day, plus expenses," I said.

Sylvia spun around.

"I have five hundred dollars. If you can prove it wasn't suicide, I'll give you another ten thousand."

"Deal."

Once again, I saw her face brighten, like the sun suddenly appearing from behind clouds. She flashed that sexy, crooked smile and sashayed over to me. The way she moved, she obviously wasn't drinking Smart Water.

As she took a seat next to me on the couch, I said: "Just so we're clear, I don't have a lot to work with, and I can't make any promises."

Sylvia crossed her legs, moving slightly closer.

"I understand. Thank you, Tex."

"So, did you know that your father got plastic surgery?" I asked.

Her forehead wrinkled, then she shook her head.

"A facelift," I said. "And not long ago, apparently. To me, that's the best and only indication that he wasn't suicidal. On the other hand, Detective Clements said there's a suicide note in his personal effects."

"A suicide note?" Sylvia repeated, stunned.

"Maybe it's legit, maybe it isn't. We won't know until we see it, but it may be our only lead. That, and tracking down his fiancée."

"His fiancée?"

Again, stunned. It felt like I was punching someone with no arms. Not my intention. But, clearly, she didn't know as much about her father as she wanted me to believe.

"You didn't know your father was engaged?"

"Engaged? No. I knew he was dating, but nothing serious."

"So you couldn't tell me who this mystery woman might be? I'm assuming it would be a woman."

"Yeah, it would be a woman." Sylvia smirked and took another drink. "How'd you find out about the fiancée?"

"Detective Clements said she came in to identify the body after they couldn't get in touch with you."

Sylvia looked away and shifted, uncomfortably. I could see her brain working.

"I was out of town—" she began.

"—Listen, I don't know what kind of relationship you had with your father. It doesn't matter to me if you weren't close, or maybe hadn't spent much time together over the last little while. It won't affect my investigation. What *does* matter to me is that you be honest...about everything."

Sylvia stood up and wandered back toward the window. Stalling, I figured. Trying to decide how much to tell me.

"I really did love him," she finally said, a bit defensively. "I know he loved me too, but we never had the relationship either of us wanted. I was a little...difficult...when I was younger and he couldn't stand it. I think he always wanted me to be more like him. I just wasn't. I was like my mother…and she left him."

It honestly didn't matter to me, but it made sense, with what little I knew about Sylvia and my impression of her father, based on his home décor.

"I appreciate the honesty."

Sylvia turned to me and nodded.

"I think those are all the questions I have for now," I said. "If you want to go get your father's personal effects, I'll look around here and see what I can dig up."

Sylvia set her glass down and went to get her coat and purse.

"Let's call you a ride," I said.

A look crossed her face. Like I'd insulted her. But then it was gone the next instant.

"I'm fine," she said.

"I'm sure you are. But it's probably not the best idea to drive to police headquarters if you've been drinking, even just a little."

After a brief pause, she reached into her purse and pulled out a phone.

* * * * *

After putting Sylvia into a cab, I took a tour of the residence. If this place was a reflection of its owner, Carl Linsky was a deliberate, highly-organized—maybe even severe—man. There was almost nothing you'd describe as personal. Minimal furniture, virtually no art or decorative objects. A neutral color palette.

The place was an old Victorian: high ceilings, smallish rooms, and not many of them. A front room, a modest-sized kitchen, two bathrooms and three bedrooms: a master, a guest room and one set up as a den. Sylvia was clearly staying in the guest room, which was a disaster compared to the rest of the place.

I didn't search her room or the guest bathroom, which also looked like a bomb had hit it. The den contained what you'd expect: a television, expensive leather furniture and shelves filled with the kind of books you'd expect: science stuff, mostly, with some Dickens and other classics, plus a number of books about chess.

There was only one thing that struck me as odd: an antique chess set on a coffee table was missing a piece. Carl Linsky was probably at least a little OCD; a missing chess piece would probably drive the guy nuts.

I moved on to the master. Not surprisingly, Linsky's bed was immaculately made. No decorative pillows. On a nightstand was a book with a lobster on the cover, titled 'Strategies for Engineered Negligible Senescence'. Sounded like a real page-turner. I read the back cover—the subject matter involved research by biogerontologists related to slowing or even stopping the human aging process. Apparently, lobsters show no sign of aging. I guess they'd live forever if they weren't so delicious.

I rooted through a dresser and a closet. Not a lot of clothes or shoes, but all high quality and low-key. Nothing hidden away in a sock drawer or under the bed. No wall safe.

Next up was the master bath. Tidy and clean. The medicine cabinet contained a variety of pain relievers. I wondered if Linsky had chronic pain issues. Or maybe he was just sixty-seven years old. Drawers were filled with supplements, all neatly organized, probably alphabetized.

I continued my search in the kitchen. High-end appliances, quartz countertops and walnut cabinets. Expensive, but austere. Functional. I took a peek in the refrigerator. It was a shrine to good health, filled with kale, bean sprouts and other practically inedible things, all starting to go ripe. In the cupboards, there were large containers of dry protein powder and more supplements. No sign of anything unhealthy or even remotely tasty.

How many health nuts commit suicide? Personally, I couldn't imagine life without the decadent joy of delicious, artery-clogging food, but it seemed like someone so dedicated to healthy eating would be obsessed with living a long life. Maybe if I'd found an empty package of double-stuffed Oreos, it would explain his sudden change of heart, but no such luck.

As I searched the kitchen, I picked up the faint scent of something especially rotten and traced it to the trash compactor. Just to be thorough, I opened it to take a look. An almost visible stench was unleashed. Carl Linsky's last meal must have been some sort of vile veggie smoothie.

But what caught my watering eye was something pink sticking up from the compost pile. I gently extracted what turned out to be a pink envelope and shook off the vegetable matter. Even through the stench, I could smell perfume. The envelope had been dowsed with it.

There was a greeting card inside. On the cover was a picture of two kittens, surrounded by hearts. Inside, the printed message read: 'Ours is a purr-fect love'. Underneath it, written in a loopy, feminine scrawl, was: '*My Beloved Carl, This card says all my heart feels but my lips cannot utter when you're near me. May these past weeks turn into nine lives together. Yours, Delores.*'

There was nothing about the card or what was written inside that fit with my perception of Carl Linsky, but as they say, opposites attract. I wondered if this Delores woman was Linsky's fiancée, or if he was the kind of guy who liked to juggle. Clearly, Delores was a smitten little kitten. If the feeling had been mutual, maybe they'd had a lovers' spat or even a breakup. People do crazy things when relationships go bad. It was worth checking into.

Carefully wiping down the envelope revealed that the card had been sent through the mail. A mostly-legible return name and address were handwritten in the top-left corner. The name was 'D. Lightbody'.

8

"Are you Delores Lightbody?"

The woman on the other side of the door looked me up and down—literally from head to toe—then her lips curled into a vaguely predatory smile.

"Yes, indeedy."

She was a good foot-and-a-half shorter than me with short, wavy rust-brown hair, a flat, wide nose and jowls. She had the face of a saint.

Bernard.

"I'm a private investigator," I said. "If you have a few minutes, I'd like to talk to you about Carl Linsky. I'm investigating his death. My name's Murphy."

She swung the door open. "Well, do come in, Mr. Murphy."

"Thank you," I said, stepping past her. The place was half Anthropologie showroom, half bordello—pink, perfumed and pillowy.

Delores closed the door and turned to give me another exaggerated once-over.

"You are very, very welcome."

Her eyes drifted down to my shoes, then, very slowly, back up my trousers and the length of my tie, over my face and up to my hair, then back down to lock in on my eyes. She was a ball of fire. Literally. I could feel heat coming off her.

"Well, this is certainly exciting," she said, "a real live P.I. I love detective novels, you know."

"Is that right?"

"I suppose I've always had a certain fascination with private dicks."

She hit that last word really hard.

"I can imagine," I said. "But I'm afraid real P.I.s aren't that exciting."

Delores pshawed.

"I don't believe that for a second. If you found the right partner to do some undercover work with, I'll bet you'd liven right up."

For someone who'd just identified the body of her dead fiancé, she didn't seem particularly broken up. She gestured toward a chair and matching loveseat. I headed for the chair. The loveseat seemed risky.

"Well, enough about me," I said. "Let's talk about Carl, shall we?"

Delores plopped down on the pillow-strewn, red velvet loveseat, arms spread out wide—an open invitation to give a belly rub.

"What if I refuse to cooperate?" she purred. "Will you interrogate me under a bare bulb?"

There were a couple ways things could go from here. Again, a P.I. of lower moral character might just offer an exchange of favors. I decided to take the slightly higher road and lie my face off.

"You're an attractive woman, Ms. Lightbody. *Extremely* attractive. But tampering with evidence—or witnesses—could get my license revoked. I'm guessing you'd be a lot of fun to tamper with, but I just can't take that risk."

She pouted for a moment, but then shrugged, resigned. The full boil reduced to a gentle simmer.

"As I said," I continued, "I've been hired to investigate Carl Linsky's death. I found your name and address on an envelope at his home. I gather you and Carl were romantically involved?"

"I was madly in love with him."

"Engaged, I understand."

She hesitated. "Well…not officially."

Hm. That put a different spin on things. Maybe Delores had been more of a stalker than a fiancée.

"Tell me about Carl," I said with an encouraging smile.

"Oh, where should I begin?"

She collected herself and took a long, exaggerated breath.

"It was a month or so ago, on a foggy San Francisco night when Carl and I first met. Naturally, it was love at first sight."

"Interesting. Had you and Carl been drinking heavily?"

"Oh, no. Carl never drank. And I was working. He came to see me about drawing up his will. I'm an estate planning lawyer."

"And that was just a few weeks ago?"

"So little time together," Delores said dreamily, "but a lifetime of memories."

This was interesting. Linsky gets his will drawn up and dies soon after. It wasn't proof of anything, but it suggested that the possibility of imminent death may have been on his mind. And, obviously, suicide is one form of imminent death.

Delores leaned forward and bit her lower lip.

"Losing him was devastating. I still can't understand why he…did what he did."

"Neither can I," I said. "I haven't found anything to indicate he was suicidal. I was hoping you could help me out with that."

"He was so full of life," Delores said, dreamy again. "He was a man of few words, but I sensed he had a strong will to live…to *really* live. To make every minute count, and to have as many minutes as possible. He was the last person I ever dreamed would…do what he did."

"Do you think there's any chance it wasn't suicide?"

Delores gave me a confused look.

"What are you saying?"

She paused.

"Surely you're not implying that it was…"—she clapped a hand to her ample chest— "…*murder*?"

It was like watching small-town dinner theater. Might as well join in.

"Well," I said, "let's just say the police didn't find any trace of banana peel up there on the bridge."

"But I can't believe anyone would want to hurt Carl." She hesitated. "Unless—"

"Unless what?"

"I really shouldn't say," she said, really wanting to say.

"Delores," I said, with a seductive smile, "don't make me put you under a bare bulb."

She giggled.

Clearly, Delores and Carl hadn't been as close as she imagined they were. I should have picked up on that when I found her card in the trash. If she had any useful information, it would almost certainly have something to do with the will she'd drawn up for him.

I sat forward and gave Delores my most smoldering look.

"Tell me about the will. Who stood to benefit from Carl's death?"

Delores makes the ‘zipping’ motion across her lips.

“I don’t suppose it’s Carl’s daughter?” I asked.

Talk about a mood breaker.

“Sylvia?” Delores spat out the name. “All that trollop cares about is her father’s money. But now she’s reaping what she’s sown.”

“What do you mean? She’s getting nothing from Carl’s will?”

Delores shook her head vigorously. “Nothing of real value. Most of Carl’s estate will go to the North Hill Clinic. The rest to a few different charitable groups and foundations.”

I couldn’t help feeling a little disappointed. I seriously doubted that the North Hill Clinic board of directors was behind Linsky’s death. If someone had wanted him dead, it wasn’t for his money, apparently.

At this point, I figured I’d gotten everything I could out of Delores. I was about to excuse myself when she pursed her lips and looked at me out of the corner of her eye.

“Of course, there is the life insurance.”

“Carl’s life insurance?”

“One million dollars,” Delores said, somewhat maliciously.

“And the beneficiary? Sylvia?”

Delores gave me a look. “You’ll have to ask her about that.”

I fully intended to. From the start, I’d wondered about Sylvia’s relationship with her father and why she was so driven to prove he didn’t commit suicide. I’d thought maybe it was denial, or maybe genuine concern, but the life insurance was an unsettling new wrinkle. Now I knew Sylvia had a clear motive for wanting her father not just dead, but *murdered.*

* * * * *

I flew back to Pacific Heights, where Sylvia was waiting for me, with a fresh drink in hand and the air of someone itching for a fight.

“His things are over there,” she said, tilting her head.

There was a manila envelope on a table. As I opened it, she described the contents:

“There wasn't much. His wallet, a set of keys—two go to the house, one to his speeder. The other two, I don't know what they go to. His North Hill Clinic ID badge. And a copy of the suicide note.”

“I'll check them out,” I said, putting the items back into the envelope. “Right now, I've got a few things I need to run by you. I spoke to Delores

Lightbody. Apparently, you two aren't exactly soul sisters."

Sylvia's eyes went dark.

"She's hideous. I don't know what kind of black magic she used on my father, but I can't think of any other explanation."

"Delores told me about your father's will," I said.

Sylvia took a drink.

"Yeah. You should have seen the big smile on her fat face. She loved telling me I was getting almost nothing."

"She also told me about the million-dollar life insurance policy."

Sylvia whirled around.

"Why are you treating me like I'm some kind of suspect? I won't get a cent of that! I'm surprised you're even bringing it up. You know life insurance policies don't pay off in cases of suicide!"

It was almost laughable. She'd hired me to prove he hadn't committed suicide. Her motives couldn't have been any more obvious. And she knew I knew.

She set her glass down and snatched up her coat.

"You can think what you want," she snapped, "but I don't have to stick around here and be insulted by the hired help."

She stormed out, slamming the door behind her.

It stung, but she was right—I *was* the hired help. And I'd violated P.I. Rule #17: *Never upset a client.* But she hadn't fired me, so she was still my client. And, on the bright side, she'd be good for the ten grand she'd promised me…if I could just prove that a pretty obvious suicide was somehow a murder.

Unfortunately, the only person who seemed to have a motive was my client.

9

I went through Linsky's personal effects, hoping to increase my number of leads, which was currently zero. I started with the copy of the suicide note. According to Detective Clements, they'd positively identified the handwriting as Linsky's and I had no reason to doubt her. The note read:

> *The pain has become unbearable. I cannot survive the endgame.*
> *Forgive me, Sylvia. Cowards die many times before their deaths;*
> *the valiant never taste of death but once.*

I'd never read a suicide note before, so I wasn't sure what to expect. Maybe I thought it should be longer, more detailed, more emotional. But, from what I knew of Linsky, it was exactly the kind of suicide note I'd expect him to write. At least he'd acknowledged his daughter. Maybe they'd both wished they could have been closer. Now it was too late.

I set the note aside and examined the key fob—for a speeder, obviously—and a ring with four keys on it. Sylvia had said two of the keys went to the house and had no idea what the other two were for. One was quite old and scratched and looked like it might fit a door lock; the other was new and smaller and might go to a drawer or file cabinet.

The wallet contained no cash, a few credit cards and a driver's license with the first photo I'd seen of Carl Linsky. Detective Clements was right when she said he had a distinctive appearance, though I'd describe it as being less like a clown and more like one of the old dwarves from The Lord of the Rings (or a wizard, if he'd had longer, straighter hair...and more of it). A narrow face with a prominent nose and chin, accentuated by a short goatee. He'd gone bald and white, leaving only a frizzy wreath around the sides and back of his head.

If he'd gotten a facelift, it must have been after this photo was taken. Here, he still had saggy jowls, droopy eyelids and puffy bags under his eyes. The only thing striking about him was his dark, almost black eyes, which were piercing…even in his license photo.

His North Hill Clinic ID was a badge tucked into a lanyard. It also had a photo, which looked to have been taken a few years before the driver's license photo. Younger Carl wasn't any handsomer. It was hard to believe he'd contributed one bit of DNA to Sylvia.

Looking at the badge, I remembered Sylvia describing her father as being 'semi-retired'. I hadn't asked what that meant. Was he still working part-time at North Hill? In my mind, the fact that he had the badge when he jumped meant one of two things: either he'd been at North Hill before he went to the bridge, or he'd wanted it found with his body. Either way, it seemed significant.

It also occurred to me that there was no office or workstation in Linsky's home. Maybe he still had an office at North Hill. If so, that might be the best place to look for any secrets he might have been hiding.

I pulled the badge from the lanyard and turned it over. There was an embedded chip on the back. If it still worked, I could use it to get into North Hill and Linsky's office, if he still had one there. Linsky had been dead for a week and, for all I knew, they'd already deactivated his ID badge and moved whatever he'd left behind into a storage closet. If that was the case, I'd need Sylvia to go ask for her father's stuff, but in my experience, that ran a huge risk of red tape. And even if they let her have her father's things, the process could take weeks or months. I couldn't afford to wait.

* * * * *

It was a short flight to the North Hill Clinic. This was the newest and biggest hospital in the Bay Area and no expense had been spared, all rounded edges and gleaming steel and glass.

I'd never been inside; I'd always avoided hospitals like the plague, in part because that's where you can catch things like the plague. It took something serious to make me enter voluntarily. Like following a lead for my first case.

Before doing anything else, I had to see if Linsky's badge still worked. I parked my speeder near a side door labeled 'Staff Entry Only', with a card reader next to it.

The ID was still active.

I opened the door and stepped into a vacant, sterile-looking hallway. Now the nerves kicked in. I wasn't sure if using Linsky's badge was technically illegal, but getting caught could be bad. They would almost certainly confiscate the ID, so that meant I'd get just one chance.

I was wearing a suit, tie and wingtips—none of them expensive, but not bargain basement, either. I was clean-shaven and had a decent haircut, so I didn't think I'd look totally out of place. North Hill was a big facility, so a new face probably wouldn't arouse suspicion. As always, the best disguise was confidence. Acting like you're supposed to be there is half the battle.

With a self-assured stride, I walked down the hallway, glancing casually at any signs or placards I passed. There was nothing to indicate which section I was in, only room numbers.

I reached an intersection. There were people moving in every direction, including a pair of nurses, chatting excitedly, who smiled at me as they passed. I looked around quickly for some kind of directory and didn't see one. I must have hesitated too long—a dead giveaway that I was lost.

"Can I help you with something?" a woman's voice said.

I turned to see one of the nurses smiling at me. She looked helpful, not suspicious, so my disguise seemed to be holding up. Unfortunately, I hadn't come up with a handy excuse in case of unplanned helpfulness.

"I, uh..." My mind had gone blank. Eventually, I would learn how to lie like a cheap rug, but I was still more boy scout than hard-boiled P.I., so I just blurted out: "I'm looking for Carl Linsky's office."

The nurse's smile evaporated, replaced by a pained expression. After a long pause, she said: "You haven't heard?"

I gave her a blank look. Not intentionally. My brain was frozen.

"Dr. Linsky died," she said, gently.

The mental cogs slowly started turning again. I looked away, my jaw tight and eyes squinting, the very picture of an uncommonly strong man coping with sudden, unexpected grief. Gazing off into the abyss of mortality gave me a few moments to get my brain into second gear.

"It makes sense now," I said, finally. "His last message. He said he had something for me, that I should come pick it up from his office. He said he might not be there. Now I know why."

I paused to collect myself.

"He must have known the end was near," I finished, in a husky whisper.

The nurse stepped forward and put a consoling hand on my arm.

"I'm so sorry."

I shook my head, unable to speak.

"Come with me," the nurse said. "I'll take you to his office."

Bingo.

I'd never pulled off this kind of thing before, and I hadn't even been trying. It might warrant a new entry in my list of P.I. Rules, something like '*When in doubt, be pathetic*'. It would need some word-smithing.

I could barely contain my glee as the nurse escorted me through the North Hill labyrinth. I'm not sure I would have found the office on my own, at least not without eventually arousing suspicion with aimless wandering. It was a good five-minute walk, including an elevator ride and a set of stairs. Along the way, the nurse asked me how I knew Dr. Linsky. To avoid another brain freeze, I flipped it around and got her talking about him, which she did right up until we stopped outside a door with Linsky's name on it.

The nurse swiped her ID badge and opened the door for me. It was a modest office, but had a large window that offered a spectacular view of the Bay, with the Golden Gate Bridge just visible on the far left and Alcatraz on the right. The sun was setting, lighting up the red-orange sky and the overall effect was more like a framed painting than a window.

I was relieved to see the office was still full of stuff. It looked like nothing had been done to it since Linsky was last here.

"Well, thank you for your help," I said, hoping she would leave. She didn't seem to be in any hurry.

"What was it he left for you?"

I glanced around, scanning for anything of interest.

"Oh, it was just…a…thing."

"A thing?" she asked.

I could hear a change in her voice. Not a good change.

"Maybe he left it in one of the desk drawers," I said.

I opened one of the drawers and started looking through it.

"I guess I'll leave you to it," the nurse said, in a way that made me want to search even faster.

"I'm sure it's here somewhere. Thanks again."

The door closed behind me. In addition to the desk, there was a bookcase and three file cabinets. I went through the desk first, but had no clue what I was looking for. None of the drawers were locked and nothing in them seemed relevant or important.

I moved on to the file cabinets. They were all unlocked and full of files labeled with numbers and names. Nothing unusual or interesting.

The last place to look was the bookcase. It held books, mostly, but there was one shelf with a few personal items. One was a framed photo of a much younger Sylvia. The photo had obviously been cropped, removing someone else who'd been standing next to Sylvia. Her mother, I guessed. The photo told me something. Despite their apparent issues, Linsky had loved his daughter. The ex-wife not so much.

If Linsky had secrets here, they were well-hidden. It would take me hours to do a thorough search…and I didn't have hours. I didn't have minutes, even.

Not even seconds.

Voices were outside the door. As I stepped back from the bookcase, I spotted a laptop bag that had been shoved into a corner. I picked it up, just as I heard the door click. The bag had a strap, so I slung it over my shoulder, stuck my thumb casually under the strap and took a step toward the door.

It opened to reveal a compact little man in a tailored suit. His angry, angular face looked like it had been carved out of dark brown pumice.

"Can I help you?" he asked, sounding not at all helpful.

"No, I'm good. I was just leaving."

"I'd like to see some ID, please."

The jig was up. I thought about stiff-arming him and running for daylight, but he looked fairly fit for an older guy. Plus, I was boxed in and he had a significantly lower center of gravity. I might get past him, but not without a fight, which would raise a ruckus and then I'd be outnumbered. Odds were, I wouldn't get out with Linsky's laptop. I might even get arrested. I'd have to talk my way out.

I produced my P.I. license and handed it over. The man took a close look and didn't give it back.

"I'm listening," he said.

"As you can see, my name's Murphy and I'm a licensed private investigator. Linsky hired me. Before he died, he told me he'd left something important for me in his office."

My story matched up more or less with what I'd told the nurse, just in case they checked. And it was more true than not. Fifty-one percent, at least. And totally plausible.

"Did you find what it was he left for you?"

"I didn't," I said. "But I'm sure I could if I had a little more time. Well, maybe a lot more time. There's a bunch of stuff to go through in here. What are you gonna do with it, anyway? Does it go to the next of kin?"

"Personal items do. Eventually. Once we've had a chance to examine everything."

Sounded like a lot of red tape to me. As I'd suspected.

Then, a mild stroke of genius.

"If you want, we can call Carl's daughter," I said. "She'll confirm that he hired me."

"Sylvia?" The man snorted with disgust. "I wouldn't believe a word out of that young woman's mouth. If I call anyone, it will be the police."

Apparently, this guy knew my client. I wondered what the story was there, but this wasn't the time to explore it.

"Well," I said with a smile, "I haven't broken any laws. But we can give the cops a call if you like."

The man looked me up and down and seemed to deflate a little. I saw it as an opening.

"Look," I said, less snarky, "I'm just doing my job. Were you and Carl friends, Dr.—?"

"Sternwood," he replied, almost reflexively.

After a moment, the man who called himself Sternwood nodded.

"I admired Carl a great deal. He was a good man. And a great doctor. It was a shame how things ended."

"Suicide is tragic," I agreed. This was good. I felt like we were connecting here.

"I must admit, I've felt a sense of guilt," Sternwood said. "He was never the same after we decided he could no longer be trusted to perform surgery."

Huh? This was new.

"Time catches up to all of us, I suppose," I said, with a solemn nod.

"I'm not sure it was age *per se*," Sternwood said. "He had started to act erratically, mood swings, fits of anger. During his final surgery, he lost control. We couldn't risk that happening again."

The man seemed lost in thought for a minute, but then snapped out of it and looked up at me.

"I'll let you go, Mr. Murphy, but I'll need Carl's ID badge."

My instinct was to deny having it. But I'd used it to enter the facility, and Sternwood must have known that. I acted disappointed, but I really just wanted him to kick me out. I gave him Linsky's ID badge—reluctantly—and he handed me my P.I. license.

"Carl's daughter will be notified when her father's possessions are made available," he said. "Whatever it is you're looking for, you'll have to get it from her."

He turned around and I followed him out into the hallway. There were no security personnel waiting, but the nurse who'd escorted me to Linsky's office was there. She'd lost her helpful glow. I nodded to her, then to Sternwood and turned to walk away.

After a few steps, I heard the nurse say: "He didn't have that laptop bag when he came in."

Looked like I was going to have to run for it after all.

10

I wasn't in peak physical condition, but with at least twice the adrenaline and a twenty-year head start, I easily ditched Sternwood and made it back to my speeder with Linsky's laptop bag.

Sternwood seemed like the kind of guy who didn't give up easily. He had my name and my office address was publicly listed, so I didn't go back to my office.

Instead, I found a nearby coffee shop, where I ordered a tall Americano and took a seat at a corner table. There was a razor-thin, expensive-looking laptop in the bag. It was emblazoned with a logo of a flaming sword in a colorful mosaic pattern, like a stained-glass window.

I opened the laptop. There was a handwritten note on the keyboard. As best I could recall, the writing matched the suicide note.

Mr. Fletcher,

If I am dead, you might choose to ignore this. However, I believe you to be a man of strong character and ask that you continue the course of action we have discussed. Everything I have learned can be found in my private room. There is also money there. Contact my daughter, Sylvia Linsky, to get my keys. She should not be told anything we've discussed, for several reasons, including her own safety.

The only thing necessary for the triumph of evil is for good men to do nothing.

Vaya con Dios,

Carl Linsky

OK, well, this was something.

I sat back and took a sip of coffee, then reread the note several times. This message was much like the suicide note. The tone was similar and it ended with a quote. Or two, if you count the Spanish song lyrics. As in the suicide note, where Linsky gave no details about a possible motive for his death, there were no details on why he might now be dead.

But this changed everything. First of all, I was considerably more open to the idea that Linsky may not have committed suicide. Secondly, what did Linsky mean by 'course of action' and 'triumph of evil'? It sounded ominous, though Sternwood had said Linsky had been acting increasingly erratic; maybe he'd gone completely delusional.

Most relevant to me was the reference to Linsky's 'private room'. That, it seemed, is where I would find his secrets. And, apparently, this Mr. Fletcher would know where to find it.

There might also be some relevant information on the laptop. I booted it up. Almost instantly, a dialog appeared with a message: *External device required.*

I searched through the bag. There was a power cord, a spare battery and nothing else. So much for that.

I stowed the laptop and then read the note again as I finished my coffee. Obviously, I needed to locate this Mr. Fletcher. It was probably safe to say that he would be local, since Linsky had left the laptop bag for him to find. But, as I'd found out first-hand, the laptop bag wouldn't have been easy to get. Unless Fletcher worked at North Hill, I suppose. But then he'd be *Dr.* Fletcher, right?

After another read-through of the note, one part jumped out at me: *Everything I have learned can be found in my private room. There is also money there.* Linsky was gathering information...and keeping it secret. And maybe Linsky was *paying* Fletcher to help him do whatever he was doing. And what type of person do you pay to gather information and keep it secret?

A private investigator, maybe?

Probably just wishful thinking, but it was worth checking into.

Which presented a problem. Back in the day, I could have looked up Fletcher's name in a phone book. Now I needed to get online.

It was only at times like this that I missed having a cell phone. I had a company phone the last couple years I worked at the Dobbs Detective Agency. It was to be charged and on your person 24/7. Word was, it was more of a tracking device than anything. Dobbs' agents handled a lot of sensitive—not to mention *lucrative*—situations and there were always opportunities for skimming, double-crossing and side action. The Colonel had a paranoid streak a mile wide and almost pathological trust issues, so he wanted to monitor every move his employees made.

This, in turn, gave me my own paranoid streak. Carrying a cell phone made me feel like I was under constant surveillance…which I was. But it was a job requirement. When I went out on my own, I vowed not to carry a cell phone or any similar device. It made things less convenient, but Sam Spade and Philip Marlowe had done just fine without them. And, sure, that was a hundred years ago…and they were fictional characters…but you get my point.

So I was making do with a barely-functional PC and a landline vidphone. Hell, I still used a fax machine.

But everyone else had a smart phone.

I looked around the coffee shop for someone helpful-looking. As I scanned the room, an older man wearing a beret and some funky eyeglasses looked up from his laptop and gave me a smile. I smiled back, then gathered up my things and walked over to him.

"Hi, there," I said. "Cool glasses."

"Why, thank you," he said.

"Could I ask a favor? My aura must be on the fritz. I think my laptop just died and my cell's suddenly out of juice. Could I borrow your phone for just a second?"

I'm not sure the guy bought my excuses, but he shrugged and picked up his phone. After a quick swipe he handed it to me.

"You're a lifesaver," I said.

I opened a web browser and entered 'Fletcher', 'Private Investigator' and 'San Francisco'. A second later, a page of listings appeared. Incredibly, the very first listing was '*Sonny Fletcher – California Association of Licensed Investigators*'. And below the heading was a familiar address.

Mine.

11

My office was in New San Francisco, the shiny new side of the city that was rebuilt after the 'nuclear incident'. I was in one of the most affordable areas, but it wasn't cheap. Luckily, it had a back room just big enough to fit a cot and a dresser, so I didn't have to rent a separate apartment. Most important, it wasn't in Old San Francisco. I couldn't imagine trying to run a business out of that slag heap.

I hadn't intended on returning to my office, but I had to chance it. I did some reconnaissance first and didn't see anything out of the ordinary. It was Friday night and the parking lot was mostly empty. Just to be safe, I parked a couple blocks away and used a back entrance to enter the building.

Stepping into the lobby, I was relieved to not see or hear a soul. I walked to a directory on the far wall and scanned it. Sure enough, right under 'Dumper & Runn Divorce Attorneys for Men', I found what I was looking for: *Fletcher Investigations – Suite 404.*

I guess it goes without saying that I hadn't paid much attention to the other tenants. One of the many things I couldn't afford was a receptionist, so I almost never left my office, just in case a client showed up. When Sylvia Linsky finally appeared at my door, I didn't ask how she'd found me. Now I was pretty sure she hadn't come looking for *me* at all.

There weren't many independent private investigators these days. The odds of two freelance P.I.'s having offices in the same building were slim to none. Sylvia may have gotten a lead to Fletcher and came here to find him. Since she ended up visiting me, that meant either she hadn't found him or she did, but didn't get what she wanted from him.

It turned out to be the former. The door to Fletcher's office was locked but, looking through the glass, I could see that he'd cleared out, possibly in a hurry. The space was littered with office scraps, and he'd left a few things of value behind. Considering that the lobby directory hadn't been updated—and knowing management wouldn't let affordable rental space stay unoccupied very long—I figured Fletcher had vacated recently.

And the timing seemed curious, in light of Carl Linsky's recent suicide and the note he'd left for Fletcher.

I returned to my office and called the property manager, a guy named Pembleton. I told him I wanted to chat and see if he could help me. He was a helpful, chatty guy. He said he knew Sonny fairly well and had last seen him a couple weeks earlier. Described him as an 'old *caballero*'.

He was surprised when I told him Fletcher appeared to have cleared out. Apparently, Sonny was one of the oldest tenants and had been leasing the space for years. He'd missed the last couple payments, but that was nothing new.

A few years back, Pembleton said, Sonny's wife had died tragically—suicide, he was pretty sure—and Sonny disappeared for a few months. When he finally showed up again, it looked like he'd aged twenty years, but he paid up his rent and went back to work.

Pembleton was being as chatty as I'd hoped, but his helpfulness had its limits. When I asked if he could put me in touch with Fletcher, he politely informed me that it was against policy to give out tenants' personal or contact info. However...as the property manager, he *could* let me check out the now-vacant office, which would soon be available to rent. He offered to meet me the next day, but when I told him it was kind of an emergency, he said he'd be right over. Chatty and helpful.

Twenty minutes later, Pembleton let me into Fletcher's office. A relatively expensive desk and several file cabinets had been left behind. They were all empty, except for a few random papers and office supplies. As I searched through them, I could feel the property manager's eyes on me.

"It's like I'm watching a movie," he finally said. "I've never seen a detective in action."

There was a chair next to the desk. I leaned down, placed my hand on the seat and closed my eyes, focusing my deductive powers.

"Five days."

"Five days?" Pembleton asked.

"Since he left. Maybe six."

"Seriously?"

I ignored him and turned my attention to a wastebasket beside the desk. It was full, with two empty bourbon bottles on top. I picked them out and set them on the desk.

"I could tell he was a drinker," Pembleton said. "But don't all you detectives drink?"

"You mean alcohol?"

"Uh, yeah."

"Not me. It clouds the mind."

"Yeah, that's kind of the point."

In the next stratum of the wastebasket was a stack of used, empty coffee cups—nine or ten, all with a logo of a red '6' on them.

Motel 6.

It looked like Fletcher's routine was to start every day with the same cup of swill. And no one in their right mind gets their coffee from a motel. Not unless you're staying there.

So, a likely assumption was that he was holed up in a Motel 6. The question was, which one? I needed something else to cross-reference.

I kept digging through the trash. Nothing useful, other than half a sandwich in a wrapper labeled 'Bread & Butter Deli'. It didn't smell particularly edible, and I wasn't that hungry anyway.

I did, however, happen to know where the Bread & Butter Deli was—on O'Farrell Street, in the Tenderloin. I didn't know if there was a Motel 6 in that neighborhood, but if there was, I'd bet this half sandwich that I'd find Fletcher there.

12

A Motel 6 was just around the corner from the Bread & Butter Deli. Pembleton would have been very impressed.

I walked into the lobby. Now what? Even if I got lucky and Fletcher was staying here, I wasn't sure how receptive he would be, so I wanted to keep the element of surprise; this ruled out having the desk clerk call his room. Fletcher might even be checked in under a fake name. I could stake the place out and wait for an old caballero to show up, but that could take hours—maybe days. Plus, I didn't know what he looked like. I decided the best approach was to storm the castle.

I started knocking on doors. Most of the rooms were unoccupied, but four people opened up for me—including one very hairy and aroused man—before I finally came face to face with Sonny Fletcher.

He cracked his door open, chain still attached.

"What d'ya want?" he mumbled. The smell of booze was eye-watering.

"Uh, yeah, hi. I'm on a scavenger hunt. I'm looking for a spool of thread, a shoehorn and the answer to the question 'Why did Carl Linsky throw himself off the Golden Gate Bridge?'."

"Mm," he said, not the least bit rattled. He turned his head to take a sip from a glass. "You a P.I.?"

Unexpected.

"Yeah. The name's Murphy."

Fletcher paused, then said: "Come in, Murphy. I'll talk to ya."

The door closed and I heard the chain slide. He pulled the door open and walked back into the room.

He wore an off-white suit jacket that may have been nice at one time, but was now rumpled and stained. Still, there was a swagger about him.

"*Mi casa es su casa*," he said over his shoulder.

"Thanks."

I took a few steps inside.

"Close the door."

I did, then took a moment to soak in the interior as Fletcher continued to soak his liver.

"Cozy," I said.

The old man smirked and finished off his bourbon, or whatever it was.

"Yeah. My travel agent got it for me."

He had a full head of longish, unkempt hair and a grizzled goatee that was more salt than pepper. Probably a dashing kind of guy, a few decades and cases of bourbon ago.

"It looked like you cleared out of your office in a hurry," I said. "You running from bill collectors or something?"

"I guess you could say that."

He turned to me and his voice went up a few notches.

"Come on! What do you want from me, huh?"

"I understand Carl Linsky hired you... before he died," I said.

"I had nothing to do with Linsky buying the farm. Bible truth."

He held a curled-up hand to his mouth and kissed it, then placed it on his chest.

"What were you doing for him?" I asked.

Fletcher ran a hand through his hair and shook his head.

"OK, I guess I can tell you now. It doesn't matter. He wanted me to find some people for him."

"Why?"

"I don't know! The man gives me some names and I go to work. OK?"

Fletcher grabbed a bottle and refilled his glass. I didn't know a whole lot about Carl Linsky, but Sonny Fletcher didn't seem like the kind of guy a fastidious old man with OCD would choose to work for him.

"Why did Linsky hire you?" I asked, hitting the 'you' a little too hard. I really hadn't meant it to sound like an insult, but that's how it came across.

"That's low," Fletcher said, his jaw tightening. He took a few steps forward, getting up in my face. I was half his age and twice his size, but it made me take a step back.

"I hadn't had a drink in almost two years! Until last week."

There was rage there, but something else. For a moment, I thought he might start to cry. But he gathered himself and turned away.

"So, what happened?" I asked.

"Look, I just tracked down two people, alright? It was a Val Davis and a Rona Morgan. And it didn't take me any time at all. I found out where they were. They were in the ground! And they hadn't been there too long."

My butterflies were back.

"These women," I asked, "how did they die?"

Fletcher didn't answer immediately. At last, he said, "I don't know. Not for sure."

"But they died recently. Just like Linsky."

"Yeah."

"And that's when you vacated your office?"

"Yeah," Sonny mumbled, "around then. Look, I...I prefer not to talk about this anymore, okay?"

Val Davis and Rona Morgan. I could probably follow up on them without Fletcher's help and I didn't want to push him too hard. I figured I might need him later. But I was pretty sure he had more to tell me.

"What about Linsky's death?" I asked.

"I don't know!"

He was done. If I didn't back off, he might never agree to talk to me again. I pulled out a business card and held it up.

"Here's my contact info. I was hired to prove Linsky didn't commit suicide. If you can think of anything that might help me, I just need something to keep the thing going."

Sonny looked up. "Wait a minute..."

He turned around and started searching for something.

"He told me to hang on to it. The *bees hop*. In case anything happened to him."

Bees hop?

A moment later, the old man found what he was looking for. He came up to me and held out a small object. It was a chess piece. A bishop.

Then I remembered. This had to be the piece missing from the chess set in Linsky's den. I turned it over, looked at it from every angle. It was nothing special. I wondered why Linsky had given it to Fletcher.

"It's just a bishop," I said.

"Uh-huh."

"Is that it?"

"Just that…and a warning. Get off this case. Judgment Day came for me. It could come for you, too. Get out, *amigo*. Get out while you can."

"I'll keep that in mind."

Fletcher turned his back to me and returned to his glass of painkiller.

"Mm-hm."

"Don't lose my card," I said.

He didn't reply.

I started toward the door. "Maybe we'll see each other around."

He didn't look back.

"Yeah, maybe."

I opened the door and paused. It felt like I should say or ask something else, but I couldn't think what.

"Hey…" Fletcher said.

"Yeah, I know. Close the door."

13

It was coming up on midnight when I got back to my office. No sign of Sternwood or cops. Thank god. I was exhausted and the cot in the back room was calling like a rickety canvas siren. After a month of doing nothing but waiting, this day had been a shock to the system.

But I couldn't call it a night just yet. Sylvia had left a message on my vidphone. It looked we'd both been busy—me tracking down leads and her throwing down cocktails.

"Hey, Tex," she breathed into the camera. "I need to talk to you as soon as possible."

She mustered a smile. It was like she had to focus to do it. At least she wasn't yelling at me. She'd gone from one kind of pissed to another.

"Could you come over to my father's house whenever you get this message, no matter how late it is? I'll be waiting for you."

It looked like she'd slipped into something a little more comfortable. Which was even more intimidating than her being mad at me.

* * * * *

Sylvia didn't answer when I knocked on the door, but it was unlocked and I let myself in. The house was dark, except for the warm glow from a small lamp next to the couch where Sylvia lay sleeping.

Her robe was half-open, revealing a silvery silk negligee and soft, pale skin. From the neck down, she was all grown-up, but with her tousled hair and flushed cheeks, her face looked almost childlike.

I stood there for a long moment, staring down at this gorgeous creature, in awe of her physical perfection…and completely mystified by what was inside her.

So beautiful. So damaged.

I leaned down to pull her robe closed, then touched her lightly on the shoulder. She stirred and her eyes fluttered open before closing again. A slow, intoxicated smile spread across her face.

"Well, lookie who it is...." she murmured.

I sat down next to her. After a sleepy pause, she stirred again.

"Tex Murphy, handsome P.I., on the case from hell."

Sylvia slowly swung her legs off the couch, knocking over a bottle of Grey Goose vodka she'd left on the floor. She ran both hands through her hair and turned to face me.

"I bet you've solved this damned mystery already, haven't you?"

I bent down and picked up the bottle.

"Not quite. I may need another day or two."

"And here I am," she went on, oblivious and slurring through her crooked smile, "Sylvia Linsky, the bereaved client whose daddy took a dive into the San Francisco Bay."

She laughed, without the least bit of humor.

"Sounds like quite a story, doesn't it?" she said, reaching for the vodka. I pulled the bottle away and set it on the side table behind me.

"Sounds like you've had too much to drink."

Sylvia's expression went sour. Childlike.

"Oh, don't tell me I've had too much to drink," she said. "I have plenty to drink about... more than you know."

"That's just the grief talking."

I'm not very good at this sort of thing.

"What do you know about grief?!" Sylvia snapped. "Huh? Did your daddy just die? Did your mommy walk out on you before you could even say your own name? Huh? I didn't think so."

She pointed unsteadily at the bottle, a silent command, and glared at me. *P.I. Rule #17.* I retrieved the bottle and handed it to her.

"Do you know what it's like to be absolutely alone?" she asked, unscrewing the cap. "That's what I am now. Alone. I don't have anybody."

I watched her take a long drink straight from the bottle.

"I'm really sorry, Sylvia."

She cut her drink short, spilling some down her chin.

"Don't," she growled. "Don't you pity me. I don't need you. I don't need anybody. Go away!"

P.I. Rules be damned. I grabbed the bottle out of her hand.

"What you don't need is any more of this," I said, gently. "What you *do* need is some beddy-bye."

I set the bottle down and then scooped her up in my arms. She let out a surprised giggle and threw her arms around my neck.

"Mr. Murphy! I'm surprised at you, taking advantage of a woman who's had too much to drink."

I headed for the guest bedroom. At least she wasn't putting up a fight.

"Not tonight, Sylvia. I require my victims to be sober enough to sign a waiver. You passed that point a long time ago."

She laid her head against my chest and went quiet. I carried her into the bedroom, which was softly lit from moonlight coming through a window, and laid her down on the bed. Her body was warm and loose as I got her situated under the covers. Her eyes were heavy as she sank into the pillow.

"Don't you like me, Tex?" she asked, dreamily.

I pulled the top sheet and comforter up to her shoulders.

"I like you. That's why I'm putting you to bed... and leaving."

Sylvia's eyes closed.

"You're no fun. Not one bit."

I brushed a lock of hair from her face. She looked calm now. Peaceful. I wondered if her parents had ever carried her to bed and tucked her in. I stared down at her for a few moments. So beautiful. So damaged.

"Goodnight, Sylvia."

I stood and headed for the door. Behind me, Sylvia breathed out a whisper.

"I like you too, Tex."

I paused at the door.

"You're not going to like anything in the morning."

14

I, on the other hand, woke up raring to go.

There was still no evidence to support Carl Linsky's death being anything but a suicide, but there were an increasing number of reasons to question it. The most interesting angle was what Sonny Fletcher had told me: Linsky had hired him to track down some people, at least two of whom—Rona Morgan and Val Davis—had also died recently.

I fired up a pot of coffee and my old desktop computer. A quick search revealed that Rona Morgan had died two weeks ago. The cause of death was not specified, but her obituary made it sound like it was sudden and unexpected. She was a 35-year-old woman who had graduated in Engineering from UCLA and worked at Gideon Enterprises before starting her own consulting business several years ago. There was no mention of marriage or children.

Her name turned up in a handful of news articles, with one making a point of saying she was a mutant. This was a relatively new thing, classifying people with genetic mutations as 'mutants'—as opposed to 'normal' people, *aka* 'norms'—and this classification was becoming every bit as divisive as gender or race.

Val Davis had died two days after Morgan, in a speeder crash. She was only 23 and already had a PhD in Computer Science from San Francisco University. After graduating, she'd been hired to do research at USF. Like Rona Morgan, she was unmarried. I could find no reference to her nationality or genetic classification.

There were no obvious connections between the two women, or

between them and Carl Linsky, other than the fact that he'd hired Fletcher to find them. But now all three of them were dead within a two-week period. A suicide, an accident and something else that didn't warrant a police investigation. Move along. Nothing to see here. Coincidence, that's all.

Except the butterflies in my stomach were going crazy.

There was a link between Linsky, Rona Morgan and Val Davis and I had to believe that, whatever the link was, it had led to their untimely deaths. Sonny Fletcher had to have known it too, and it scared him off the wagon and into a Motel 6.

Finding out what the connection was would be the only way to convince anyone else that Linsky's death was more than a simple suicide.

After pouring a third cup of coffee, I took another look at the note Linsky had left for Fletcher. I should have asked the old detective about the 'private room' Linksy referred to in the note. I could pay Fletcher another visit, but I think I'd spooked him and he may have already cleared out. But I might not even need to check.

The word 'room' made me wonder if I should take another look around Linsky's home. I hadn't been looking for a secret room before. And I'd already planned on going back first thing in the morning. I had some questions to ask a sober Sylvia.

* * * * *

I'd gotten an early start and it was still mid-morning when I got to Linsky's home. Not surprisingly, Sylvia was still sleeping off the Grey Goose.

I crept quietly through the house, assessing the layout for any unaccounted space that might hide a secret room. No dice.

There was no basement or cellar, but maybe there was an attic or crawlspace. Now that I was looking for it, I found a large panel in the ceiling at the end of a hallway. There was a small hook on the panel, but it was twelve feet off the floor. Linsky probably had a tool he used to reach it, but if he did, it was nowhere to be found. Luckily, my above-average height and wingspan allowed me to reach it standing on a chair. I pulled down carefully and caught a ladder as it slid out through the opened panel.

I climbed up into Linsky's attic. The dimly-lit space contained an assortment of packing boxes, rolled up rugs and the like. It was fairly spacious but, to my eye, somewhat smaller than the main floor. My heart rate went up a few ticks.

There were cobwebs and thick layers of dust covering the attic's contents, but the floor had been swept recently. Maybe it was to erase footsteps in the dust, but there was really only one place for a hidden room. I crossed to the far wall and took a peek behind an old box spring.

There was a door. Locked.

I slid the box spring aside and fished out Linsky's keys from my pocket. The old, scratched key slid easily into the lock. I turned it and pushed the door open. The room beyond was pitch-black. I felt around until I found a light switch and flipped it.

It was just a tiny office space. Nothing high-tech. A desk, a chair, a large file cabinet, a space heater. But something else in the room grabbed my full attention: most of one wall was covered by a huge bulletin board, and most of the bulletin board was covered with photos, post-it notes and scraps of paper covered with handwritten notes.

My first thought was: *this is a murder board.*

At the top of the bulletin board, written in large block letters, was the word OVERLORD. Below it, in the center of the bulletin board, was a line of eight large squares, each about 6x6 inches, alternating black and white, like a row of a chessboard.

A photo of a woman was pinned over the square on the far left; I recognized her from the photo that had been included with her obituary: it was Rona Morgan. Below her square was the letter 'A' and a drawing of a rook chess piece.

On the square next to Rona Morgan's was a photo of Val Davis. The letter 'B' and a knight were underneath it.

The next three squares had post-it notes on them, all different colors, each with a '?' symbol written on it. Below them, respectively, were the letters C, D and E and a bishop, queen and king.

A photo of Carl Linsky was pinned to the sixth square. Below this square was the letter 'F' and another bishop.

Pinned on the square to the right of Linsky's was a photo of Linsky and a man I didn't recognize. Below it was the letter 'G' and another knight.

The final square had another mystery post-it note above an 'H' and a second rook.

Above his own photo, Linsky had attached what looked like a credit card. It had a logo identical to the one I'd seen on Linsky's laptop—the flaming sword over a mosaic pattern. Taking a closer look, I saw the letter 'F' printed on the card, the same letter written below Linsky's photo.

I stepped back and tried to take it all in. Apparently, Overlord, whoever—or *what*ever—that might be, was the connection between Linsky, Morgan and Davis. And there were five other people involved—the mystery man in the photo with Linsky and four others, as yet unidentified.

After I'd examined everything on the bulletin board, I took a seat at the desk. Six file folders were laid out; four of them had different-colored post-it notes stuck on the front. I glanced back at the bulletin board. Unless I missed my guess, these four folders corresponded to the four unidentified people on the bulletin board.

I flipped through the folders, starting with the color-coded ones. Each contained a long list of names, some crossed out, others highlighted and cross-referenced to additional materials contained within the folders.

In the two folders without post-it notes, there were lists of names, but most all of them had been crossed out. 'Val Davis' was one of the remaining names in the first file; 'Rona Morgan' was in the second.

It was a lot to process. But it seemed clear that Linsky was trying to identify a single person from the lists in each file. He'd narrowed it down to a few and then given the remaining names to Sonny Fletcher to track down. That's how Fletcher had found out about Davis and Morgan.

Based on the layout of the bulletin board, Linsky had reason to believe there were eight people involved with this Overlord. He was one, he'd identified two others, Davis and Morgan, and he obviously knew a fourth person personally—the one in the photo with Linksy. If I could find the mystery man—and he was still alive—maybe he could tell me who or what Overlord was and, more importantly for my case, why people connected to it were dying. I pulled the photo of Linsky and the mystery man off the bulletin board and put it on the pile of files.

I then turned my attention to the desk drawers. In the very first one I opened, I found what looked like an external hard drive. As with Linsky's laptop and the 'F' card he'd attached to the bulletin board, it had the flaming sword logo on it. My heart skipped a beat. Maybe this was the external device required to access Linsky's laptop.

Which I had brought with me, in hopes that something like this would turn up.

I retrieved the laptop bag, pulled out the laptop, plugged the device into one of its USB ports and then booted it up. Sure enough, instead of the 'External Device Required' message, another dialog appeared: *Insert Passcard.*

There was only one thing I'd seen that might fit the bill.

Excited, I jumped up and grabbed the 'F' card Linsky had attached above his photo, then sat back down and took a closer look at the external device. There was a slot on the side, which the card slid right into.

My excitement was short-lived. A login dialog appeared with 'linsky@stg.net' in the user name field and a blank password field.

This was one of the many things that made me despise modern technology. All the damn passwords. I could never remember mine and I wasn't alone. At the D.D.A., it was a running joke that the best way to hack the average person's computer was to look around for a post-it note with the login info written on it. I started to search for just such a post-it note.

Apparently, Linsky was a little more careful than the average person. I went through everything. No luck.

Then it hit me.

Fletcher's 'bees hop'. Linsky had given it to him, in case anything happened.

I sat back at the desk, took a deep breath, then typed in BISHOP and hit enter.

The screen flickered, then another message appeared: *Access Denied – Account Expired.*

Well, shit.

I'd gotten the password right, but whatever 'Account Expired' meant, it didn't seem like I'd be getting anything from Linsky's laptop. I turned it off, then stowed it, along with the reader and the passcard, in the bag.

Back to my search of the desk. In another drawer, I found a stash of meds. There was Human Growth Hormone, several different steroids and even some of those little blue pills. For someone who'd committed suicide, Linsky sure seemed obsessed with defying age and living long and hard.

There was also a blister pack of Fentanyl buccal tablets. The word 'opioid' was on the label, so this was some kind of heavy-duty painkiller. It had been prescribed by a Dr. Klaus about a month ago. I wondered if that was when Linsky had his cosmetic surgery.

One last prescription bottle contained Triazolam, apparently a sleeping pill. This was also prescribed by Dr. Klaus, but just ten days earlier.

There was nothing else of interest in the desk drawers, but there was an old-fashioned phone—a landline—on the desk. It had speed dial numbers. Maybe I could find out who Linsky made frequent calls to.

First though, I picked up the phone and pressed REDIAL. I figured it might go to Sonny Fletcher's office—or maybe the Motel 6—but it was worth a try. After several rings, it picked up and an automated voice said: "If you know the extension of the person you're trying to reach, please enter it now. Or, press 1 to leave a message."

I started looking around the desk, searching for a number Linsky might have written down. There was nothing. The only place I hadn't looked was under the phone. I picked it up and saw the back of a notepad. I flipped it over and saw 'x107' written down.

I quickly punched in the three numbers. The automated voice said: "Please hold."

A moment later, I heard a woman's voice: "You've reached Wanda Peck. I'm unable to take your call, but please leave your name, number and a message, and I'll return your call."

There was a beep. I paused, not sure what I should say, if anything at all. I had no idea who this Wanda Peck was, who she worked for, or what part she might play in the case. On the other hand, the only way to find out would be to talk to her.

But what should I say that would get her to call me back? Not knowing her connection to Linsky made it tricky. I didn't want to scare her off, so maybe I shouldn't mention that I was a P.I. Or that I'd been hired to look into Linsky's suicide. Or that this was turning into a murder investigation. Maybe keeping it vague and intriguing would pique her interest.

"Yeah, hi, Wanda? A friend gave me this number and said I should call. It's pretty important, so I'd rather not leave a message. Please call me when you can."

I wasn't sure when I'd be back at my office, so I gave her my name and Sylvia's cell number, as well as my office number.

After I hung up, I tried the speed dial buttons and was disappointed to find out he hadn't set up any of them.

I put Linsky's files and the photo of him with the mystery man into the laptop bag. As I was leaving, I automatically did what I always do when I leave my office—I pushed the chair into the desk. But it didn't go in all the way. Something under the desk was blocking it.

Curious, I pulled the chair out and took a look. There, where Linsky would put his feet if he were seated at the desk, was a small fire safe. I grabbed it and set it on the desk. It was locked, but didn't require a combination…just a key. And I happened to have one.

Linsky's small key unlocked it. Inside was a passport, a social security card, a banded bundle of one hundred-dollar bills and a few documents, including a vehicle title, a property deed…and a life insurance policy.

I read through the policy. Sylvia Linsky was the sole beneficiary. And the payout was a million dollars. Tax-free.

I thought back to Linsky's suicide note. He'd said 'Forgive me, Sylvia.' It struck me that maybe he wasn't asking her to forgive him for leaving her without a father; maybe it was because the only money he was leaving her was his life insurance, and committing suicide would nullify it.

Either way, I could understand why Sylvia felt like she was getting a raw deal.

There were a hundred C-notes in the bundle. Ten thousand dollars. Linsky had probably left it to cover Sonny Fletcher's expenses. It wouldn't take a whole lot of rationalizing to justify taking it. Fletcher was off the case and, in effect, I was taking over the investigation. Plus, Sylvia had said right up front that she didn't have money to cover my expenses and, I now knew, she never would…unless the life insurance paid off. This cash would guarantee that I'd get what I was owed.

After some internal debate, I decided to take a thousand dollars—for expenses—and leave the rest in the fire safe. I could get to it in an emergency. In the unlikely event Sylvia ended up with the million dollars, this could be my cut. And if things didn't work out, we could split it. That would cover me and at least be something for Sylvia.

Everything went back into the fire safe. For now, this would be my little secret.

15

'Twas almost eleven and all through the townhouse, not a creature was stirring. Time to make coffee.

I had Carl Linsky pegged as an herbal tea kind of guy, and herbal tea is basically a hot, watery veggie smoothie, as far as I'm concerned. I was right; he had a ton of tea, but also a bag of whole coffee beans in the refrigerator—fair trade and organic, of course—with a grinder and a French Press stashed in a cupboard.

It's a well-known fact that the three best things to wake up to are frying bacon, a warm body and fresh-ground coffee. For just a moment, I imagined how nice it would be to wake Sylvia up with all three, before figuratively slapping myself repeatedly.

The smell of roasty-toasty caffeinated goodness worked its magic. The coffee had just finished brewing when Sylvia emerged from the guest room. Even fresh out of bed, disheveled and sleepy in a fluffy pink robe—and undoubtedly hung over as hell—she was devastatingly beautiful.

"Hi," she said, averting her eyes self-consciously.

"How you feeling?" I asked.

"I'll let you know when I wake up. Probably not great."

She got herself a cup of coffee and held it up to her face with both hands. After a brief steam facial, she took a sip.

"Thank you," she said.

"I hope black is OK. There's no cream or sugar."

"It's fine. I meant thanks for last night. I'm sorry about yesterday."

I poured myself a cup.

"No need to apologize. This is a hard thing to go through."

"And you're the one person who's helping me get through it," Sylvia said, softly. "The last person I should be freaking out on."

I moved closer and topped off her mug. She smelled good. Her hair was perfectly tousled and she'd put on just a touch of makeup. I couldn't help but feel flattered, though maybe I was just flattering myself and it had nothing to do with me. Women like Sylvia Linsky have that effect.

"So, I've made some progress on your case," I said, moving back to a safe distance.

Sylvia perked up. "Really?" A tone of genuine surprise.

"Really. Did you know your father had hired a P.I.?"

Sylvia's face did a few things at once. After a few moments, she said: "No. Well, yes, later. After. I found his name and number here. I didn't know he was a detective until I called. But he didn't answer or call back. I haven't talked to him, so I didn't know my dad hired him."

"But that's how you ended up at my office, right? You came looking for Sonny Fletcher and he wasn't there?"

She nodded.

"Well, you could have saved me some time," I said. "Fortunately, I found out about Fletcher on my own and tracked him down. And through him, I learned that your father was working with some other people, two of whom have died in the past couple weeks."

Sylvia's face went blank and she shook her head, confused.

"What?"

"They weren't suicides," I said. "Or homicides. At least not officially. But the timing is a little suspicious."

"So, you think—?"

"—I don't know what to think. Not yet. I need to find one of the other people your father was looking for. Alive, ideally. Do you have any idea what he was working on?"

"No."

"Have you heard of Rona Morgan or Val Davis?"

"No."

"Does the word Overlord mean anything to you?"

She shook her head. I hadn't expected her to have information about her father's apparently top-secret activities, but I had to ask. She had a lousy poker face, so this assured me that she was completely out of the loop.

But there was one thing she might be able to help with. I opened the laptop bag and took out the photo of Linsky and the mystery man I'd taken from the bulletin board.

"Do you recognize this man?"

Sylvia took the photo and kind of flinched when she looked at it. Maybe it was seeing her father, or maybe it was the other man. Hard to say.

"Yeah," she said. "His name is John Klaus."

Klaus.

The name of the doctor who had prescribed pain meds and sleeping pills for Linsky.

Sylvia handed the photo back, like she wanted it away from her.

"Did they work together?" I asked.

"I'm not sure. I mean, they were both surgeons, but I don't think they worked together. They were old friends."

"So you know Klaus pretty well?"

Sylvia turned away and refilled her mug.

"No, not well."

If we'd been playing an actual game of poker, I would have bet my entire stack that she was bluffing. Clearly, she knew Klaus pretty well. And didn't want to talk about it. But I needed information on him and it seemed like Sylvia had some.

I was about to approach the subject like a Fugu cook approaching a blowfish—with extreme caution—when I heard a melodic beep coming from the guest bedroom. It was a phone ringing. Sylvia's cell, most likely. I looked at her, but she made no move to go answer it.

Something clicked in my brain and I remembered giving Sylvia's number to Wanda Peck. With no time to explain, I rushed to the bedroom. Sylvia's phone was charging on the nightstand. Sure enough, the caller ID was the same number displayed on Linsky's attic phone when I'd hit redial.

I unplugged the cell, hit the green button and said: "This is Murphy."

"We need to talk," a woman's voice said. "In person."

I turned around. Sylvia stood in the doorway, staring like she'd caught me trying on her panties.

"I'm free when you are," I said.

"The sooner, the better," the woman replied. Then she gave me an address with special instructions and hung up.

16

The special instructions Wanda Peck had provided made me feel like a backdoor man. Mostly because she said: "Don't come through the front."

I figured she'd tell me why when I got there. For now, I was just eager to meet her. Being the last person Carl Linsky called made her a person of interest.

Seeing her face-to-face made her a person of even more interest.

In the space of twenty-four hours, I'd met two of the most attractive women I'd ever seen with my own eyeballs. But while Sylvia was a barely-contained wildfire, Wanda Peck was a frozen waterfall—remote, serene and intensely composed.

The address had led me to a nondescript building, a generic office complex with no obvious signage. Ms. Peck met me at a side door and got right to it.

"Are you the Poisoned Pawn?"

She was using one of my tactics: hit them with a point-blank question and watch the reaction. I wasn't sure exactly what she'd said, so my reaction was a blank stare. It was probably enough of an answer, but my response sealed the deal.

"Sorry. Did you say *poison pond*?"

She ignored the question and switched gears.

"Who gave you my name and number?"

"No one," I said. "I called you from a phone belonging to a man named Carl Linsky. You were the last person he called from that phone before he jumped off the Golden Gate Bridge."

I hoped this would get a reaction out of her. I wasn't really surprised when it didn't.

"At least we're getting off on the right foot," she said. "I recognized the number you called from. If you'd lied about it, this conversation would be over."

I was glad we were getting off on the right foot. I liked her foot. And her legs. All of it. I hoped we'd end up working closely together.

She stepped back and ushered me inside.

"Why the side door?" I asked.

"Less visible. There are people monitoring who comes and goes here. Depending on what your situation is, you may not want these people to know you came here."

I doubted anyone would care about me showing up, but whatever.

Wanda led me to a bank of elevators. She was tall and slender with perfect posture, almost regal, her height accentuated by a perfectly-tailored dress and heels. She had a whole lot of wavy, golden hair worn up in an elaborate style, showing off a lovely neck.

"What do you know about Capricorn?" she asked, as we waited for the elevator.

"Not much. I'm a Pisces myself. Pisces are passionate and intuitive, but can be overly trusting."

She rolled her eyes. It wouldn't be the last time. The elevator dinged and opened. We stepped inside and Wanda pressed the button for the eighth floor.

"What's your connection to Linsky?" she asked.

"What's yours?"

Wanda crossed her arms and leaned back against the wall.

"Do you even know where you are?" she asked, a bit condescendingly.

"Literally? Or metaphysically?"

"This building. This organization. Do you know what it is we do?"

"Nope. That's why I'm here."

Which was true. I had no clue who Wanda Peck was. For all I knew, she was one of the people Linsky was trying find. Or maybe she was the Overlord. Seemed like she'd make a good one. Or, it suddenly occurred to me, maybe she was the reason Rona Morgan and Val Davis were dead. Maybe she invited me here to find out what I knew before killing me off in some unsuspicious way. By breaking my heart, probably.

"Tell you what," I offered. "I'll go first. I'm a private investigator.

Linsky's daughter hired me because she says her father wasn't suicidal and wants me to prove it. Mostly, I suspect, so she can collect his life insurance. Everything points to it being a straight-up suicide and the cops have closed the case. But, frankly, I think there's more to it than meets the eye."

The elevator stopped. Wanda stepped out and turned right without a word. I followed her to a nicely furnished office—sleek, modern and high-tech—where she gestured to a chair and closed the door behind me.

"A lot of people come to us because the police can't—or won't—help them," she said, as I took a seat.

"So, what is it you do?"

"CAPRICORN is a civilian agency focused on fighting discrimination. We started out twenty years ago during the rise of the Alt-White. Then it was the Muslim Purge. And now we've got this second generation of Mutants. There's always someone to hate and a lot of people eager to hate them. So, we infiltrate organizations, try to expose and destabilize them, occasionally bring legal action or get legislation passed. We're privately funded, meaning we have no real authority, but we have significant resources, so we fight the good fight."

"Well, I support everything you just said. But what does it have to do with Linsky?"

Wanda moved to the front of her desk and leaned back against it.

"Full disclosure," she said, "I'd never heard Carl Linsky's name until you just mentioned it. I got a call from his number—the one you called from—but never talked to him. He just left a message."

"Which said…?"

"Among other things, that we should look into the deaths of two women."

"Rona Morgan and Val Davis, I assume. Did he say why?"

Wanda shook her head. "No. But he was certain they'd been murdered and the police wouldn't investigate."

"Did you call him back?"

"Several times, but he never answered. Now I know why. Do you have more details on what he was talking about?"

"Some. I think Linsky and the two women may have been working on something, but separate from each other. There was a fourth person who Linsky knew personally, and four others he was trying to identify."

I pulled the photo of Linsky and Klaus from the laptop bag.

"This is the fourth guy. I'm trying to find him. His name is John

Klaus."

Wanda sat up.

"Klaus? John Klaus was working with Linsky?"

I handed her the photo. She examined it closely, then set it aside.

"Do you mind if I hold onto this for a bit?" she asked.

"Not at all. Now that I've got a name, I don't need the photo. What I need is to find Klaus and it sounds like you might be able to help. I'm just hoping he's not already dead like the others."

Wanda drummed her fingers thoughtfully on the edge of the desk.

"That might explain it. Klaus hasn't been seen for a while. We hadn't considered the possibility of him being dead. If he is, it hasn't been reported. Maybe he's hiding out."

Just like Sonny Fletcher, I thought.

"So, who is John Klaus?" I asked.

"He's a big player behind the scenes in the Law & Order Party. He's been on our radar for a while."

I didn't follow the news—especially anything to do with politics—but I'd heard of the Law & Order Party. You couldn't avoid it. From the little I knew, it sounded like Law & Order was everything bad about politics…on steroids. I wasn't sure how Linsky's death would have anything to do with politics, but I was open to all possibilities at this point.

"I'm guessing you and your organization aren't big Law & Order supporters," I said.

Wanda smirked, regally.

"They're fascists. Their leadership is white, rich and ultra-conservative. They're openly anti-Mutant. Some party members have publicly stated that Mutants are subhuman and should be sterilized, if not actually euthanized, to save the gene pool."

If anyone else had said this, I probably wouldn't have believed it, but Wanda didn't strike me as someone who exaggerated. If it was true, it was scary as hell. And, apparently, common knowledge. I probably should have been aware of it, but I really did have zero interest in politics. I'd heard a quote that summed up my attitude perfectly, that politicians were like diapers—they should be changed often and for the same reason. Maybe it was the system that inevitably corrupted them, or maybe you had to be a narcissist or sociopath to want a career in politics. For me, it didn't matter who was in office. It would always be the same.

"Do you have anything other than this photo?" Wanda asked.

I dug into the bag for Linsky's laptop and handed it to her.

"There's this. I think Linsky was using it to work remotely on whatever his secret project was."

"That's the Gideon logo," Wanda said, referring to the flaming sword embossed on the laptop. She seemed surprised. Maybe a little shocked. "Where'd you get this?"

"It was in Linsky's office at the North Hill Clinic. I think he left it there for me to find."

Wanda gave me a skeptical look.

"I thought his daughter hired you *after* he died."

"Yeah, well, he left it for someone *like me* to find."

"Have you seen what's on it?" she asked, opening the lid.

"I tried. There's a reader you have to attach and a passcard, both of which are in the bag, but it said the account had expired. Do you think you could get past that and see what's on the hard drive?"

"Maybe," she said, setting it off to the side. "If you want to leave it with me, I'll see what we can do."

"Sure. I just need you to do me a favor. I, uh, kind of stole it. If you could call Dr. Sternwood at the North Hill Clinic and let him know it's in the hands of the authorities, I'd really appreciate it."

With just a hint of a smile, Wanda nodded.

"Anything else?" she asked.

I took a second to think. There had to be something. I was enjoying our visit.

"Oh yeah," I said, "the thing Linsky and the two women were working on was for someone or something called Overlord."

"*Overlord*," she repeated, thoughtfully, then glanced at the laptop. "I wonder how that fits with Gideon."

She looked back at me.

"You've heard of Gideon Enterprises, I assume."

"They do security, but that's pretty much all I know about it," I said.

"It's the largest, most powerful corporation that most people know almost nothing about. They contract with everyone from governments to drug lords—anyone with huge assets and sensitive information to protect. Our own government is their biggest client, which means Gideon operates with little to no outside oversight."

So, Gideon Enterprises was one of the biggest black-ops groups on the planet. If Linsky and the others were working for them, maybe the corporation was behind the deaths, like some pirate captain killing off the scabs who'd buried his treasure. Or maybe it was a competitor of Gideon's. Or someone else trying to cover things up.

One thing was certain: I was on this case for just one reason—to prove Carl Linsky hadn't committed suicide—and if a big, powerful group like Gideon Enterprises was responsible for his death, I didn't stand a realistic chance of proving it.

I looked up and saw Wanda staring down at me with an expression that was somewhere between sympathy and pity. It was like she was reading my mind.

"You're going to need some help."

17

Wanda Peck had an excellent poker face and kept her cards close to her chest. If we ever played strip poker together—and I sincerely hoped that someday we would—I'd have to come to the table layered up. I was pretty sure I'd be *au naturel* before she had her socks off.

The rest of our meeting provided no more answers. She said she didn't know what or who Overlord was, but I couldn't tell if she was holding out on me. If she had any other info on Rona Morgan and Val Davis, she didn't share it, though she seemed inclined to agree that their deaths—and Linsky's suicide—were suspicious.

I decided to give her the laptop bag and everything in it. I didn't have the resources to extract info from Linsky's laptop or vet the lists of names I'd found in Linsky's attic. The people he was trying to identify were very likely in those lists, but I'd be racing against some faceless enemy who would almost certainly zero in on them before I did.

The only race I had any chance to win was the John Klaus Derby. No one else had been in Linsky's attic and Sonny Fletcher hadn't mentioned Klaus's name. Finding him before someone else did—and alive—might be the only way to keep this case going.

Unfortunately, Wanda had said he'd disappeared, either Jimmy Hoffa-style or into hiding. Whichever it was, she didn't think he'd be easy to find. Maybe impossible. She was right that I would need some help and she seemed capable of being extremely helpful...if she felt like it. Giving her all the evidence I'd found was a gesture of trust and good faith. She reciprocated by giving me her private number.

"Does this mean what I think it means?" I asked.

"Probably not," she said.

* * * * *

I hadn't eaten solid food in a day and a half, so I made a quick, ill-advised stop at Weenie World and ordered an off-menu abomination called the 'Three Dog Bite'—known colloquially as the 'Three Dog Night Sweats'—an unholy trinity of jalapeno and cheese-filled polish dogs, wrapped in bacon and deep-fried, served on a bed of Loaded Tater Tots and drizzled with their secret Woof Sauce.

Back at my office, I gave Sylvia a call on my untraceable old vidphone. After our chat that morning, I was sure she was holding something back about Klaus. I doubted it was a list of his favorite hiding places, but you never know. She didn't answer, so I left a message asking her to call me back.

For now, I'd need to do some digging on my own. I fired up the computer and dug into my deliciously toxic lunch.

Online information about John Klaus was scarce. His name came up with a surgical practice called the Bel Viso Center, where he was a surgeon on staff. Bel Viso was ultra-exclusive and didn't provide a physical address or phone number—only a website for online consultations. I could probably figure out a way to get in, but it would be a lot of effort and probably a waste of time. I doubted he was hiding out in his office.

There was no reference to Klaus's home address or other contact info, not even if he was married or had children. No criminal record. No social media presence.

With nowhere else to go, I followed a link to the official Law & Order Party website, hoping to find something about him there. After a thorough search, I found nothing on Klaus, but learned more about Law & Order than I ever wanted to.

Their name said it all. They advocated recriminalizing all drugs (and hinted at a new prohibition of alcohol), clearing out the homeless (with no details of how they planned to do this or what they'd do with them), banning online porn (by policing internet usage) and creating a task force to root out and deport all illegal immigrants and 'other undesirables'. While not explicitly stated, undesirables included Mutants, LGBTQs, welfare recipients and the disabled.

Sounded like a police state to me.

And yet, unbelievably, there was no shortage of avid support. A whole lot of average Joes, and even a few reputable public figures, were ready to goosestep through the streets under L&O banners. The next presidential election was three years away and, despite being a third party, the polls had Law & Order at a fifty-two percent approval rating, higher than either of the two major parties. With some state and local elections coming up next year, it was looking like the Law & Order Party might get a foothold across the country.

One office up for grabs in 2038—less than a year out—was the Governorship of California. L&O's candidate was a poster boy named Robert Knott. He was following in the proud tradition of former actors-turned-politicians and looked the part, with chiseled features, sun-weathered face, steely blue eyes and roguishly wavy blonde hair.

Some faces you just want to punch. Robert Knott had one of those.

After an hour of swimming in the Law & Order cesspool, I'd had all I could take. It was literally making me sick to my stomach. And the Three Dog Night Sweats wasn't helping.

Worst of all, I was no closer to knowing where to look for John Klaus. With nothing more constructive to do, I poured myself a couple fingers of Pepto and switched my search to Gideon Enterprises.

According to its Wikipedia page, the company had been founded by an Englishman named J. Saint Gideon, who read like a character straight out of a James Bond movie. His background was in 'British Intelligence' and he had helped develop the world's largest surveillance network. He'd nearly died and was left crippled from a 2013 terrorist attack.

A few years later, he founded Gideon Enterprises, which started out providing traditional online security—firewalls, encryption, cyber-terrorism prevention, etc.—and eventually became the world's most sought-after provider of security systems. Over the past decade, the organization had expanded into newer technologies. Apparently, Gideon Enterprises was now overseeing global networks for satellites and drones.

Gideon was still president of the company, but a CEO named Frank Schimming was now the acting head, leaving Gideon to pursue other interests, including chess—he was a Grandmaster—and philanthropy. The company had made him a trillionaire and he gave away a lot of it, primarily to a variety of educational institutions and human rights organizations. There was no mention of any personal relationships.

I thought back to the name I'd seen on Linsky's bulletin board: *Overlord.* It seemed like a perfect word to describe both Gideon Enterprises and its founder, who also happened to be a world-class chess player. But there was nothing in the company bio related to medical technologies. What kind of security project would require the input of doctors or surgeons like Linsky and Klaus?

I typed in 'Gideon Enterprises & Overlord' and got a few hits that linked to blogs and forum discussions with lots of misspelled words and exclamation points. The general consensus was that Gideon Enterprises was 'Big Brother' and the word 'Overlord' appeared only in that context. I poked around for a while, but found no references to Overlord being a specific project or person.

There was no shortage of conspiracy theories, however. One article claimed that Gideon Enterprises was a secret partner in the most recent nuclear treaty between the U.S. and Russia. The theory was that Gideon already provided the security for the U.S. weapons systems and, in exchange for Russia's compliance and cooperation, they would upgrade the antiquated Soviet infrastructure. As part of the deal, the two superpowers supposedly agreed that, should a situation arise, they would join forces against any other country with nuclear capabilities and Gideon would broker the alliance. In the poker game of Armageddon Hold 'Em, Gideon Enterprises was in the dealer position.

A search of 'Gideon Enterprises & Carl Linsky' turned up nothing. 'Gideon Enterprises & John Klaus' brought up a handful of entries, but nothing that directly connected the two, only through references to the Law & Order Party.

Searching 'Gideon Enterprises & Law & Order Party', on the other hand, turned up hundreds of pages of links. It was a widespread assumption that the two organizations were in bed together and about to screw the hell out of California, then the U.S., then the world.

As I was reading, my vidphone beeped. I checked the caller I.D., expecting it to be Sylvia returning my call, but it wasn't. It was a private number. Probably a telemarketer, but with only one case on my docket and the investigation stalled, I was taking all calls.

I answered and a man's face appeared onscreen. We'd never met, but I immediately recognized him. And it sent a chill through me.

It was J. Saint Gideon.

18

I stared at the screen, probably a little glassy-eyed and slack-jawed. I'd just been reading about this genius secret agent trillionaire and how his corporation might be planning to forcibly fornicate with the planet; now he was on my crappy little vidphone screen.

Gideon introduced himself in a crisp, slightly nasal English accent and asked if I would like to come visit him. I was too stunned to form a coherent sentence, but managed to get out a "Yeah".

He flashed a wide smile, said "Excellent", and gave me an address.

"Are you free this afternoon?" he asked.

"Yeah."

"Then I will see you shortly," he replied. "Shall we say six o'clock?"

"Yeah."

He nodded and then ended the call. I hoped I'd made a good first impression.

* * * * *

The address Gideon gave me was in Bolinas, an unincorporated community about fifteen miles northwest of the city. It was nestled on the shores of Bolinas Bay, surrounded by the Point Reyes National Seashore preserve, making it was one of the most exclusive areas around. Its residents were famously reclusive.

As I made the short flight, I felt a strange mix of excitement and paranoia. I had to admit, I was a bit star-struck. The most famous person

I'd met was Justin Bieber and he hadn't really impressed me, to be honest. But the best part of meeting Gideon had nothing to do with his celebrity; it felt like I'd hit the investigative lottery. There was no guarantee that he could—or would—provide information about Carl Linsky or John Klaus or Overlord, but at least I'd have a chance to ask.

At the same time, in the back of my mind, I had alarms going off. How did Gideon know about me? Why did he want to see me? It seemed likely that Linsky, Morgan and Davis had all been working for or with his company...and were now dead. What exactly was I getting myself into?

Gideon's home was palatial, exactly the kind of residence you'd expect a trillionaire to live in. The entire estate seemed to shimmer, like a mirage coming off hot pavement, except this was no mirage. It had to be doming security—a brand-new bit of technology I'd never seen, only heard of. As I approached, the ripple effect vanished and the grounds came into sharp focus. Apparently, it was now safe for me to land.

I spotted flashing lights on a flat rooftop and steered toward them. I landed my Lotus and climbed out. No one was waiting for me. There were two doors on opposite sides of the landing area. I looked back and forth between the two, waiting for someone to show up.

Then I heard Gideon's voice. It was coming from a tiny drone hovering nearby.

"Welcome, Mr. Murphy. I apologize for the impolite reception."

Out of the corner of my eye, I saw one of the doors open.

"If you would, please enter through the open door and take the lift to the mezzanine."

The drone escorted me through the door and to the elevator inside. The panel in the elevator had four buttons. I pressed the one marked 'M'.

Gideon was waiting when the elevator doors opened and I was surprised to see him in a wheelchair. Then I remembered reading about how he was almost killed in a bombing years ago, and that it had left him crippled. Still, robotic exoskeletons had made wheelchairs obsolete...at least for those who could afford it. And Gideon could afford it.

Not only was he using a wheelchair, it wasn't even motorized. It was an antique, the seat made of wicker, with worn-out holes in several spots, and he had to push the two large wheels to move it. I wondered why he didn't have something state-of-the art, maybe even a hover chair.

He looked up at me brightly and extended his hand.

"Pleasure to meet you, Mr. Murphy."

He was a handsome man, probably in his early sixties, well-preserved. His sandy hair was combed back like a classic Hollywood film star. Gary Cooper came to mind. His hair matched his outfit—a silk robe with a cravat and leather slippers.

"Likewise, Mr. Gideon."

We shook hands and then he spun effortlessly and rolled himself away. I followed him into the mezzanine, which was large and lofty and lavishly decorated. Stained glass windows cast colors across the walls and floor. It was a very impressive space, which contrasted sharply with the small man wheeling himself into the midst of it.

"Cozy little flat you've got here," I said.

"You must find it ostentatious," Gideon replied without looking back. "I admit I do as well. It's certainly too much home for only one person."

One person?

"You don't live here alone, do you?"

He rolled his wheelchair next to a small, antique couch and then spun around to face me.

"I'm afraid so. I suppose my disability has given me an aversion to reliance on others. My fortune has provided me with a fully-automated, self-sufficient existence. I want for nothing. Except, perhaps, human companionship."

"Don't you worry, being here alone? I mean, given your condition?"

As I asked the question, I realized how condescending it sounded. But Gideon chuckled and shook his head.

"Gideon Enterprises defines state-of-the-art, with regard to security systems. I am surrounded—perhaps imprisoned—by the very finest electronic moat. No, I don't worry about my safety, though I thank you for your concern."

He gestured to the couch and I sat down.

"Now, to what do I owe this welcome visit?" he asked.

"You invited *me*, Mr. Gideon."

"True, but my understanding is that *you* are the one with questions."

I wanted to find out how I'd gotten on his radar, but we'd get to that. Before he got too comfortable, I intended to assess his poker face.

"Tell me about Overlord," I said.

He raised one eyebrow, ever so slightly.

"Overlord," he repeated slowly. "An unpleasant word. It evokes images of slavery, at least to my mind."

The eyebrow settled back into place.

"Conversely," he continued, "Overlord was the code name of the Allied offensive on D-Day. Which, of course, led to the liberation of Europe. To which context are you referring?"

"Neither, actually. I think it has something to do with a project being funded by your company."

"Oh, no. Gideon Enterprises is no longer mine, I'm afraid."

Gideon took a deep breath and slowly exhaled.

"I'm sure that Frank Schimming would be a better source of information than I."

"Schimming's the CEO, right?"

Gideon smiled grimly.

"Yes, thanks to my exploitable lack of business acumen. My complete trust in him was repaid with his usurping my position as head of Gideon Enterprises."

"But you're still president."

"Yes, yes. But I have no more real authority to run my company than the King of England has to run his country. I'm merely a figurehead, nothing more."

"Why don't you just sack him, as you English say?"

Gideon smiled again.

"Even if I could, what would be the point? My time has passed. I'm as outdated as this antique," he said, patting the armrests of his wheelchair. "Such is the cutthroat nature of business. Though I dare say the world itself has become nothing more than a business, run by a select few."

"I'm not sure I agree, Mr. Gideon. I think there are a lot of people out there who care less about money than making the world a better place."

"Oh? And you, my fine friend?" He leaned forward and tapped me on the knee. "How do you intend to make the world a better place?"

"I don't know. Keep an open mind, respect others, buy Girl Scout cookies."

His eyebrow went up again.

"You think this will make a difference?"

"If enough people care, it just might catch on."

Gideon gave me a look, like I was a kid telling him about the Red Ryder BB Gun I hoped Santa would bring me.

"Ah, yes. I was like you at one time. Idealism costs nothing and I lived on it for many years. But its taste is bittersweet. It's in large part the reason why I can no longer walk."

He gripped his shriveled legs, stared down at them, then glanced back up at me.

"You'd like to hear what happened, wouldn't you?"

That wasn't why I was here…but I kind of did.

"I don't want to make you feel uncomfortable."

Gideon lifted his hands from his legs and slid them along his armrests.

"Oh, I've been in this damned cage for more years than I care to remember."

Grabbing both wheels, he turned away and pushed himself across the room.

"I've had to grow accustomed to it," he said, as he pulled up to an ornately-carved armoire. I watched as he opened it, revealing a row of decanters and several sets of glasses. He spoke as he poured what looked like liquid gold into two of the glasses.

"It was 2013. I was in Geneva to attend a covert meeting of UN operatives. There were fourteen of us. And at least one was a traitor armed with an explosive device. I was the only survivor."

The full glasses went onto a tray, which he placed on his lap.

"Did you ever find out who it was?" I asked.

"No."

Gideon turned and wheeled himself slowly back toward me.

"It could have been any of a score of countries or organizations," he added.

This didn't seem like the time to tell him I didn't drink, so I took the glass he offered me.

"I don't suppose it matters anymore," he said, picking up his glass. "It was the beginning of the end. There are no heroes anymore, only villains of varying degrees."

"There are some people still fighting the good fight," I said. "What about CAPRICORN?"

Gideon waved his free hand.

"Oh, CAPRICORN does their best, but they're merely fighting the good fight. No, greed and corruption have the upper hand."

He paused to take a sip, then took another deep breath.

"When I was younger, I sincerely believed we could achieve a semblance of global order and harmony. But that was only the foolish dream of a...youthful idealist."

He smiled sadly.

"Once I was crippled, I was no longer of use. I was turned loose into the world, a cruel and deadly steeplechase where survival was a matter of social Darwinism. I was—"

He went silent for a few moments, then swallowed hard, his eyes glistening.

"—I was lost. I believed that my handicap had denied me my destiny."

Gideon stared into his glass.

"Years and years passed before I realized that I still had much to offer."

His face suddenly brightened and he looked up.

"With little more than a plan, I laid the foundations of Gideon Enterprises. Among the new mutant population, I found other social misfits whose skills and talents had been overshadowed by their physical abnormalities. Those were difficult times. We were openly ridiculed. Finding investors and financing was an often-humiliating series of rejections. How could someone like myself, a cripple, ever hope to accomplish such a venture?"

His empty hand clenched and he flashed a fierce grin.

"But eventually we *did* succeed, becoming the wealthiest and most powerful corporation of its type in the world. I had recaptured the idealism of my youth, the belief that through sacrifice, commitment and hard work, anything was possible."

Gideon paused and I watched him deflate.

"But then it happened again. In the blink of an eye, all those years of investment and careful nurturing were torn from me by thieves and liars masquerading as board members and stockholders. And now, towering over them all," he said, his voice rising, "is Frank Schimming. His disregard for integrity is matched only by his worship of dividends and profit margins. And, once again I'm unwanted, unneeded and facing a purposeless existence.

"So, you listen to me!" he almost shouted, eyes boring into mine. "If you insist on striding through life, arms laden with hope, you will only meet with one devastating disappointment after another!"

He broke off his stare and raised his glass to take another sip. His hands were trembling. After a moment, he set the glass down and took a couple deep breaths. The anger and frustration drained out of him, replaced by embarrassment.

"Oh, Mr. Murphy. Please forgive me."

"No need to apologize, Mr. Gideon."

Another sad smile.

"It's good of you to indulge me. It's just that I receive so few visitors these days. I suppose this is what happens when one withdraws from the world. Now, please, tell me what I can do for you."

"Well, first," I asked, "why did you call me?"

"We have a mutual friend. She said I might be of assistance to you."

I doubted he was referring to Sylvia and it seemed unlikely that he was friends with Delores Lightbody or Detective Clements. Only one woman knew about the Gideon Enterprises logo on Carl Linsky's laptop.

"So, you know Wanda Peck?"

Gideon smiled.

"I do. We've worked together…in the past. Another idealist, like you, in her own way."

"Do you know a man named Carl Linsky?"

"Only by reputation. Former head of neurology at North Hill Clinic. I read about his suicide in the news feed."

"So, as far as you know, he wasn't working for Gideon Enterprises?"

"Not to my knowledge. Again, Frank Schimming would be the one to ask."

"How about Val Davis or Rona Morgan?"

Gideon nodded.

"Rona Morgan was a dear friend, a brilliant engineer and a key contributor to the success of Gideon Enterprises. She left the company to start her own business and we hadn't spoken in some time, but I was devastated to hear of her death. The other person I don't know."

I was nearly to the end of my list of names and had come up empty. There was only one left.

"I don't suppose you know who John Klaus is, do you?"

Gideon's reaction was immediate and similar to Sylvia's and Wanda's. Like he'd gotten a deep whiff of something rotten.

"Yes. Unfortunately."

"Not a big fan, I take it."

Gideon took a long drink, like he was washing the bad taste out of his mouth, then wiped the corner of his mouth with the back of his hand.

"He and the other members of the Law & Order Party are the worst of the worst. It is they, not the Mutants, who are subhuman. If they come into power, it will be like Nazi Germany all over again. They must be stopped. I will spend every last dollar to fight against them."

Gideon took a breath, calming himself.

"Why are you trying to find Klaus, if I may ask?"

"He and Carl Linsky were friends, apparently. And I think they were working together. Klaus is the only person I know about who may still be alive and have information about what he and Linsky were working on."

Gideon was quiet for a moment, distracted by a thought. Then he said, more to himself than me: "It must be related."

He looked up.

"I suspect there's at least one other person who could help you. And he or she would undoubtedly be a better source than John Klaus. Did Ms. Peck tell you about the letter?"

Whoa, wait. The letter?

Gideon was a charming, interesting guy, but up to this point he hadn't told me anything that would help my case. Maybe he had something to offer after all.

"John Klaus was mentioned in it," he continued. "I believe the other woman was, as well. What was her name? Davis?"

I nodded, my heart rate jumping up a few notches.

"Whoever wrote the letter must have been unaware of my ouster at Gideon Enterprises. He or she wrote to warn me that the Law & Order Party might be attempting to infiltrate my company. From what you've told me, I wonder if the content of the letter might be related somehow to your investigation."

"Do you have the letter?"

"No, I gave it to Ms. Peck."

"I'll definitely follow up with her. Sounds like I need to talk to whoever wrote that letter. But you keep saying 'he or she'. You don't know who wrote it?"

Gideon shook his head.

"No. Whoever it was called themself the Poisoned Pawn."

19

The *Poisoned Pawn.* Wanda Peck had asked me if I was the Poisoned Pawn. Now I knew why.

Gideon told me what he remembered of the letter, but there weren't a lot of specifics and nothing related to Carl Linsky. As for the reference to John Klaus, the Poisoned Pawn suspected that Klaus might be trying to help Law & Order take control of a project being funded by Gideon Enterprises, but not how or why.

If I hadn't had other things to do, I could have spent hours chatting with Gideon. He was charming and interesting, and probably had a few great stories to tell. I got the feeling he was enjoying having some company and it made me sad that he was so obviously lonely. He invited me to stay for dinner, but I politely declined. I was eager to contact Wanda, ask her about the Poisoned Pawn letter and maybe figure out who had sent it and track them down.

I thanked Gideon for his time and saw myself out.

* * * * *

Night had fallen while I was in Gideon's mansion. As I flew my speeder back toward the city, the skyline was sparkling under a waxing red moon. I felt excited and energized. In two days, I'd gone from an unemployed nobody to meeting the trillionaire founder of one of the most powerful corporations in the world. And my investigation had gone from an open-and-shut suicide to a potential conspiracy of epic proportions.

But I had to remind myself that my job was to prove Linsky was murdered. Nothing more. At least now, I had reason to believe it wasn't just Sylvia's wishful thinking.

My working theory was that Linsky and seven other people had collaborated on a project, and it was likely funded by Gideon Enterprises or someone with ties to the company. Assuming that Linsky, Morgan and Davis had all been murdered, it implied that either the project had been completed and they were no longer needed—and were being eliminated to keep the project secret—or, maybe someone was killing them to *prevent* the project from being completed.

At this point, I was reconsidering whether or not I wanted to find John Klaus. He sounded like bad news. Plus, if Law & Order was behind the deaths, the last thing he'd want to do is help me. He might even take exception to me nosing around. Probably best to steer clear.

At least I'd found another lead. The anonymous letter-writer—the Poisoned Pawn—was now the most likely source to help prove that Linsky had been murdered.

* * * * *

It was Saturday night and the area around my office building was a ghost town. There was a bounce in my step as I hustled up to my office. Now that I had Wanda's personal number, I expected I could get in touch with her despite the late hour. Hopefully, the contents of the Poisoned Pawn letter would give me a new lead.

I unlocked my office door and stepped inside. The light was flashing on my vidphone, indicating that I had one or more messages.

As I moved toward the desk, I heard a sound and caught movement out of the corner of my eye. As I turned to look, something smashed into the back of my head. My knees buckled and I crumpled to the floor. My vision blurred…blackness closed in. As I lost consciousness, I heard an indistinct whisper.

The last thing I saw was a hand holding a hypodermic needle.

Part II:

Pawns

20

I'm leaning back in my chair, eyes closed, feeling completely at peace. Reliving the shock of that night thirteen years ago—being attacked, seeing the needle, hearing the whisper—should make me feel afraid or anxious, even angry, but it doesn't.

"Focus now," St. Germain says softly, "only on the whispering voice. What is it saying?"

It's like I'm there, in my old office. I see it clearly in my mind's eye, everything in perfect detail. But the whispering is faint, out of focus.

"Your hearing intensifies," St. Germain murmurs. "Everything slows. Go deeper. Focus."

I don't know how he's doing it, but it's working. Like filtering static. Gradually, two distinct syllables emerge.

Wer-sah…

These syllables come at the end. It's like remembering part of a name; the rest of it is connected, just barely out of reach…

Geh-wer-sah…

The whispered words are like a figure materializing out of the mist, slowly taking form…

Things.

I suddenly hear that word, distinctly and clearly. It's the first word the whispering man says…

Things cuh geh-wer-sah…

My conscious mind is starting to connect all the pieces…

Things could get wer-sah…

...an Australian accent...

Things could get worser.

A wave of panic hits me and I feel myself shooting to the surface like a scuba diver running out of air. St. Germain is still talking, but now my ears are pounding, drowning him out.

I open my eyes and struggle to sit up. I'm groggy, like coming out of a nightmare. I've never been under hypnosis before. Maybe I've come out of it too quickly and I'll end up with a case of the metaphysical bends. But, like emerging from a dream, it all fades away within a few moments.

"What is it?" St. Germain asks with concern.

"Things could get worser," I say. "That's what the voice said."

"And that means something to you?"

"I've only heard someone say that once before. It was when Chelsee and I were abducted."

I shake my head, clearing the cobwebs, and reach for my glass.

"But that took place years after this."

"2043," I say. "Six years later."

"Was it the same man?"

"I don't know," I say, after a drink. "I didn't see this one's face."

"What about the voice? Did it sound the same?"

"This voice sounded deeper. But they both had Australian accents."

"Curious," St. Germain murmurs.

I take another drink, still rattled. Dalton Fiske was the man who'd abducted me and Chelsee, but I never knew he existed before that night. There was, however, another nasty Aussie that I met during the Linsky case—I haven't gotten to that yet—and if he's the one who jumped me, maybe there was a connection between him and Fiske; they'd both used the same odd phrase, which seems beyond coincidence. Maybe Fiske had been working for Gideon Enterprises. Or Law & Order. Or maybe 'things could get worser' was just a weird thing Aussies say.

"Could the man who abducted you and Chelsee be the one?" the Count asks. "The one who tried to kill you tonight?"

"I'm pretty sure he's too dead to be doing anything."

St. Germain mulls this over, then says: "This new revelation could, however, prove a connection between your first case and events that occurred much later."

He watches me finish off my scotch.

"It's fascinating to hear so many names from the past," he says, wistfully. "CAPRICORN, may it rest in peace. The Law & Order Party, may it burn in hell. Robert Knott. Gideon. All key players in the most defining period of this generation. I must admit, I'm surprised to learn that your case drew you into that tangled web. But, then again, perhaps I shouldn't be."

I refill my glass.

"I was just lucky to get out alive," I say. "And I wanted to stay that way, which is one reason I never talked about the case after it ended. Not until that night when I told Chelsee the whole story. Well, most of it."

"You do have your secrets," St. Germain says. "If I'm not mistaken, Robert Knott's mysterious disappearance came shortly after this."

"Yeah. Crazy coincidence."

"I don't suppose you know anything about that." A sly smile.

"I might. But we don't want to get ahead of ourselves," I say, returning the sly smile.

St. Germain nods, thoughtfully.

"I met J. Saint Gideon once, you know, many years ago...before Geneva. I admired him greatly. By all accounts, he was not only brilliant, but a man of impeccable character."

I shrug.

"We're all at least a little peccable. Wasn't it Ming the Merciless who said: 'Absolute power corrupts absolutely'?"

"Ah, yes, Flash Gordon, Episode 1: Planet of Peril," the Count says with a smile. "Actually, it was Lord Acton who said it. Another fascinating man."

St. Germain is lost in a happy thought for a moment, like he's remembering all the good times he and Lord Acton shared back in the 1800's.

"The actual quote is: "Power tends to corrupt, and absolute power corrupts absolutely," the Count says, after he snaps out of his reverie. "He also said: 'Great men are almost always bad men'."

"Well, lord knows that's been my experience."

"J. Saint Gideon included?"

I wave a cautionary finger.

"No spoilers."

"Fair enough."

St. Germain raises his glass of scotch, like he's making a toast.

"Pray, continue."

21

That night in my office was the first time I'd ever been knocked unconscious. Looking back, it wasn't all that bad—probably wouldn't even make my current list of top five cold-cockings. It was quick and precise, meant to put me out, not do any unnecessary damage. Professional, not personal. But at the time it was the most painful, traumatic experience of my life.

Ah, the innocence of youth.

I wasn't out for long–just a few minutes. When I came to, my head was throbbing. I reached back and felt a large lump plumping up at the base of my skull. Trying to stand triggered a shower of sparkles, so I sat back against the desk and took a few moments to assess the situation.

I couldn't fathom who had jumped me, or why. I'd uncovered a few little secrets, but—other than a little petty theft—I wasn't causing any trouble. And who knew I'd even found out anything? The only people I'd confided in were Wanda Peck and J. Saint Gideon and I didn't think either of them had any reason to send someone after me.

As for the motive, they clearly didn't intend to kill me. When I could finally stand up, I checked my pockets. Nothing was missing, including my wallet with the thousand dollars still inside it. This wasn't a robbery, obviously. So, did I just happen to show up while they were searching my office? Or was this a warning that I was getting too nosy? If that was the case, I'd expect to find some sort of message to make sure I didn't miss the point.

The office appeared to be exactly how I'd left it. If whoever jumped me had searched the place, they'd been very tidy. Not that there was anything to find. My file cabinets were empty monuments to optimism, still waiting to be filled with all my amazing future case files. My desk was mostly a place to sit and play Parcheesi. And my computer contained nothing more top-secret than Nana Murphy's 'Don't Ask, Don't Tell' Casserole recipe.

And, fortunately, I'd left all of Carl Linsky's things with Wanda Peck. Of course, they wouldn't know that.

There was no message left behind. No warning to 'Stay off the case…or else!' So this wasn't a threat. Maybe they were just looking for Linsky's laptop.

But then I realized there *was* something missing. When I'd entered the office, the message light had been flashing on the vidphone. Now it wasn't. Whoever was here had played and then erased the message or messages. I had to hope that it hadn't been anything important. I could—and would—call Sylvia and Wanda to see if they'd left the vidmail messages. But first I needed to clean up.

Looking in the washroom mirror, you wouldn't know I'd just had my clock cleaned—eyes slightly unfocused, but that wasn't unusual.

I grabbed a clean sock from my dresser, filled it with ice from my mini-fridge, then returned to the desk. With the makeshift icepack pressed to the back of my head, I started making calls. The first was to Wanda Peck's private number. It went to her vidmail, so I left a message, asking her to call me back.

The second call was to Sylvia's cell. She picked up and flashed her sexy, crooked smile.

"Hello, handsome," she said. "Sorry for all the messages. I was just hoping we could get together this evening. What are you up to?"

I couldn't remember the last time a woman other than my mom was this happy to see me. I felt a little zing in my gut, or thereabouts.

"Just working on your case," I said. "Speaking of which, do you have John Klaus's contact info?"

Sylvia's smile faded.

"There are some things I need to tell you," she said, lowering her voice. "But I'd like to do it in person. When can I see you?"

"It depends. Maybe later tonight. I'll have to get back to you. In the meantime, where are you?"

"At my father's house."

Maybe I was being paranoid—getting cold-cocked can have that effect—but I was suddenly worried about Sylvia. Whoever jumped me had seen the messages she'd left on my vidphone. I had no reason to think they'd go after my client, but I wasn't sure why anyone was doing anything. Best to err on the side of caution. But I didn't want to freak her out either.

"Maybe you should get out of the house tonight," I said.

Sylvia gave me a confused, amused look.

"Why's that?"

"It's been a stressful week for you. It might be good to get your mind off things for a bit. Maybe meet up with friends for a drink. I could join you later."

"So you're a therapist, too?" she asked with a smile. "A man of many talents."

"You have no idea. I'm also a fabulous dancer. It's a proud Murphy family tradition."

Sylvia laughed. "That is something I would love to see."

"Play your cards right and you just might."

She looked away and thought for a moment.

"Dancing sounds fun. Maybe I'll do that. And then I'll make you come get me."

"It's a deal."

"OK," she said. "I'll wait for your call."

I hung up, adjusted my icepack and leaned back into my chair. I was relieved that Sylvia would be on the move. Now I just needed Wanda Peck to get back to me. Until then, there wasn't much to do.

I thought through the list of people I'd talked to since my investigation started, trying to think of who else might have called me. Delores Lightbody, possibly, but I doubted she had anything new to share, outside of more sex-starved double entendres.

Sonny Fletcher came to mind. He'd given me the leads on Rona Morgan and Val Davis; maybe he had other names. And I had more information now, more questions. I could swing by the Motel 6 and, if he hadn't checked out, try to loosen his tongue with some 80-proof lubricant.

But not until Wanda called.

Or…maybe I could get Fletcher on the phone. He probably wouldn't answer if I rang his room—it might even scare him off, if I hadn't already—but maybe he'd call me back if I left a message for him at the front desk. I booted up my computer and found the number for the Motel

6. A harried-looking young man answered.

"Motel 6. Could you please hold?"

He didn't wait for a response.

As I killed time, I brought up the email on my computer—a time-killer if there ever was one. I hardly ever got emails outside of online bills and junk mail, though I had to admit some of the junk mail was pretty entertaining. This time, however, there were two items of actual interest.

The first was 'A Personal Message from Robert Knott, Law & Order Party Candidate for Governor'. I opened the email. To my utter shock, it wasn't a personal message at all; it was a form letter, inviting me to a $50,000 per plate fundraising dinner, to be held that evening at the Savoy Hotel. Or I could just click the convenient link to donate any amount to support the cause to 'Strengthen America'. The last thing I wanted was an inbox full of neo-Nazi propaganda. I sent the mail to my phishing folder.

The other item had been sent by 'SF' and the subject line was blank.

SF, I thought, *Sonny Fletcher?* I opened the mail and read it.

Murphy,

I warned you to get off the Linsky case and didn't tell you why, but you have the right to know.

Believe it or not, I was like you once—young, driven, invincible. But a few years ago, it cost me the most precious thing in my life. My wife was murdered by a man named Slade. For me, he was the Angel of Death.

I've lived with fear and regret and shame ever since, but I tried to find reasons to keep going. As I told you, I was sober for two years, until a week ago, while I was tracking down the names Linsky gave me. I saw a sign from the Angel of Death. A sign that was meant for me to find. At that moment, I knew my Judgment Day was drawing near.

Meeting you made me take a hard look at myself. It's time I faced my demon. Slade feeds on fear, but not this time. I will avenge what he did to me or die trying.

I know this will probably fall on deaf ears. I still remember what it was to be young. I only ask you to do one thing: Don't end up like me.

I was still on hold with the Motel 6 desk clerk. I reached over and hung up. I wondered if I'd ever see Sonny Fletcher again.

22

Wanda Peck called a few minutes later and asked me to come meet her as soon as possible. Same place, side door.

I left the office with significantly less pep in my step than I'd come in with. Sonny's message alone was enough to dampen the mood. Throw in a surprise beating and the resulting paranoia, and the cheery mood from an hour earlier was long gone.

I'd never been married, or even really in love, so I could only imagine how agonizing it would be to lose a wife, much less have her murdered, with the added torture of feeling like you were responsible for it. The fact that Sonny had carried on—and even gotten sober for a while—showed what stuff he was made of. I hoped I could be that strong if I ever lost the woman I loved more than anything.

My head was on a swivel all the way to my speeder. And my head didn't want to swivel. It was hurting. A lot. A painful confirmation that I was no longer just investigating the case—I was up to my neck in it. Whoever the bad guys were, they were now aware of my existence. If there was a silver lining, it was that my attacker could have killed me, but didn't.

As I flew over the city, I remembered something my property manager, Pembleton, had said about Sonny—or, more specifically, Sonny's wife; he'd heard she committed suicide. But, in his email, Sonny had said she was murdered…by a man named Slade.

Considering Sonny had crossed paths with Slade while looking for Linsky's associates—who I believed had been killed, but in ways that deflected suspicion—I wondered if it was at least possible that this Slade person was involved in the deaths of Rona Morgan, Val Davis and, somehow, Carl Linsky.

* * * * *

Wanda ushered me in the side door. The hallway was lit with florescent lights that ratcheted up the pounding in my head. We stepped into the elevator and I leaned back against the wall—gently—closing my eyes.

"You OK?" she asked.

"Not really. I've got a huge goose egg."

"Huh," Wanda said. "I figured you'd come up with something. You seem like a resourceful, persistent fellow."

"No, I mean a literal goose egg. On the back of my head. Someone jumped me in my office."

Wanda went silent. After a few moments, I cracked my eyes just enough to take a look at her. She was staring at me with a brand-new expression. She was worried.

"Who?"

"I didn't get a chance to ask."

I could see her running through possibilities in her head. Maybe she had an idea of who it could have been. She had to know more than I did. But if she had any suggestions, she kept them to herself.

The elevator doors opened and we headed down the hallway toward her office. More florescent lights. It felt like my skull was going to explode.

"Do you have Linsky's laptop bag?" I asked through gritted teeth.

"The laptop's with our hardware guy."

"I don't care about the laptop. I want the pain pills."

I staggered into Wanda's office and fell into a chair. A minute later, she tapped me gently on the shoulder. I opened my eyes to see her holding a small, white tablet in the palm of one hand and a bottle of water in the other.

"Put it under your tongue and let it dissolve," she said.

It could have been a strychnine pill and a bottle of Benzene, for all I cared. I stuck the tablet in my mouth and laid back, praying to the Pain Gods that it would kick in quickly.

After a few minutes, my head went mercifully fuzzy. I couldn't recall the name of Linsky's painkiller, but whatever it was, it made me wonder if

John Klaus was also a veterinarian. This thing would numb a hippo in heat.

As the pain subsided, I sat up and took a deep breath. Wanda was in her usual spot, leaning against the front of her desk, arms crossed.

"You should go get checked out," she said.

"Yeah, I should have health insurance, too," I said, forcing a grin. "I'll sleep it off, be fine tomorrow."

"Your call. I'm not your mother."

I didn't mean to, but couldn't help giving her a little once-over.

"No, you are not."

She gave me a thoroughly disinterested look, then tossed something at me. It felt like I moved in slow motion, but I managed to snag it. I was impressed. I hoped Wanda was, too. It was Linsky's bottle of sleeping pills.

"In case you can't sleep," she said. "So you met with Gideon?"

"I did. Unfortunately, he seems to be out of the loop on all this."

Wanda nodded.

"I was afraid of that. Frank Schimming's done a thorough job of putting him into quarantine."

"Gideon did say something about receiving a letter, and that he gave it to you. The one from the Poisoned Pawn. I seem to recall you asking me if *I* was the Poisoned Pawn."

"I had no idea who you were," she said with a shrug. "It was worth a try."

"What did the Poisoned Pawn have to say?"

"Not much, to be honest. Just that he'd been hired to work remotely and anonymously on some potentially-dangerous new technology, made even more dangerous by the fact that Law & Order—possibly with John Klaus's help—was making a move to take it over. No specifics on the technology. He wasn't even certain that Gideon Enterprises was funding it. There wasn't enough information to get any traction. But then—"

Wanda twisted to reach for something on her desk.

"—you showed up with this."

She handed me the photo of Linsky and Klaus I'd found in the attic.

"We took a closer look at the photo," she continued. "Linsky and Klaus are both wearing badges with the letters 'STG' on them."

"So Gideon Enterprises *wasn't* funding the project."

"Not officially," Wanda said with a grim smile. "We had to navigate a maze of corporate entanglements—and there are a surprising number of companies with those STG initials—but we're quite certain this particular

STG is the 'Security Technologies Group'. And it's a very, very, *very* distant relative of Gideon Enterprises."

"Which the Poisoned Pawn probably wouldn't know."

"Yes, but maybe he has a laptop like Linsky's, with the Gideon logo. Which could explain why the first letter went to J. Saint Gideon."

"Wait, the *first* letter? There are more?"

"A second message came directly to us. The Poisoned Pawn believes that Law & Order may have a—quote—'hit list', and that it includes the STG team members and a few other people."

A hit list.

If there was a *literal* hit list, it might not be proof that Linsky was murdered, but it might be as close as I would get. If I could get my hands on it and get the police to investigate, I might have a fighting chance to get Linsky's cause of death changed and resolve my case.

"We need to find the hit list," I said, stating the obvious.

"If there really is one," Wanda replied. "We don't know for certain who the Poisoned Pawn is, or how good their information is."

"Don't know *for certain*? You have an idea who it might be?"

"After what you told me, I'm afraid Carl Linksy may have been the Poisoned Pawn."

I tilted my head back and closed my eyes. Not what I wanted to hear. But, considering what I'd found in his attic, it made sense. He seemed to be the only one who'd been putting pieces together.

"OK," I said, eyes still closed. "Regardless, it's not much of a stretch to think there could be a hit list out there, is it? I'm almost certain Morgan and Davis were murdered. Linsky too, though that one is a little trickier."

I thought back to Sonny's email.

"This is a total longshot," I said, "but I just came across the name of someone who might be part of all this. Does the name 'Slade' ring a bell?"

Wanda thought it over, then said: "No. Just Slade? No other name?"

I sat up and opened my eyes.

"My source also called him the Angel of Death. Again, I'm just speculating, but it sounds like he might be a hired killer. And his M-O might be committing murders that don't look like murders."

"Who's your source?"

I debated whether or not to tell her. It probably didn't matter. I'd told her most everything else. And it was possible—maybe even likely—that I'd never see Sonny again.

"A P.I. Carl Linsky hired just before he died. He's the one who turned me on to Rona Morgan and Val Davis. His name is Sonny Fletcher."

Wanda shook her head, indicating that the name was unfamiliar.

"His wife died a few years ago," I said. "A suicide, apparently, but Fletcher said this Slade guy murdered her. He didn't say Slade killed Morgan or Davis—or Linsky—but it's not like we have any better leads."

Wanda made a couple notes.

"I'll look into it, see if I can find out who he is," she said. "In the meantime, I think we have just one viable option for finding the hit list, if there is one. And that's where you come in."

"How's that?"

She gave me a long, hard look.

"You know who Robert Knott is?"

"Sure. He's Law & Order's candidate for governor."

"Not after tonight."

"What do you mean?" I asked. "Isn't he at some big party fundraiser right now?"

Wanda pushed away from the desk and walked slowly around it.

"He is. But he's leaving town right after. Leaving Law & Order… leaving everything. He's convinced the party leaders are onto him."

"Onto him?"

"Robert contacted me some time ago. He was deeply concerned about the increasingly radical direction of the party. He had also heard rumors of plans to amp up public support for more law and order. More violence, maybe even an assassination or two."

"And you believe him?"

"The Law & Order Party will do anything to take control. Which is why Robert offered to help us bring them down. Unfortunately, he must have aroused suspicions. He thinks he's being bugged and tracked. He may even be the one they intend to assassinate."

"And how, exactly, do you think *I* come in to all this?"

Wanda braced herself on the chair behind the desk and fixed her eyes on me.

"As you said, he's at a big party fundraiser, along with all the Law & Order bigwigs and most of their security detail. It's our best and maybe only window to get into Law & Order Headquarters."

"So you're gonna break into Law & Order Headquarters?"

"Not me. *You.*"

"Whoa," I said. "That kind of thing is way above my pay grade."

"They know me and everyone else I would trust enough to do this."

I appreciated the vote of confidence. But what she was proposing made me feel the exact opposite of confident.

"They might know who I am, too," I pointed out. "For all I know, it was Law & Order thugs who jumped me."

Wanda thought this over.

"I suppose it could have been. But even if it was, I doubt they'd be expecting you to show up at their headquarters a couple hours later. And they'd have no reason to believe you know anything."

She leaned forward, her expression softening.

"I know it's a lot to ask, but this could change everything. Law & Order has to be stopped. Robert said he has vital information that could help us do that, but he had no way to smuggle it out. It's locked away in his office. And maybe this supposed hit list is part of it. But after he disappears tonight, we'll have no chance of getting it."

"And how am I supposed to break into his office? I'm a private investigator, not James Bond."

"I can walk you through it. It shouldn't be that difficult. It'll just take a lot of guts."

Oh, sure. Play the guts card.

"This could also give you what you need to prove Carl Linsky was murdered," she added. "But it's much bigger than that. As they say, the only thing necessary for the triumph of evil is for good men to do nothing. I've done some homework on you, Tex. You're a good man. And I wouldn't ask you to do this if I didn't think you were up to it."

I liked to think I didn't have a lot of buttons, but she was pushing every single one of them. There are few things more irresistible than a gorgeous woman asking you to play the hero.

I sat back and thought it over. The prospect of finding proof that Linsky was on a hit list and simultaneously sticking it to Law & Order, with the added bonus of impressing Wanda, made the potential rewards outweigh the risk.

"OK," I said at last. "Tell me what to do."

23

"Move fast," she said.

Wanda was giving me an overview of the building's layout. I'd hoped she had a plan for a stealthy, well-equipped entry, but no such luck. I'd have to come through the main lobby, get past an armed security guard in a reception area behind bullet-proof glass, and enter an ultra-high security scanner that wouldn't let me through if I was carrying a cell phone, weapon or any other potentially useful equipment. I would be on my own in every sense of the word.

Great.

* * * * *

The Law & Order Party complex was just a few miles away, on Hunters Point. It had started to pour rain in buckets and, with the fundraiser on the other side of town, there was little traffic, both on the ground and in the air. Still, I was amazed to find a parking spot right in front of the building.

I checked my watch: less than an hour left before the fundraiser ended. And if I was to still in the Law & Order Headquarters after midnight, odds were I'd end up a pumpkin with my guts kicked out all over their front porch. I had to get in and out as quickly as possible.

I could see into the lobby from the street. As I walked up to a set of large glass doors, it looked like no one was inside. I pushed the doors, then pulled, but they were locked. There was a revolving door as well, but it didn't move either when I pushed it. There was a card reader next to the doors. Apparently, only card-carrying neo-Nazis were allowed inside after-hours.

I put my face to one of the glass doors and took a closer look. There was a security booth at the far end of the lobby that looked deserted. No one in sight. I tapped on the glass and waited for a moment. Nothing. I made a fist and started banging on the door.

Inside the booth, a head popped up and froze, like a meerkat. I waved. Still frozen. I waved again and pointed at the door. The meerkat finally moved, reaching a hand up to rub its eye. Just one eye. The other was covered by an eye patch.

After watching the man rub his eye for a few moments, I banged on the door again. He stretched, leisurely. Maybe I'd woken him up. I was about to bang again when a voice crackled through a speaker next to the door.

"Can I help you?"

"I'm here to see John Klaus. It's an emergency."

Wanda and I had come up with this ruse. We figured Klaus was at the fundraiser, but his name might get me inside. She suspected he was one of the party heavyweights, so a lowly security guard might go out of his way to accommodate a Klaus associate.

"Mr. Klaus isn't here," the meerkat answered through the speaker.

"I know. He was at the fundraiser, but he's on his way."

Security guards aren't paid to think and this one was no exception. I could almost feel his brain gears grinding.

"I don't think he'd want me to wait out here in the rain," I said.

For all the guard knew, Klaus and I were best buddies. I didn't think he would risk pissing off someone who could get him fired.

I was right. The doors clicked.

I pulled one open and stepped into the lobby. It smelled like a Denny's, minus the cigarette smoke. I followed my nose to a long banquet table covered with several coffee dispensers and the remains of a happy hour buffet. Maybe the festive fundraising evening had kicked off here.

As Wanda had described, there was a high-tech, full-body scanner next to the security booth, similar to the ones used in airports, except this one was bigger and closed off at the back. I would need to enter, get scanned and wait for it to open to get beyond the lobby. And I figured the security guard could shut the scanner down at any time, so a brute force approach was out of the question. I would need to talk my way past him or get rid of him. Either way, I had to put him at ease.

I strode confidently toward the security booth. Normally, I'd give him a big, warm Tex Murphy smile, but I was playing the role of a Law & Order thug, so any smile would have to be vaguely sinister. I wasn't sure I could pull that off, so I opted for a steely-eyed stare.

The guard gave it right back to me, albeit it at half power. I wondered if his security pals ever kidded him about 'keeping an eye on the place'. I knew I would.

"Kind of a ghost town tonight," I said. "You draw the short straw?"

The guy wasn't in the mood for chit-chat.

"Let's see some I-D."

I didn't think that would be a good idea. For every reason imaginable. I had hoped I could charm my way in, but it clearly wasn't going to happen. So I took the exact opposite approach.

"What's your name?" I asked, in an unmistakably threatening tone.

We locked eyes for what seemed like a long time. I felt my eyes starting to water, but kept them open. Now they were burning. Finally, the guard blinked.

"Rice. Harry Rice."

I pushed an image of fuzzy, mold-covered Chinese food out of my head.

"Harry Rice," I repeated, as if adding it to the Law & Order hit list. "It's good to see you take your job seriously, Harry. Mr. Klaus will be pleased to hear it."

I didn't wait for a response. I spun on my heel and walked back to the banquet table. As I'd done at North Hill Clinic, I moved like I owned the place. I'd been faking the confidence, of course, but now an idea had popped into my head.

At the banquet table, I checked the coffee canisters and found one that wasn't empty. As I poured two cups of coffee, I glanced at Harry, saw him yawn and sit back down. He didn't seem especially worried about me.

Excellent.

I turned my back to him, fished the prescription bottle of sleeping pills from my coat pocket and dropped two into each cup. I then made a show of looking for cream and sugar and added them to one of the cups.

A cup in each hand, I returned to the reception area.

"What Mr. Klaus would *not* be pleased to hear," I said, "is that a security guard is taking naps during his shift."

The guilty look in Harry's eye was a dead giveaway. I'd busted him. And my ominous tone left no room for negotiation: drink the coffee or else.

"Black? Or cream and sugar?" I asked. "I'm good either way."

I didn't know if he'd be suspicious, but I figured giving him a choice would make him less so. I was relieved when he opted for the cream and sugar, which would help mask any bitterness from the sleeping pills.

"Thanks," Harry said, reaching through a small opening to take the cup.

I watched him until he took a sip.

"How much longer you on the clock?" I asked.

"Till midnight."

I checked my watch, then said: "Better drink up."

Harry nodded and took another sip. I raised my cup and pretended to drink as I turned away.

A minute later, I took a seat in one of the lobby chairs and waited. It was now coming up on 11:30 and I was running out of time. I had to hope the sleeping pills were as powerful as the painkillers.

They seemed to be. I was halfway through a Law & Order pamphlet when I heard a clattering sound. I looked up to see Harry on his feet and staring at me through an almost-closed eye.

"What'd you do?" he mumbled, before crumpling out of sight.

I jumped up and hurried to the booth. The area was enclosed, with only the small opening and a single door on the back side that could only be accessed after going through the scanner.

Which shouldn't be a problem, as long as I didn't set anything off. Trying to ignore the clock ticking in my head, I removed everything that had ever tripped an airport scanner: belt, shoes, wallet, watch, keys. I took off my coat and put everything into a pile on the floor. After one final check, I stepped into the scanner.

The front opening sealed shut and I heard some mechanical sounds. Five seconds went by. Ten. Then a green light flashed and the back of the chamber opened.

Getting past the scanner and guard had been the hard part… theoretically. There could be additional security inside, but Wanda had thought odds were good that they'd have all hands on deck at the fundraiser, leaving a skeleton crew at headquarters.

Remembering Wanda's instructions, I moved quickly and located Robert Knott's office, which was not far from the lobby. Wanda said his last message to her had been vague and cryptic, presumably because he thought it might be overheard, but the gist of it was that he'd left the information in a 'safe place' and that 'only *you*'—meaning Wanda—'could access it'. Neither of us knew exactly what that meant, but Knott had to know that she would never be allowed in his office, so Wanda thought it might refer to something only she would know about. If necessary, I would call her from Knott's office phone.

Now I just needed to get into Knott's Office. The door was locked and a card reader next to the door had a flashing light which, I suspected, meant it was connected to an alarm system. I couldn't risk setting off an alarm by kicking in the door.

Maybe Harry Rice could help.

I returned to the security booth. Being on the 'safe' side of the scanner, the door to enter the booth didn't require a security badge. Harry was lying on the floor, snoring soundly. I searched him and found a passcard on a retractable reel. Hopefully, this was an all-access pass.

Sure enough, Harry's card unlocked the door to Robert Knott's office without triggering the alarm and I stepped inside. At first glance, it looked like the office of a movie producer, rather than a politician. The décor was more Old Hollywood than New San Francisco, with an antique desk and chairs, potted ferns, and artsy collectibles. The walls were covered with a number of vintage and more recent movie posters, as well as photos of Knott with a variety of famous faces.

Now where was the 'safe place'?

I had to assume he was being literal, and that it wouldn't be out in plain sight. And probably not just tucked away in a typical hiding spot. To me, that ruled out the desk and filing cabinets. I checked my watch. 11:29. Someone could show up any minute. And someone would definitely show up by midnight, when Harry's shift ended. I figured, to be safe, I had twenty minutes at most.

So I trashed the place.

I dumped out the potted plants, tore up the chairs, moved the desk, rolled up a rug. I went through a shelf full of books, flipping through them and tossing them aside. After ten minutes, I'd scoured the entire room and come up with nothing.

Looking around, I focused on the posters and photos. Maybe I should have started with those. Maybe when Knott had said a 'safe place' he had been literally literal, as in an actual *safe*. Like a wall safe.

I felt equal parts stupid and relieved when I found it. Behind the poster of a movie titled 'Only the Young Die Good' was a small safe. It had a keypad with numbers 0 to 9. This had to be the safe place, but what the hell was the code to open it?

There was a vidphone on Knott's desk that had somehow survived Hurricane Murphy. If there was anyone in the building who was conscious and sitting by a phone, they might notice that someone was making a call from Knott's office, but I had to chance it. I dialed Wanda's number. She answered on the first ring, her face appearing on the screen.

"Tex?"

"Yeah," I said, checking my watch and trying not to yell out of sheer panic, "I'm in Knott's office and I found a safe. Now I need the code."

Wanda's face went blank. She stared back at me, silent.

"I'm running out of time here!"

"I…I don't know," she stumbled. "I'm trying to think. He never gave me a code."

"He must have. There's no other way to get in the safe."

I could see she was racking her brain. I waited as long as I could. It was probably about ten seconds. Then I said: "What exactly did he tell you? Can you remember?"

"He said I was only one who could access the information. That's it."

Now we were both silent.

Only Wanda could access the information.

Wanda. If the keypad had letters, I'd try entering her name. But it only had numbers.

Then it hit me.

The buttons on the vidphone.

I looked down.

'W', along with X, Y and Z were on the 9 button.

'A' was on the 2 button.

'N'…6.

'D'…3.

'A'…2.

I ran back to the safe and took a moment to steady my hand before punching in the numbers. *92632*. A click. I pulled the handle.

The safe opened.

"Tex?" I heard faintly in the background. Wanda, still on the vidphone.

"I got it!" I called out.

There was only one item in the safe: a flash drive. I grabbed it, closed the safe and hurried back to the desk. I held the flash drive up to show Wanda, then said: "See you shortly," and hung up.

In a haze of adrenaline, I ran back toward the lobby. Everything was perfectly silent, except for Harry's snoring. No sign of anyone.

I couldn't believe I'd pulled this off. Now I just had to get out.

I almost went back through the security scanner before remembering that I now had a flash drive in my pocket. I ran back inside the security booth, stepped over Harry and placed the flash drive by the small opening. For just a moment, I felt bad for Harry. He probably wouldn't get a Christmas bonus.

After going through the scanner, I grabbed the flash drive and stuck it in my pants pocket. I didn't bother to put on my other things, which I'd left on the floor outside the scanner; I just scooped them into my jacket and tied it up, like the sack on a hobo stick. In my stocking feet, I ran to the front doors and leaned into one of them.

It didn't move.

I pushed harder. Locked. I lowered my shoulder and rammed the door. It didn't budge.

I looked for a card reader, but couldn't see one.

Harry had unlocked the doors from inside the booth. Still holding my bundle, I ran back across the lobby, dropped my bundle, almost forgot to take the flash drive out of my pocket—again—and then stepped into the scanner.

It was longest ten seconds of my life.

The light turned green. I hurried into the security booth and looked around frantically.

I finally found what I was looking for. Pressing the button triggered a click I could barely hear from across the lobby. I ran back out, through the scanner, grabbed the flash drive and bundle and sprinted for the doors.

A moment before I hit the door, I heard another click. The doors had locked again, but I double- and triple-checked anyway.

Shit.

It was hard to think straight. I was so close. Just a few inches from making my escape. And the clock was ticking. Any second, someone could show up and I'd be screwed. I had to come up with something. Maybe I could put something heavy on the button back in the security booth. But, no, that probably wouldn't keep the doors unlocked. The button would need to be pressed while I was by the door.

Which was impossible.

At least without enough time to rig up some MacGyver contraption with a burning candle or some other ingenious thing.

Or…

Maybe I had it backwards.

Harry had been a big help. I needed just one more favor from him. I set my things by the door, ran back to the scanner and, after yet another agonizing wait, returned to where Harry lay sleeping. He wasn't especially heavy, which was good, since I had to pull him out of the booth, take off most of his clothes, and then drag him through the scanner and all the way across the lobby.

I propped him up against the door and then completed my fourth lap around the Law & Order obstacle course. Back in the security booth, I pressed the button and heard the faint click. Very, very slowly, Harry tilted away, his dead weight forcing the door open a few inches.

I sprinted back across the lobby, grabbed my things, stepped over Harry, hit the door and splashed off into the night.

24

I lifted off and headed due west, speeding in a straight line out over the ocean. As the lights of the city faded in my rearview mirror, the white-hot adrenaline gradually dissipated, leaving a strange sensation that was equal parts relief, satisfaction and dread.

I'd never taken that kind of risk before, putting myself in honest-to-god danger and winging my way out of it. Kind of a near-death experience. And totally worth it. I felt like Bilbo discovering the one chink in the armor of the Law & Order Smaug.

But there would be hell to pay.

If Law & Order found out what I'd done—which seemed inevitable—they wouldn't just swat me away like an annoying little gnat; they'd want me smeared across their windshield. All I could do now was keep moving and stay out of traffic.

I couldn't go back to my office, not for the foreseeable future. Wanda said her offices were probably being watched, so that was out, too. If Carl Linsky's home wasn't already on the radar, I had to assume it would be…and soon. Maybe I needed to take a hint from Sonny Fletcher and hole up in a cheap motel.

It wasn't a bad idea, actually. Of all the places I could go in the city, the Motel 6 would be as safe as any. Part of me wanted to blow town, get some distance from Law & Order, but I had to get the flash drive into Wanda's hands. To arrange that, I'd have to call her.

The Motel 6 had phones, coffee and beds.

Plus, I could check in on Sonny.

I really hoped he was still alive, in part because I wanted to find out more about Slade, but mostly because he was one of the good guys. I was starting to wonder how many of us there were left.

I banked my speeder around and headed back toward the city.

* * * * *

In the Motel 6 lobby, I used the courtesy phone to call Wanda. For once, *I* was the cool one. She'd been going crazy, or as crazy as she ever got, waiting for me to call. She agreed we shouldn't meet at her office and gave me a new address. We would meet in an hour, which would give her enough time to make sure she wasn't being followed.

Paranoia was going around like the flu. Or more like Ebola. Out of the blue, I thought of Sylvia and felt a surge of panic. If she hadn't been in danger before, she might be now…or would be soon. She had left messages on my vidphone—messages seen by whoever jumped me. She was the one who'd started asking questions about her father's death. Maybe they would want to shut her up. Or go through her to get her father's incriminating information. Or…use her to get to me.

I felt a sudden need to get her someplace safe.

When I'd called a few hours earlier, it looked like she would do what I suggested and go out on the town. I hoped she had…and that she was still somewhere other than her father's house.

I punched in Sylvia's number on the motel's courtesy phone and she answered immediately, but asked me to hold on until she found a quieter spot. She'd been drinking, but seemed relatively coherent and happy to hear from me.

"Finally!" she said, over a dull roar. "Are you gonna come see me?"

This could be tricky. Sylvia needed to know that she might be in danger, but convincing her could be an issue. She wasn't the kind to back down or get bossed around. I admired that, but it could make her a pain in the ass. Sprinkle in a bunch of intoxicated overconfidence and she might do the exact opposite of whatever I told her, just to prove a point.

"Yeah, I'll come pick you up," I said. "Where are you?"

"We're at The 628. I'm with a friend. And we want to see you dance!"

That would have to wait.

"I'll come find you," I said. "Don't leave until I get there, OK?"

"Are you kidding? I can't wait to see your sweet moves!"

I hung up, then called 411 to get the address for The 628. After doing some math, I decided I had time to make one more quick stop before picking up Sylvia and then making my rendezvous with Wanda.

I headed up to Sonny's room. Even if he was still alive, he could have checked out of the motel and disappeared forever, so I was a little surprised and a lot pleased when I heard music coming from inside his room. I knocked on the door and heard him answer: "Yes?"

"Sonny? It's Murphy."

"It's open. *Adelante*."

My Spanish was as fluent as my Language of Love, which is to say, not at all. But I got the gist and pushed the door open. Sonny was on the far side of the room, seated at a table.

He looked like a new man. His shirt was a black, western cut with a distinctly Latin flair. His white and wild hair was pulled back into a tight ponytail, which turned him from a grizzled old *borracho* into a wizened old bullfighter.

"Sonny…*hombre*! You look good," I said.

He seemed very calm. Peaceful, even. A song was playing on an old radio—a sad-sounding ballad, sung in Spanish. Sonny had one hand resting on his stomach. The other was on the table, loosely gripping an empty shot glass. There was also a second shot glass and an expensive-looking bottle, half-full of something. Tequila, maybe. I wouldn't know.

He gestured to the chair across from him and I sat down, still taking in the drastic change.

"*Qué pasa, compadre*?" I said.

A slow smile spread across Sonny's face.

"Murphy, I've come face to face with my demon."

That could only mean one thing.

"Slade?" I asked.

Sonny nodded, still smiling.

"What happened?"

"Pour me a drink."

I uncorked the bottle and filled his shot glass. When I finished, Sonny picked it up and held it to the light, his eyes soft and dreamy.

"In the depths of my despair," he began, "I had a vision... a vision of redemption. I realized I couldn't pass on without confronting what I feared most in life."

He threw the shot back and set the glass down, then continued: "I tracked him down and tailed him. Found the lodge where he was staying. I broke in."

He paused and smiled at me.

"I'm still a good detective." He blew lightly on his fingertips.

"And Slade was there?"

"No," he said. The smile faded. "Not at first."

He pointed at the bottle. I poured another shot. Sonny's face got tighter.

"I had to take something from him," he said, his voice low. "Something important. Even though nothing he had could replace Maria."

A moment after he spoke his wife's name, the singer in the background sang the same word: *Maria.*

"But I found something, Murphy. And I know it's important… because it was hidden."

He raised the hand resting on his stomach.

"Here."

Sonny's hand was covered in blood. I glanced down and saw the lower half of his shirt was soaked.

"You're hurt!"

Between his glistening fingers was a card. I'd seen it before, or at least one just like it. It looked identical to the one I'd found in Linsky's attic. He held it out until I took it. An STG passcard, except this one was marked with an 'E'; Linsky's was an 'F'.

"We need to get you to the hospital," I said.

"No, there's no need. I've had my last drink, *amigo*."

I didn't want to believe it. But I could see he was right. He was too far gone. The calm, the peacefulness, the dreamy eyes…he was almost done bleeding out.

"Well," he said, "maybe there's time for one more. *Uno mas*."

I nodded and refilled his glass. He picked it up, then paused.

"Now one for yourself."

"I'm not really a drinker," I said.

He cocked his head and smiled.

"For me."

I looked into the face of the dying man. The weathered skin, the crinkled eyes, the spots and grey hairs earned over a lifetime. A lifetime that was almost over. At any moment, the light would go out of his eyes.

"All right," I said.

As I filled the other shot glass, he set his on the table. When I finished pouring and looked up, his head was tilted forward, eyes open, seeing nothing. Perfectly still.

I've never been religious but, in that moment, I hoped he was somewhere else, his wife waiting with open arms. The song on the radio came to an end. I picked up my glass and said: "*Salud*," then drained the shot.

Sonny's last drink was my first.

25

I stared at the empty husk of Sonny Fletcher, feeling the alcohol burn its way down my throat and into my gut. I'd never watched someone die before.

At least he'd died well. Avenged, in his own way. I picked up the passcard he'd taken from Slade and wiped the blood from it. I barely knew Sonny, but it was suddenly very important to me that I make his death meaningful, take the baton and get to the finish line, whatever that was.

I'd come into all this to help Sylvia claim her father's life insurance. It was much more than that now. The stakes were higher—probably much higher than I could imagine. There were a few good guys and a lot of bad guys involved. Sonny was one of the good guys and he was dead. I'd been attacked. The bad guys were winning and destroying everyone who stood in their way. I couldn't stand by and do nothing.

I felt bad leaving Sonny where he was. If I'd had more time, I would have done a thorough search of his room, then made an anonymous call to 911. As it was, I'd been here longer than expected. I'd have to hurry to meet up with Sylvia and make my rendezvous with Wanda.

After finding Sonny's room key, I turned off the radio, turned out the lights, hung a 'Do Not Disturb' sign on the door and left.

* * * * *

It was almost 1:30 a.m. and Valencia was in full swing. The street was packed with hundreds of impaired young partiers wearing every kind of outfit imaginable, the air thick with vape smoke and a cacophony of drunken laughter, yelling and music. The 628 was one of dozens of nightclubs and bars in this part of town. I didn't drink or do drugs, listened to classic jazz, and my preferred styles of dancing were the Tango and Samba, so this had never been my scene.

It took forever to find a spot to park my speeder and then work my way through the crowds to The 628. There was a line outside, which I had no intention of standing in. There was one beefy-looking guy checking ID's at the door and I didn't feel like explaining myself. I got close and waited for him to turn away, then hustled past him. He yelled for me to stop, but I'd already been absorbed into the huge crowd and I didn't think he'd risk leaving the door unattended to come after me.

The inside of the club was an acid trip…at least what I would imagine an acid trip to be. Pounding techno music, an ecstasy-fueled mass of writhing bodies and seizure-inducing kaleidoscopic lights. Just the thing for my aching head.

I knifed through the sea of people until I found Sylvia. Grabbing her arm, I put my mouth to her ear and said we needed to get out. NOW.

I was surprised when she didn't resist. She just nodded and turned to say something to her friend. I grabbed her hand and plowed my way to the front door. The beefy guy saw me and moved to block the exit. I cocked my head in Sylvia's direction; he looked at her, then back to me, nodded and stepped aside.

A few minutes later, we were back in my speeder, lifting off from the street. Out of the corner of my eye, I could see Sylvia glancing over at me, but she stayed quiet. I'm sure I was putting off vibes she hadn't felt before: annoyance, anxiety, anger…topped off with my first taste of alcohol and the twinges of another skull-splitting headache.

It wasn't until we were high above the city that she finally spoke.

"This isn't the way home," she said, cautiously…but playfully.

"Things have changed. For both of us."

"Let me guess. You're falling madly in love with me?"

I could hear the sexy smile in her voice…and I didn't mind it. But I couldn't cross that line. She was my client and I needed to keep her safe. That's it. I just wasn't sure how to tell her that without throwing her into a panic. I decided not to dance around it.

"I have reason to believe you could be in danger."

A long pause. I had to remind myself that Sylvia had no clue what was going on. This would have confused her even if she hadn't been drinking.

"But nothing's happened to me."

"That doesn't mean nothing will," I said. "And it reflects poorly on me if my clients get bumped off during a case."

"But why…?"

"It's a long story," I said.

Sylvia was quiet for a moment.

"Well, tell me," she said, the sexy smile coming back. "I'm paying your tab, after all."

She wasn't taking me seriously. The alcohol probably wasn't helping.

"It's not about the money," I said.

"Then what is it? I'm just a client, right? I'm sure there were plenty before me and there'll be plenty after me."

She turned toward me and put her right hand on my thigh. It made me flinch.

"Look, Sylvia, there's this code I follow, the Rules of a P.I. And one of very first rules is 'Don't Fall for a Client'."

"That wouldn't happen, would it?"

She smiled and tightened her grip.

"You're not helping," I said.

She moved in even closer. When she spoke, I could feel her breath on my cheek and in my ear.

"So, tell me," she whispered, "are there any rules about *kissing* a client?"

I cleared my throat.

"That falls squarely under the aforementioned rule."

"But you've thought about it."

I ignored her. She laughed.

"So break a rule," she said. "How many rules are there?"

"Thirty-seven. So far."

"Thirty-six out of thirty-seven isn't so bad." She leaned back in and whispered: "I won't tell a soul."

I kept my eyes on the airspace ahead.

"I'll make you a deal," I said. "Let's get through this and then we'll talk about it, OK? For now, I need you to keep your hands to yourself, quit smelling so good and get back into your own seat."

After one final squeeze of my thigh, she sat back and folded her arms. I waited a few moments, letting things cool down before I spoke again.

"I'm not sure how much I want to tell you right now," I said. "You just need to trust me."

I turned to her.

"Can you do that?" I asked. "Please?"

I waited until Sylvia nodded, grudgingly, then dug into my pocket for the pain pills and handed them to her.

"Get one of these out for me."

She fumbled with the blister pack for a minute, then asked: "Where are we going?"

"Someplace safe."

Her hand was unsteady as she held out one of the pain pills. I took it and stuck it under my tongue. She reached over and put the blister pack in my palm, closed my hand over it, then put her hand over mine. And didn't let go. She wasn't good at following directions, but I let it slide.

As we flew to the coordinates Wanda had given me, I gave Sylvia just enough details to help her understand the seriousness of the situation. There was still no proof—or a reasonable explanation for how it was done—but I was pretty sure her father had been murdered. And he wasn't the only one. There would probably be even more before this was finished.

I also told her I'd been jumped and that I was worried someone might come after her to get to me. By the time I finished, there was fear in her eyes. It gave me no pleasure, but I needed her to let me keep her safe.

Just like I'd do with any other client—even a big smelly one, I told myself.

26

The spot Wanda had chosen for our rendezvous was in a section of the old city inhabited mostly by mutants. It was a relatively safe haven for the severely disfigured—the scar tissue of humanity—whose very existence offended the delicate sensibilities of 'normal' people. Everyone referred to it as Freaktown…even the mutants.

The meet-up point turned out to be an old multilevel parking structure that had somehow survived the 'nuclear incident'. It had been built back before speeders, so the only place to land was on the flat roof.

"So *this* is somewhere safe?" Sylvia asked. "Freaktown?"

"We have to meet someone first."

I climbed out of my speeder and took a look around. It was much quieter here than back on Valencia. I could hear voices and laughter and music coming from the streets below, but the volume was turned way down.

There were a dozen other speeders parked around us, but no people up here. No sign of Wanda. I checked my watch: 2:07 a.m. She was running late.

Sylvia got out and walked around to my side. She lit a cigarette and leaned back against the speeder.

"You were right," she said.

"About what?"

She took a breath, steeling herself.

"The insurance. That's why I hired you."

Not a surprise. But it was good to hear her own up to it.

"There's nothing wrong with that," I said. "I appreciate you being up front about it."

She turned to me with a pleading tone her voice.

"You have to know how it was with me and my dad. I did things to help him…things he never knew about. I loved him. I tried to protect him."

"Protect him? From what?"

"John Klaus."

She took a drag, then turned her head away to exhale the smoke.

"He's a bad man," she said quietly.

I glanced at her. She glanced back, like she'd been caught in a lie.

"Look," she said, "I didn't want to tell you about this, but I want you to know I trust you. And I want you to trust *me*."

I nodded, encouraging her to continue. Then it was like a dam breaking.

"I made mistakes when I was younger, OK?" she said. "Klaus doesn't just do plastic surgery. He runs a service. With young women. Clients. He makes them look perfect—for free—in exchange for…other stuff… spending time with men. And most of them are rich, powerful. It's an easy trap to fall into. And then you can't get out."

She paused to take another drag.

"And he trapped you?"

"He threatened to expose me. I didn't care. I just wanted out. But then he threatened to make trouble for my father. So…I had to make a deal with the devil."

Sylvia looked down at her cigarette and flicked ash off the end. When she spoke, her voice was thick.

"I agreed to do some things…get involved with someone. I didn't know at the time, but Klaus wanted to blackmail this person."

I glanced at her and saw her eyes brimming with tears, her jaw set tight.

"So, I did what he asked."

She went quiet for a long moment.

"And then he told my father anyway."

The cigarette dropped from her hand and she ground it into the concrete with the toe of her shoe. All at once, she made a soft choking sound and turned toward me. I couldn't have stopped her, even if I'd wanted to. I took her in my arms.

She had kept this bottled up for a long time and now there was no holding it back. She pressed her face against my chest and sobbed.

From what I knew about Carl Linsky, he wasn't the compassionate, understanding type. This explained the distance between him and his daughter and maybe why he'd essentially disowned her. I felt bad for Sylvia. A youthful indiscretion had changed her life forever. And then she'd done more bad things to protect her father. Part of me wanted to ask what she'd done and who she'd done them to, but it wasn't my business. It had to be hard as hell for her to talk about this.

"Thanks for telling me that," I whispered. "I'm really sorry."

Sylvia gradually stopped shaking and went quiet. It had been like a thunderstorm—intense, but brief—and now the rain had let up, but the air was still heavily charged. She didn't move away from me. I didn't let go. She had one hand on my chest. I felt her other hand slip under my jacket, along my hip, to the small of my back.

Her lower body pressed hard against me. It sent a surge through me, from head to toe. The softness of her hair, the smell of her perfume, even the traces of alcohol and tobacco smoke on her breath, all combined to make me suddenly lightheaded. She slowly turned her face up toward mine. Her eyes were glistening.

And then she kissed me. Hard. Another dam bursting. For both of us. My hand slipped into her hair, grabbing a fistful. I spun us around and she moaned into my mouth as I slammed her against the speeder. Nothing else mattered. I had never wanted anything so desperately.

Our hands were all over each other, grabbing, squeezing, searching for buttons and zippers. And then I heard a voice:

"Sorry I'm late."

It was like having a giant bucket of ice water dumped over my head. Sylvia and I broke apart like magnets suddenly reversing polarity. She turned away to straighten herself up. I stuck a hand in my pocket to rearrange the furniture.

For her part, Wanda seemed awfully amused.

"Looks like you didn't mind waiting," she said. "Who's your friend?"

I had to clear my throat before I responded.

"This is, uh, Sylvia. Sylvia Linsky."

My client finally turned around, looking relatively composed. She looked Wanda over, took a quick glance at me, then back to Wanda.

"Carl Linsky's daughter?" Wanda asked, giving Sylvia pretty much the same once-over. "Your client?"

She didn't need to remind me.

"Yeah," I said. "So, what's going on?"

So smooth.

Wanda smiled.

"I have to say, I'm really impressed, Murphy. Clearly, you're handy. And, you know, good at…pulling things off."

"I'm sorry," Sylvia cut in, "who are you?"

"I'm Wanda," Wanda said, gazing back at her with a cool smile. "Pleasure to meet you, Sylvia. Now I need to borrow your…private investigator…for a minute, if that's OK."

This didn't seem to be going well. Especially considering what I was planning on asking these women to do. But first things first. I pulled Sylvia to the side.

"Wanda is kind of a…secret agent," I said.

"Kind of?" Sylvia replied.

"I promise I will tell you everything as soon as I can. Right now, she and I have something important to discuss. It won't take long."

Without a word, Sylvia spun away, digging for another cigarette. I watched her walk off, then turned back to Wanda.

"OK," I said, "that got really weird, really fast. I don't even know what happened."

"I could explain it, if you've never had 'the talk'."

"I might take you up on that. My 'talk' consisted of my dad giving me a biology book and three days to study for the test. But that's neither here nor there."

I pulled out the flash drive I'd taken from Robert Knott's office and held it up.

Wanda raised an eyebrow.

"I was going to ask if that was a flash drive in your pocket or if you were just happy to see me," she said.

Something told me I was never going to live this down.

"Do you have a laptop here?" I asked.

"No. Even if I did, I assume the drive contents are encrypted. If that's the case, it will take a little time. Robert may be the most paranoid man I've ever met."

"With good reason to be, apparently."

Wanda nodded.

"In the meantime," she said, "you might want to stick around this part of town. I doubt anyone will look for you here. And there's someone you might want to talk to. Jorge Valdez. He runs a place called the Rank & File, just a couple blocks from here. He used to work for Gideon Enterprises and might have some useful information. They're open all night and he's there now."

"OK, I'll go see him," I said. "But I need you to do one more thing for me."

"Name it. I owe you a big one."

"Take Sylvia with you. Get her someplace safe. And keep her there."

Wanda tilted her head and gave me a cockeyed look.

"That *is* a big one."

I was still holding the flash drive. I waggled it around, like a doggy treat.

"Fine," she said, snatching it out of my hand.

"I don't know what else to do with her. I think she could be in real danger and she's stubborn and young enough to think she's invincible. I could take her somewhere, but I don't think she'd stay there. And if I wasn't on Law & Order's radar before tonight, I sure as hell am now. I may not be able to protect myself, much less her. And she's the only person they could come after to get to me."

"So you like her."

"She's my client."

"And you like her."

"That's not the point."

"I already told you I'd do it," Wanda said. "Once I've looked at what's on this flash drive, I'll contact you through Jorge."

She looked over at Sylvia and took a deep breath.

"Now, let's go get a tranquilizer dart into your girlfriend."

27

I made a mental note to start carrying tranquilizer darts. Sylvia was resistant, to put it mildly. It didn't help that she and Wanda hadn't exactly hit it off. It wasn't until Wanda stepped in and made it clear I couldn't solve Sylvia's case if she didn't cooperate that she finally gave in.

I probably would have done the same if I was Sylvia. I hated being told what to do. Always had. If someone told me to do something—even if I was already planning on doing it—I'd usually do something else, just on principle. I'd lost more than one job because of it. It was probably my fatal flaw. That, and math.

I had no intention of staying in Freaktown, and not because Wanda told me to. I wanted to get back to the Motel 6.

* * * * *

Sonny's room was exactly how I'd left it. A moment frozen in time. I'd never really thought about death in any personal way, but the passing of the old caballero hit a nerve. He'd ended up alone, beaten to a pulp by life, with nothing left but his work. The same work I did and would do till I dropped dead. I wondered if I was seeing a 3D snapshot of my own future.

It was quick work, searching the room. Sonny traveled light, with just a few changes of clothes, a couple books and several tools of the trade, including binoculars, a GPS tracker and a lockpick set. I had conflicted feelings about taking the tools, but I could use them and I'd think of Sonny every time I did. Maybe he would have wanted me to have them.

There was only one thing left to search: Sonny himself. He could be carrying something important, something that might give me a lead on Slade, but I'd never searched a dead body before. I had to remind myself that it wasn't Sonny anymore—just a thing that looked like him.

I emptied his pockets and laid what I found on the table. There was a wallet, containing the usual things—driver's license, credit cards, a little cash…and an old, creased photo of a woman that had to be his wife, Maria. A rosary. A half pack of Lucky Strikes. A zippo lighter. And a book of matches.

The zippo was silver, old and scratched, and etched with an ornate letter S. I opened it and flicked the thumbwheel. A flame appeared. Fully functional, full of fluid.

So why was there also a book of matches?

On the back side of the matchbook was written: '*Your Home Away From Home—Clean Rooms, Air Conditioning, Color TV*'. On the front, the words '*Big Surf Lodge*' and a phone number over a drawing of the ocean framed by eucalyptus trees.

There was also a smudge of blood.

I opened it and saw that none of the matches had been used. The matchbook looked new. Sonny hadn't been carrying it for very long. And I remembered him saying he'd tracked Slade down to his 'lodge'. It seemed an odd word at the time; now it made sense. The confrontation with Slade must have taken place at the Big Surf Lodge.

I decided to keep the zippo—another thing to remember Sonny by. I stuck it and the matchbook into my pocket and took one last look around. The only thing left to do was call 911.

But then I reconsidered. As much as I wanted to do right by Sonny, he had been shot or stabbed, so there would be a police investigation that I didn't want to get dragged into. As much as I hated to do it, it might be best to let things play out as if I'd never been there.

Using toilet paper from the bathroom, I wiped down everything I'd touched. Then I removed the Do Not Disturb sign from the door and left.

* * * * *

It was almost 3 a.m. when I walked into the Rank & File, in search of Jorge Valdez.

The joint was part head shop, part internet café. In the front, on my left, was a long glass-fronted counter, full of every imaginable type of chess paraphernalia and a variety of other games, as well as cigarettes and hookahs. To my right was a soda fountain and juice bar. The rest of the space was a lounge area, filled with gaming stations, tables where you could play chess the old-fashioned way—against a fellow human—and high-tech booths where virtual opponents appeared as holographic 3D projections.

The lights were turned down, so the faces of the dozen or so patrons were glowing from their respective screens, displays and backlit game boards. A soft techno groove was playing in the background.

From behind the glass counter, a man was staring at me in a way that could only be described as *smoldering*. Roguishly long and curly black hair, swarthy skin and a fiercely-trimmed goatee. He could have stepped straight out of a Telemundo tele-novella…if it weren't for the cysts covering his face like bubble wrap. They looked like un-lanced boils. A mutant, obviously.

As I approached, he shifted his seductive gaze from me to a chess board on the countertop and stroked his goatee like a scheming villain as he contemplated his next move.

"How's the game going?" I asked.

"Welcome to the Rank & File," he said in a low, slow voice, like the gatekeeper to a demonic orgy. "Do you play?"

"Not very well. I can never remember how those little horseys are supposed to move."

He looked up slowly, his mouth curling into a sneery smile.

"I think you may be in the wrong place."

"Maybe. Unless you're Jorge Valdez."

Valdez's smile got wider.

"I assumed you were Murphy. Wanda described you perfectly."

"Oh, yeah? How's that?"

"Tall, dork and handsome."

It wasn't the greatest compliment, but I'd take it.

"Any word yet?" I asked.

He shook his head…slowly, like everything else he did, and said: "Should be soon. In the meantime, can I interest you in a game?"

"Only if you were a woman and we were playing strip chess."

"I could put on a dress."

I laughed, politely.

He shrugged, but his smile got even curlier. I couldn't tell if he was just yanking my chain or wanted to actually yank my actual chain. I smoothly changed the subject.

"Got any coffee?" I asked.

Eyes locked on mine, he tilted his head in the direction of the juice bar.

"Help yourself."

As I crossed the room, I caught a little guy staring at me from one of the gaming stations. He turned his head quickly and stared into a monitor. He was severely bald and ghostly pale, with a face like a baby Frankenstein. I kept one eye on him as I got a cup of coffee.

The blend was surprisingly good. If Jorge wasn't so creepy, we could engage in some witty banter about him being related to Juan Valdez, the iconic Columbian bean picker. But I was happy to leave him to his game while we waited to hear back from Wanda.

Baby Frankenstein kept his eyes glued to the monitor. Maybe I was just being paranoid. I did stand out, being the only norm in the joint.

I looked over at Jorge and did a double-take. Right where I'd been standing was a full-body apparition. It took me a second to recognize who it was, in part because the figure was standing up and not in a wheelchair. It was J. Saint Gideon. Or, more precisely, a hologram of him.

His voice was faint, but I recognized the clipped English accent. Jorge moved a chess piece and then the hologram flickered and vanished.

I walked back to the counter and asked: "Was that who I think it was?"

"In the flesh," Jorge answered. "Or, rather, not in the flesh. We have an ongoing game."

"Wanda said you used to work for him."

"Yes, I did…until the purge."

I thought back to what Gideon had told me about getting shut out of his own company by the new CEO.

"Schimming?" I asked.

Jorge nodded. "Got rid of all the mutants."

"So is Schimming in bed with Law & Order?"

"Ah," Jorge smiled, "the Fourth Reich. I think Schimming is in bed with anything that gets him money and power. Gideon has been a friend of the mutants from the beginning, unlike most people in his social strata. Purging us may have been nothing more than a power play—Schimming showing Gideon who the new boss was."

A cell phone beeped. Jorge picked it up and read a message, then reached for a laptop.

"You've got mail," he said to me. "More secure than a phone call. Our mutual friend doesn't want to take any chances. It will take a minute for me to decrypt her message."

As he typed on the laptop, I thought I'd try my sneak attack tactic. Wanda thought Carl Linsky had most likely been the Poisoned Pawn, but we couldn't know for sure. Jorge seemed to know a lot, probably more than he was letting on. It was worth a try.

"Are you the Poisoned Pawn?" I asked.

Jorge didn't bat an eye.

"No."

"Any idea who it could be?"

"No. But the pseudonym they chose is interesting."

"How so?"

"A poisoned pawn refers to an apparently unprotected piece whose capture leads to dire consequences."

"So it's like…bait? For a trap?"

"In a manner of speaking. OK, here you go."

He turned the laptop toward me. A brief message was onscreen. Wanda said that Robert Knott's information was very good for her, not so much for me; there was no mention of Carl Linsky. But she said Knott had made his escape and listed coordinates for where I could find him. That was it.

Before giving the laptop back to Jorge, I used it to look up the coordinates. Knott hadn't been kidding about going far away. It was about as far as you could go without leaving the country.

And, according to the map, the two towns closest to where he was headed couldn't have been more perfect, considering he'd come down with a serious case of cold feet and was probably smart to head for the hills:

Coldfoot and Wiseman, Alaska.

28

I considered making a stop to check out the Big Surf Lodge before I left town. I was reasonably sure that was where Sonny had his fatal run-in with Slade. But there were at least two good reasons to hold off. One, I had no idea what Slade looked like, so there was no way to identify him. I suppose I could ask around, but that would probably be a bad idea. The second reason was that he was a killer and I wasn't. I didn't even own a gun.

For now, my best bet was to track down Robert Knott and find out everything he knew. He'd been on the inside at Law & Order, so I hoped he could connect some dots. He might even know about Slade.

* * * * *

I was in the air at 3:45 a.m. At top speed, it would take about twelve and a half hours, give or take, to get to Anchorage. I put my Lotus on auto-pilot, fully intending to fall asleep and stay that way as long as possible. I sat back with my eyes closed for an hour. Despite my utter exhaustion, I couldn't nod off.

Feeling desperate, I pulled out Linsky's sleeping pills. Two of them had zonked Harry Rice almost immediately. I took one. It didn't take long before I started feeling foggy. I closed my eyes and leaned back.

A few minutes went by. Then an hour.

I took a second pill. And waited.

* * * * *

Eleven hours later, I still hadn't gotten any sleep. Something was seriously wrong. I should have been out cold. But I wasn't. I hadn't taken a third pill. For all I knew, that would take me straight from awake to a literal coma.

About four hours in, my head had started throbbing again. A pain pill had kept it tolerable, but now I was down to three doses left. For the first time in my life, I could imagine what it was like to be an addict.

I'd watched the sun rise out the passenger side window. It was getting low in the sky out my *driver* side window when Anchorage finally came into view. And now, in addition to my headache and total exhaustion, I had a painfully empty stomach and an even more painfully full bladder.

I'd also left the relatively balmy Bay area without proper attire. Fortunately, I found a large truck stop that turned out to be a one-stop shop, with a decent selection of cold-weather gear and a public restroom.

There was even a charging station for my speeder, which was fortunate. I should have thought ahead and charged my battery before making the long flight, but foresight was never my strong suit. I'd never flown my speeder this far and it was now running on fumes.

It would take a couple hours to recharge, which would cut things close; I had maybe three hours of daylight left and a remote cabin would be almost impossible to find after dark.

What the truck stop *didn't* have was any food that looked remotely edible. With time to kill, I set out on foot. I figured a walk and some fresh air, along with a good, hot meal, might help give me a second wind.

Anchorage was a picturesque little place, built up between a bay known as the Cook Inlet and a towering range of snow-capped mountains. Everything was older, slower and quieter than I was used to, which was good, considering my mental state. People I passed by gave me friendly nods and smiles, which I also wasn't used to.

Eventually, I struck Yukon Gold when I ended up at Kriner's Diner, where dinner was a winner. It was a tiny little joint off a street called Fireweed Lane. If that wasn't enough to recommend it, they had plenty of strong, fresh coffee and the kind of menu that makes me tear up.

I ordered 'Uncle Park's Politically Incorrect Corned Beef Hash & Eggs'. My server said it was politically incorrect because it defied government guidelines for portion control. I'm a bit of a corned beef hash enthusiast and this was possibly the best I'd ever had, made all the more delicious by the spicy hint of insurrection.

The food in my belly helped a little and the coffee almost cleared my head. I would have been happy to stay there all evening, chatting up the locals and abusing the free refill policy, but I had a fugitive, ex-neo-Nazi gubernatorial candidate to find. I left a tip as hearty as my dinner and headed back to the truck stop.

* * * * *

There was just one road north of Anchorage. I flew over a few little clusters of buildings, then there was a whole lot of nothing until Coldfoot. And Coldfoot was just slightly more than nothing—basically another truck stop. From there, I flew about ten miles east-northeast over rugged, hilly, pine-covered terrain.

I'd almost run out of daylight when I finally caught sight of a cabin. This was the only structure I'd seen in miles, so I figured it had to be Knott's place. It was made of rough-sawn timber and had been there a while, but was in good repair. There was a Tuff Shed not much smaller than the cabin off to one side and a Tesla speeder parked out front that probably cost ten times what I paid for my Lotus.

Almost certainly the right place.

I landed a non-threatening distance away and stepped out with my hands up in the air. I had to assume Knott would be armed, with a trigger finger as itchy as his feet were cold. But there was no hostile reception.

Hands still up, I walked slowly to the front door and lowered one arm just long enough to knock. No answer. I waited a minute, knocked again, then checked the door. It wasn't locked.

I opened it slowly and called out:

"Hello? I'm coming in. I'm friendly! Wanda Peck gave me your address! Don't shoot me!"

I stepped inside and looked around. It was a cozy place. Nicer on the inside than the outside. There were candles and lanterns, but also lamps and a TV, so there had to be a generator and satellite equipment somewhere. No way would there be any public utilities all the way out here.

Even if I hadn't seen Knott's speeder outside, I would have known he'd been here recently. On a stand by the front door, I saw a cell phone, wallet, key fob and a Law & Order ID badge. There were dirty dishes in the sink and the previous day's newspaper on the coffee table. As for where Knott was now—especially without his speeder—I had no clue.

It suddenly occurred to me that he might be here…and dead.

I took a quick look in all the rooms and was relieved to not find a corpse. After that, I took a more leisurely tour of the place, not searching *per se*, just getting a lay of the land. About half the square footage was in a great room, with a large window offering a scenic view of the surrounding forest and distant mountains. There was a bearskin rug on the floor and rugged landscape paintings and several animal heads mounted on the walls. The furniture that looked rustic, but probably cost a boatload.

One perfectly adequate bathroom. A decent-sized kitchen with all the necessary appliances. All in all, a comfy spot to go off the grid.

There was just one bedroom. A large dog door, covered with a panel, had been cut out of the wall next to the bed. So maybe that's where Knott was, out walking his dog. Or looking for more animals to decapitate.

It was getting dark now, so I turned on a lamp in the great room, picked up the newspaper and sat down to wait.

* * * * *

A few minutes later, the front door burst open. Robert Knott stepped through, leveling a loaded crossbow at me, his jaw set and eyes squinting like some backwoods Dirty Harry.

"Who the hell are you?" he said.

I dropped the newspaper and jumped to my feet, hands in the air.

"Wanda Peck sent me."

"How do you know Wanda?" he growled.

I gave him a quick summary I'd rehearsed on the flight up: "We're working together. My name's Murphy. I'm a P.I. and I was hired to investigate the death of a man named Carl Linsky. I think someone connected to Law & Order may have killed him. Wanda and I teamed up to try to prove it so I can close my case and she can get enough dirt to expose the Party."

Considering the circumstances, it was a pretty coherent overview. Knott lowered the crossbow. I relaxed and slowly dropped my arms.

"Then I guess we're on the same team," he said, slightly less growly.

He took a few steps closer, still giving me the squinty eyes.

"So Wanda managed to get into my safe," he said.

"*I* did, actually. She decrypted your flash drive, but I did the dirty work. You didn't make it easy. They have this thing called mail. You should try it some time."

Knott looked me up and down. Apparently, he decided I was on the level and finally eased up.

"Just gathering that information almost got me killed," he said. "Hell, it probably will. They're gonna find me sooner or later. But I'll tell you one thing: they know I'm not gonna go down without a fight."

He raised his crossbow and fired. A bolt sank into one of the walls with a thud. He tossed the crossbow onto a chair and walked to an antique cabinet. Inside were several bottles of liquor.

"Wanda probably told you, they've been watching me for a while now," he said, pulling out one of the bottles. "Security was tight before. Then it got to where I was afraid to do anything. Email, phone calls, everything I did on my computer. I'm sure it was all under surveillance. I was lucky to get what I did and put it on the flash drive."

"So, why'd you do it?" I asked. "How do you go from being the Law & Order candidate to trying to take them down?"

Knott walked past me, into the kitchen, got two glasses, then brought them back to the great room and handed me one.

"A candidate is just sugar coating on a pill," he said. "The party sets an agenda and all I did was make it a little easier for the public to swallow."

"What's Law & Order trying to force feed us?"

He poured a drink for me. I was about to politely refuse when I felt a faint throb at my temples. The headache was coming back. At this rate, I'd be out of pain pills by tomorrow night. The thought of being without them gave me a panicky feeling. Maybe alcohol would tide me over. It was worth a shot. Literally. I raised the glass and drank half of it.

"What did you say your name was?" he asked.

"Murphy," I answered, trying not to choke as the fire water scorched my throat. "Tex Murphy."

"Well, you may not believe what I'm gonna tell you, Tex."

He took a long drink and wiped his mouth with the back of his hand. "Law & Order is gonna do what nutjobs have been saying the government would do for the last thirty years. They're gonna put implants into people."

"Seriously?"

"Dead serious. It's gonna allow them to identify and track everyone."

"They can already do that. You know, cell phones?"

Knott made a laughing sound that wasn't at all funny.

"Tracking people is just the start with these implants. Eventually, they think they'll be able to control people with them."

Control?

About a million questions popped into my head. If what Knott was saying was true—and it was really hard for me to believe it might be—this was end-of-the-world stuff. But it would be a plausible explanation for Carl Linsky's suicide.

"You have proof of this?" I asked.

"Hell, no. Only a few people know what's going on. I thought it was crazy at the time. But now I'm pretty sure it's happening."

I took another drink. It was helping my head.

"Have you heard of STG?" I asked.

Knott shook his head. "What's that?"

"It might be the group that's developing these implants. Wanda Peck says they're connected to Gideon Enterprises. Do you know if Frank Schimming is in with Law & Order?"

"I think Schimming's on just one side—his own. He hedges his bets. Right now, the smart money is on Law & Order."

"Wanda also said Law & Order might have some kind of a hit list," I said. "Know anything about that?"

"Just that I'm on it."

"Any idea who else is?"

Knott shrugged.

"I only heard one name: Greg Call. He was the person they seemed most concerned about. Not sure why."

Greg Call.

That was a new name to follow up on. But I was more concerned about someone else.

"Have you heard the name 'Slade'?" I asked. "I think he may be the one putting the hit in hit list."

Knott shook his head, then reconsidered. "But maybe I saw him."

He moved toward the front door and got his phone from the stand.

"I took a few pictures," he said. "Anyone I didn't recognize. I figured Wanda could identify them. But I didn't get a chance to transfer the photos to that flash drive."

Knott came back, watching the phone as it booted up.

"I'd also like to find out more about John Klaus," I said.

Knott looked up, sharply, from his phone.

"No, you don't. Klaus is the reason I'm here. Just pray you never cross paths with him. If there's such a thing as pure evil, he's it."

"So why does Klaus want you dead?"

Knott turned his attention back at his phone.

"Because he's corrupted the Law & Order Party and I couldn't go along with it anymore. It used to be about making our country safe, globally and domestically. Strengthening our military and local law enforcement. Strong, but fair. To every legal U.S. citizen. But now, Klaus *is* the Law & Order Party and his agenda is all about hatred of mutants and dividing people to gain power and control."

"I can see why you wouldn't be on board with that," I said, "but it still doesn't explain why you're on Klaus's to-do list."

Knott smiled grimly, eyes still on his phone.

"I was planning on quitting the race for governor and coming out publicly against the party. I never told anyone, but it was like he smelled it on me. I think he was going to have me murdered, blame it on mutants and use my 'assassination' to rally even more support."

"Wow. That *is* evil."

"That's not even the worst of it. I think his ultimate plan is to exterminate the mutants."

"Well, that's just insane. People aren't gonna allow that to happen."

"It *is* insane," Knott agreed. "But it's already started. This mind control project is just the beginning. There's some other big plan that's been in the works for a while. I don't know what it is—and I get the feeling it's still years away—but I've heard it referred to as a giant 'reset button'."

Wanda had said Knott was the most paranoid man she knew. He didn't strike me as a conspiracy nut, but everything he was telling me sure sounded like it. And most of it didn't matter for my case. For now, I'd be happy to get a photo of Slade.

As I watched Knott scroll through his phone, I thought of another thing to ask him about. He hadn't heard of STG, but maybe he'd heard about something related to it.

"Do you know anything about an Overlord?" I asked.

Knott stopped cold and glared at me.

"You know about Overlord?!"

The next instant, Knott's chest exploded.

29

I stood there, frozen, as Robert Knott went down. A second later, all hell broke loose.

I don't know if it was instinct or terror, but my knees buckled and I dropped to the floor. Gunfire erupted all around me, raking the walls and blasting the décor into pieces. The lamp shattered, plunging the room into darkness. A few moments later, the firing stopped and everything went deathly quiet.

Knott hadn't put up as much of a fight as he'd hoped. I had nothing to put up a fight with...except the crossbow. And crossbow training wasn't part of the P.I. curriculum. Even if I could figure out how to use it, it sounded like I was seriously outnumbered. There was more than one gunman out there. A crossbow wouldn't save me.

As my eyes adjusted to the darkness, I looked around. I was numb with shock. While my brain tried to focus, I belly-crawled as quietly as I could toward Knott's body and picked up his phone. Then I kept going toward the door, where his other things had spilled onto the floor.

Now I had a phone, wallet, key fob and ID...but no plan. There were at least two people out there, so they would undoubtedly be making their way to the front and back doors. And I wouldn't stand a chance once they got me in their sights.

Then I started to smell propane. Coming from the kitchen. Knott probably used a propane tank for his stove or to heat his water, and one of the assassin's bullets must have hit it. Maybe I had a plan after all. A stupid plan that could go horribly wrong, but it was better than nothing.

I resumed belly-crawling into the kitchen. As I got closer, the smell of propane got stronger. I kept slithering through the kitchen, until I was just outside the bedroom. I looked around, making sure I was clear of any windows, so they couldn't see me.

"I give up!" I yelled, as loudly as I could.

After a long pause, I heard a faint voice calling from outside.

"Come out with your hands in the air!"

"I can't!" I yelled back. "I'm hit! It's bad! I can't move!"

I waited for a response. Maybe they were deciding what to do.

"I don't have a weapon!" I added, helpfully. "Just please don't kill me!"

The smell of gas was really strong now, stinging my eyes.

I crept into the bedroom and up to the dog door I'd seen earlier. It was good-sized, large enough for most hunting breeds, and covered with a panel. Gently, I pulled a small knob and lifted the panel out of its slot. The opening would be just big enough for me to squeeze through.

But not yet.

I reached into my pocket. Waited for another minute. Finally, I heard the front door get kicked in. I poked my head out through the flap on the dog door, and looked back and forth. No sign of anyone.

I slid through, as silently as possible, and then turned back to face the dog door. The Big Surf Lodge matchbook was in my hand. I pulled a match, ready to strike it.

A few seconds later, I heard the back door burst open.

"There's a gas leak!" I heard a man yell. "Hold your fire!"

I lit the match and then held it to rest of the matches. As they ignited, I pulled open the flap on the dog door, flung the burning matchbook inside and rolled away.

I wasn't sure exactly what would happen. I was pleasantly surprised.

The place blew up.

The open doors must have diffused the propane, so the house didn't blow into pieces, but the interior fired up like a furnace. I heard screaming as I got to my feet and sprinted for my speeder. A man on fire came staggering out the front door. It looked like there had been only two men and they were both caught in the explosion.

I got to my speeder and jumped in. A moment later, I was rising up above the blazing cabin and kept going until it looked like a little campfire.

Part III:

Knights

30

"So that's my best campfire story," I say, lighting a cigarette. "Knott's Inferno."

I probably could have skipped all the details, but it was my first legitimate near-death experience, so it was kind of a big deal. Plus, St. Germain is eating it up. He looks as tickled as a fat kid at a soft-serve ice cream dispenser.

"I must say," he says, almost out of breath with delight, "I suspected there was much more to you than met the eye, but I never dreamed you would be the keeper of such secrets. The one person in the entire world who knows the true fate of Robert Knott. Astonishing!"

"Well, I do live to astonish."

"Mr. Knott's sudden disappearance was quite the sensation back in the day, though now he's nothing more than a curious footnote in this city's history."

"Hard to believe the star of classic films like 'Only the Young Die Good' could be so easily forgotten."

St. Germain chuckles.

"I'll admit, he's a less compelling character than, say, Jimmy Hoffa or D.B. Cooper."

"Or Amelia Earhart," I say. "My personal favorite. That's a case I'd like to crack someday."

The Count purses his lips and gives me a conspiratorial look.

"I assure you, there are *some* who know the true circumstances of her disappearance. It was common knowledge in certain circles."

I take a drag off my cigarette and size up my guest. He's implying something, but I'm not sure exactly what. Amelia Earhart went missing in 1937. One hundred and thirteen years ago.

St. Germain waves his hand, dismissing the subject.

"A tale for another time. Tonight is about you, Mr. Murphy. And, as much as I'm enjoying your story, we must keep in mind that the point of telling it is to determine who tried to kill you earlier this evening."

"Well," I say, "it wasn't Robert Knott."

"Clearly," St. Germain says with a smile. "But it was *someone.* And you've introduced a number of possible suspects that match the criteria."

"What criteria is that?"

St. Germain reaches for his glass of scotch and gazes into it before speaking.

"I should give you some context. About ten years ago, I began to suspect that there was a malignant force at work; a spider at the center of a web that was gradually spreading to every corner of the globe. I have spent the past decade trying to identify this nameless, faceless person. So far, he has eluded me. On occasion, I've gotten hold of a thread, but can never trace it back to its source. At times, I've even questioned whether or not I'd imagined his existence. But recent developments have made me certain that he is not only real, he presents the gravest threat imaginable. And I fear we are near his endgame; within weeks—perhaps even days—the world could change forever."

"How? What's the endgame?"

"If my suspicions are correct, a kind of Nuclear Winter. I can share the details later, but they're irrelevant for our purposes here. Our goal is to try and identify him. And, whoever he is, he has the vast resources necessary to realize his plans."

"By 'resources', you mean cash."

"Among other things. He must also have the most advanced technology available, access to top secret networks, and political influence at the highest levels. He would also have an almost maniacal desire for control, but I'm also inclined to believe he is not well-known. Relative anonymity would be vital to him. A very few people would fit this profile. But let's start with wealth. Our adversary would certainly be very rich, so that's how I began my search. How many billionaires would you guess there were in 2037?"

"No idea. 10?"

St. Germain smiles and swirls his scotch around.

"Over four *thousand*."

"Geez."

"Geez, indeed. Based on wealth alone, that's a very long list of suspects."

I watch the Count take a sip.

"When it comes to narrowing down suspects," I say, "I always use the '3 M's': means, method and motive—*could* they have done it, *how* did they do it and *why*. Any idea what this 'spider's' motivation is?"

"I don't. But it must be something specific…something beyond merely acquiring more wealth, or power *per se*. John Klaus, for example, appears to have been motivated by anti-mutant sentiment. I'd not heard his name before, but he certainly fits the criteria. Frank Schimming, as well. Another candidate is someone who's name may have come up during your Martian case: Collier Stanton."

"Tom, Dick and Harry. Actually, they were all dicks."

"So?" The fat man arches an eyebrow, expectantly. "Could any of them be our adversary?"

"I can tell you it's not Collier Stanton. As for John Klaus, we'll get to him in a bit. And Frank Schimming was on the Moon Child for the big New Years' Eve blowout."

"Hm," St. Germain says, disappointed.

"One other little tidbit," I continue. "The 'big plan' Robert Knott referred to—the giant 'reset button' Law & Order was involved with—that turned out to be the Moon Child."

"Intriguing," St. Germain says, genuinely surprised. "Another link between your cases. I have a question or two about that. But first things first. Those implants Knott referred to…"

"I don't want to ruin the surprise," I say with a smile.

St. Germain raises his glass.

"Fair enough. Though, if you'll humor my playing armchair detective, I would deduce that your headaches and insomnia could have been caused by just such an implant."

I stub out my cigarette.

"A solid deduction. But, believe it or not, that didn't occur to me at the time. I figured I had a concussion or something. I was a bit on the naïve side."

"One of your charms."

"Well, I got a lot less charming as the investigation went on. Looking back, it started with the headache I got from being jumped that never really went away. But it went to a whole new level when Sylvia kissed me. It was the first time I lost control. And it got worse, like I was in a constant state of fight or flight. I'd never been an angry, violent person, but those things started coming out in me."

"Sleep deprivation can have that effect. It can drive one insane, even cause death. Humans can survive much longer without food than without sleep."

St. Germain catches himself and gives me an apologetic smile.

"But enough of me prattling on. What happened after your fiery escape?"

I take another drink and settle back into my chair.

"As I said, it hadn't occurred to me that I might have one of the implants…until after I talked to Knott. It finally hit me as I was flying back to civilization—still unable to sleep—that something was really wrong. Which made me think of Carl Linsky. If he'd gone through what I was going through, I could see why he might throw himself off a bridge."

"Did you consider going to a hospital?"

"Not really. I hate hospitals. And I doubted anyone would take me seriously. *Yeah, so, I've got an implant in my brain that's keeping me awake. Could you please get it out?* They probably would've stuck me in a padded cell."

"Well, when you put it like that. So, what did you do next?"

"With everything Knott had told me, I'd pretty much decided that the STG project, Overlord and Law & Order's implants were all connected. And everyone who'd worked on the project—and could or would help me—was either dead or about to be, so I needed to find one of them…and fast. And after Sonny showed up with the bloody STG passcard, I was fairly certain there was one person who had those names. Slade."

31

I made the flight from Alaska back to New San Francisco without a stop, pushing my little Lotus as hard as it would go. A strong headwind added extra time and it was almost lunchtime when I got back in town. I hadn't eaten since Anchorage, but now my appetite was gone. I'd been awake for nearly sixty hours, not counting the few minutes I'd been unconscious after getting jumped.

Ordinarily, I would have waited until after dark before going to the Big Surf Lodge, but time was of the essence. After a quick stop to look up the address and take a bio-break, I flew fifty miles down the coast, to a spot off the Pacific Coast Highway, just north of Santa Cruz.

The Big Surf Lodge was like something on a vintage postcard. In addition to a large lodge, there was a row of rustic old cabins with wood shingled roofs, surrounded by cypress trees, set on the edge of a cliff offering a majestic ocean view.

At first glance, it looked as if Slade might have cleared out after the confrontation with Sonny. There was just one vehicle in the parking lot: an older car—the four-wheeled kind—and not a nice one. Slade would certainly have a speeder, which meant he probably wasn't here, either temporarily or permanently. There was only one way to find out.

The not-nice car must have belonged to the kid at the check-in desk inside the lodge. He was tall and thin and hadn't shaved. Maybe ever. He had an excuse-me moustache and a tassel of blonde hair hanging off his chin like corn silk. Despite wearing a tie, there was nothing professional about him. Probably a relative of the owners.

He barely acknowledged me as I walked in. I didn't take it personally; a general lack of social skills, along with hunched posture and a vacant look, seemed pretty typical of almost every kid raised with a cell phone.

Speaking of which, I had Robert Knott's phone, which contained a photo of a man he thought might be Slade. I'd gone through the photos during my flight and found one that looked promising.

I figured the best way to engage the kid at the desk was to just stick the phone in front of his face. A normal adult might have found this awkward, if not downright antagonistic, but the kid focused right on it, maybe expecting an awesome cat video. But it was just the photo. I wanted to see if he would react to it.

He did. It wasn't much. Just a little flinch, then a quick glance at me.

"Is he staying here?" I asked.

The kid shook his head so nervously, he might as well have said: 'Yessir! He sure is!'

"Which cabin?"

"He's not here," the kid squeaked. "I mean…I've never seen that guy before."

I stared him down. His face looked somehow vacant and terrified at the same time.

"I get it," I said. "He's scary. Maybe he threatened to hurt you if you said anything. But I'm going to find him and nothing you say will convince him that you didn't help me. So you might as well. And then I'd get into your car and drive somewhere far away."

The kid didn't move. Except for his eyes, which suddenly couldn't stay focused on one spot. Probably a sign that his brain was switching out of read-only mode and actually trying to think through this unexpected predicament.

I, meanwhile, had a sudden and inexplicable urge to grab him by the collar and smash his head repeatedly into the counter. I guess the lack of sleep was starting to affect my usual cheery demeanor.

"If you don't start talking," I said, trying not to clench my teeth, "I'll tie you up so it'll be easy for him to find you."

I leaned forward, until I was just inches from the kid's face and growled: "*Which…cabin?*"

It was like a twig snapping.

"He rented 'em all. I think he's staying in number six."

The kid looked like he might start crying. I felt bad for him. Almost enough to not want to punch him.

"Anything else I should know?" I asked.

No response, but I could see he wasn't holding out on me. He just stood there, silent and unfocused, a tear trickling down his cheek.

"Go," I said. "And I wouldn't come back for a while."

He ran. Straight out to his car. A squeal of tires and he was gone.

I'd gotten what I needed from Knott's phone, so I dropped it on the floor and stomped on it. No sense in carrying around a potential tracking device. Plus, it felt good.

So now I knew Slade was staying here, in cabin number six. Best case scenario, I'd find a spare room key, Slade wouldn't be there, then I'd find a hit list and leave before he got back. There were only about a million things that could go wrong, none of which had been factored into my decision-making prior to this moment.

If Slade was there, I'd have to defend myself. And if I needed to defend myself, I was in serious trouble. I'm not a fighter. I could hold my own with an average Joe, but not a professional killer.

First things first. I went behind the front desk and found a box labeled 'Cabin Keys', but it was empty. Unfortunate. That meant I'd need to break in to his cabin. I took a quick look around the office, hoping to find a weapon of some kind, but the motel owners seemed to be the artsy, pacifist types.

I walked out of the lodge. The only sounds were birds chirping and surf pounding on the beach below. Slade must have chosen this place because it was so isolated. Anything unusual or out of place would be easily recognized. Like my speeder, for example.

The absence of other vehicles made me hopeful that Slade wasn't in his cabin, but even if the coast was clear, he could show up at any time. If he did, it might tip him off if he saw an unfamiliar speeder parked outside. Just to be safe, I decided to move it. I found a good hiding spot down the road where I could land in the trees, then walked back to cabin number six.

After taking a long listen at the front door, I went around the perimeter, peeking into every window, until I was sure the place was empty. There was a back door, facing the ocean, and I checked that one first. Locked. Returned to the front door. Also locked. Tried the windows. No luck.

Well, maybe a little luck. The old cabin doors hadn't been retrofitted with modern hardware or security panels and I had Sonny's lockpick set in my pocket. Picking locks wasn't my forte, but after a few minutes of prodding, jiggling and cursing, I finally managed to get the back door open.

The interior was classic Monterey shabby chic—an ocean-y pastel palette, tile, things made of whitewashed driftwood—and worn to perfection. At first, I wondered if Slade might be staying in one of the other cabins. The only things that gave him away were a coffee mug in the sink, a few provisions in the refrigerator and cupboards, and some clothing in a closet. I had to give him one thing: he was tidy.

As I searched the place, I started to get a feel for who Slade was. His clothes were neatly hung and arranged, indicating a pretty healthy streak of OCD. They were expensive and made for a man a few inches shorter than me, but wider through the upper body. A check of the bathroom revealed that he took shaving very seriously and had a thing for skin products.

The bed was made up perfectly and tightly enough to bounce a quarter off it. Military background, maybe. There was also a pair of handcuffs attached to the metal frame—for business or pleasure, I couldn't say. Maybe both. Or maybe they were one and the same for him.

There wasn't a lot of area to search. After fifteen minutes, I'd gone over every square inch and hadn't found anything important, much less a hit list. Slade had left nothing incriminating, or even useful, behind. No paperwork, no weapons. Nothing to identify him. He probably carried everything vital around with him. Which meant I would have to confront him to get my hands on what I wanted. I was starting to think I would need to come back later with a better plan and more firepower.

I was finishing up my search in the front room when I heard aggressive footsteps crunching toward the cabin. There was a clear line of sight from the front door to the back; I wouldn't have enough time to make it out the back door without Slade seeing me. I could try to take him by surprise, maybe knock him down and run for it, but he was almost certainly armed and I'm not faster than a speeding bullet. That left one option.

Hide.

The first hiding place I thought of was under the bed. As a key jingled in the front door lock, I moved as quickly and quietly as I could into the bedroom and was about to hit the floor when I realized I'd left the closet doors open. If my suspicions were correct about Slade's OCD, he would notice and be on instant alert. I had to close them.

Which would take precious seconds. Enough to change the plan. I stepped into the closet and pulled the doors shut behind me.

Good thing.

Just a moment later, Slade came straight into the bedroom. My heart was beating so hard I could feel it in my ears. I closed my eyes and clenched my fists until I got my breathing under control. When I opened my eyes, I peered through slats in the closet doors, which provided a partial view into the room.

Slade was taller than average and powerfully built, with blue-black Superman hair and a handsome face that was plumply hydrated, wrinkle-free and immaculately shaved. He was wearing a long overcoat and carrying a briefcase. I watched him attach the briefcase to the handcuffs on the bed frame, then take off his overcoat, fold it neatly and lay it on the bed. He took out a cell phone, pressed a button on the side of it several times, and put it on the nightstand. Then he walked into the bathroom, pulling off his black turtleneck. A moment later, the door squeaked loudly as he pushed it almost shut, then water turned on in the shower.

My instinct was to run for it. I could slip out now without Slade ever knowing I was here. I could go buy a gun, or three, and come back with a little more leverage. But he could be gone by the time I got back. And if he found out the kid at the desk had headed for the hills, he might decide to relocate altogether. This might be my only window of opportunity.

And his briefcase, which almost certainly contained what I was looking for, was *right there.*

I stepped out of the closet and closed the doors softly. A quick look at the briefcase revealed a three-digit combination lock that I didn't have the combination for. I double-checked the handcuffs; the only way to free up the briefcase would be with the handcuff key…or a blowtorch. And I was fresh out of blowtorches.

I checked the pockets of Slade's overcoat, but they were empty. I'd already gone through every drawer in the cabin during my search and hadn't found any keys. Which meant they were probably in the pockets of Slade's trousers…which were in the bathroom.

I walked up to the bathroom door, debating whether or not to risk making a grab at his clothes. Steam was billowing through the cracked door. Between the squeaky door and the release of steam that would come from opening the door—not to mention not knowing exactly where his clothes would be—I couldn't risk it.

I'd never tried to pick handcuffs, but it had to be possible. All you needed was a bobby pin, at least from what I'd seen in the movies. I returned to the bedroom and went to work.

As I'd done with the back door lock, I used the lockpick set, poking and prodding, with no clue what the mechanism was inside the handcuffs, or how to manipulate it. My nerves were bad and my hands were shaking, which didn't help. It felt like an hour passed, though it was probably a minute or less.

Then a phone buzzed. Loudly. I almost dropped the lockpick.

It was Slade's cell phone on the nightstand. I looked down and saw the caller ID: *Unknown*. After the second ring, the water in the shower turned off. I dropped to the floor and slid under the bed.

The bathroom door squeaked open and bare feet padded out.

"Yeah," Slade said flatly.

I could hear a man's voice, but not clearly enough to make out any words.

"Just got back," Slade answered. He had an accent. Australian.

"Yeah. Number six. One of my lucky numbers. I enjoyed that one."

I could hear the malicious smile in his voice. The mention of 'number six' made me think of the cabin, but it seemed much more likely he was talking about a sixth person. A sixth *victim*.

Slade was quiet for a minute, listening to the man on the other end of the line.

"Got it," Slade said. "I'll get on it tonight. I have some unfinished business to take care of first. An old friend showed up unexpectedly. He got away with one of the passcards."

An angry, unintelligible outburst from the other man.

"Calm down," Slade interrupted. "I know where to find him. I just couldn't be in two places at once. I'll get it back."

After a few parting words, the call ended. Slade set the phone down and then muttered two angry, four-letter words—one that started with an 'F', which I rarely used, and a 'C' word that I would *never* use. He tromped back into the bathroom, grabbed a towel, then walked to the kitchen.

It was now or never. I slid out from under the bed and slipped into the bathroom, careful to avoid bumping the door. Slade's clothes were hung on the back of the door. I fished through his trouser pockets and found a set of keys…and his wallet. I took both and was about to open the bathroom door when I heard the pad of footsteps coming closer.

Almost without thinking, I turned around and stepped into the shower. Luckily, the curtain wasn't transparent and was half-closed, just enough to cover me. I literally held my breath as Slade entered the bathroom, vigorously toweling off his hair. He grabbed a bathrobe from a hook on the wall and stepped back out, leaving the door open.

After a few moments, I stepped gingerly out of the shower and stood by the open door, listening hard. I heard a cupboard open and close. Slade was back in the kitchen. Hopefully he was making himself something to eat and would stay there for a bit.

I snuck out of the bathroom and tiptoed to the bed. Held my breath again as I unlocked the handcuffs. I picked up the briefcase, my palms sweating, then moved to the bedroom door and listened again. A cracking sound, then the sizzle of a frying egg.

I tiptoed out, finally getting to the back door. Grabbed the handle. Opened the door as quietly as I could. Resisted the impulse to throw the door open and run. Stepped outside. Pulled the door slowly shut. Somehow had the self-control to take soft steps until I was a good distance from the cabin.

Then I ran.

32

I'd run more in the past three days than the rest of my adult life put together. Adrenaline is a hell of a thing.

I sprinted all the way back to my speeder and piled in, gasping for breath. The set of keys I'd taken included a speeder fob so, unless Slade had a backup, he couldn't come after me. At least not for a while. I probably should have taken his cell phone, too, but I'd been a bit distracted. At least I had his wallet, which could come in handy for proving his identity to Wanda and maybe even the cops.

After I'd flown a safe distance away, I landed my speeder and took stock of my ill-gotten booty. Slade's wallet contained a California driver's license and one credit card, both in the name of 'Norton Richardson'. There was also a few hundred dollars in cash, which I had no problem confiscating. The only other item was a lottery ticket. I had to laugh, thinking how great it would be if I hit the Mega Millions jackpot with Slade's numbers.

I turned my attention to the briefcase. If there's such a thing as a military-grade briefcase, this was it. A sledgehammer probably wouldn't be enough to break into it. A blowtorch might do the trick, but then I'd risk incinerating the contents. Obviously, figuring out the lock would be preferable.

The lock had a button, three tiny LED lights and three dials, like on a bike lock, which could all be set from zero to nine. With no clue what the combination would be, I pressed the button to see what would happen. The three LED lights lit up in red, flashed once and went dead again.

Slade seemed like the kind of guy who wouldn't use something so obvious as his birth date for a combination, but it was worth a try. I checked the driver's license. The birth date was 01/06/1990. That would make him forty-seven, which seemed about right. But I needed three numbers. Would it be 0-1-0? 1-6-1? I tried all the combinations of 0, 1, 6 and 9. Each time, the LED lights flashed red.

Then I remembered Slade saying that six was 'one of his lucky numbers'.

Lucky numbers.

I took another look at the lottery ticket. The numbers were: 6-10-19-27-31. With the first one being a six, I had to hope these were *all* of Slade's lucky numbers…and that he might just use them for something like, say, a nine-digit code.

I turned the first dial to 6, the second to 1 and the third to 0, then pressed the button.

One of the LED lights turned green.

Yes!

I reset the dials to 1, 9 and 2, then pressed the button. A second LED turned green.

7, 3, 1. Button.

All three lights flashed green and the lock clicked. Indiana Jones music played in my head as I opened the case. So much for Slade's numbers being lucky…at least for him.

Going through the contents of the briefcase, I was a little disappointed that there weren't any weapons for me to confiscate, but I was pleased to find three passports, all with his photo but different names and nationalities. Slade wouldn't see these again.

There were also three of the STG passcards, identical to the one I'd found in Linsky's attic and the one I'd gotten from Sonny, except for having different letters on them—A, B and H. There was no hit list, *per se*—I guess I'd envisioned something like a shopping list, with a header reading 'People to Kill' and a list of names with some crossed out—but there were eight manila envelopes, each of which contained information about a specific person. Val Davis. Rona Morgan.

And Carl Linsky.

I did a mental fist pump. In context, this was a smoking gun. It was more than enough to convince Wanda that Linsky had been murdered. Maybe enough to convince the cops to change his cause of death. I needed to get in touch with Detective Clements.

I checked the contents of the other five envelopes. The first contained information on Greg Call, whose name I'd gotten from Robert Knott. The next two were for men I hadn't heard of: Bosworth Clark and Samuel Q. Jones.

The fourth was a bit of a surprise. J. Saint Gideon. But the fifth was, literally, the last person I could have expected.

Me.

* * * * *

After a quick look at the contents of the envelopes, I decided I needed a favor from my only contact in the police department. And the odds of that happening were slightly less than winning the Mega Millions. Detective Clements had no reason to help me out; I'd been lucky to get the bare minimum of information about Carl Linsky's suicide from her. Plus, it was the weekend, so it might be impossible for me to even get in touch with her. But maybe someone else could.

I flew my speeder to a café on the other end of Santa Cruz. There was an antique payphone inside and I used it to call Wanda Peck. I needed two favors from her, the first of which was to use her CAPRICORN cachet to track down Clements and pass along my request.

The second favor would take a little time, so I told Wanda where I was and we set a time to meet. Knowing that Slade couldn't have followed me, this place was as safe as any. After I hung up, I got a table and let Slade pay for my lunch.

The adrenaline had worn off, leaving me deliriously exhausted, with a raging headache on top of it. I took one of the last of the precious pain pills and ordered a double shot of tequila.

I still wasn't hungry, but eating had seemed to help when I was up in Alaska, so I ordered the biggest gut bomb on the menu: a shredded beef chimichanga with mango-habanero salsa.

After downing the booze, I pulled out the envelope containing my information and read through it. They'd put together an impressively comprehensive overview of my mundane existence. Not surprisingly, it was the thinnest file of the bunch. They knew my personal history and family members, where I worked and lived, how long I'd been there, typical schedule, known associates...even the places I ate. I'd never made a secret of any of this. Still, it was disturbing to have total strangers know so much about me.

I assumed this info had been used to set up the ambush in my office, which meant Slade was almost certainly the one who'd jumped me.

It had now been three days since I last slept and felt like I was dying. Again, I thought of Carl Linsky and wondered if he'd experienced the same thing I was going through. I couldn't imagine what another sleepless night or two would do to me.

At least now I had a chance of finding someone who would know about the implants and how to get mine out of my head. Slade had said his last victim was 'number six'. Assuming I was already in the victim category—and that the eight folders represented the entire hit list—that meant there were two people to go. If Slade hadn't gotten to J. Saint Gideon yet, there was only one other person left standing for me to find. And their info was in one of these folders. The question was: which one?

I'd asked Wanda to get in touch with Detective Clements and see if she could use her law enforcement network to help narrow the list of candidates. In the meantime, I went back through all the files, paying special attention to the ones with information on Greg Call, Samuel Q. Jones and Bosworth Clark.

I was just finishing up when Wanda and Sylvia entered the café. They both seemed happy—and relieved—to see me, each in her own way. Under normal circumstances, this would have been the stuff male fantasies are made of. Wanda was her usual regal self, all crisp and tailored in dark grey; Sylvia was all warm and soft, wearing a long, clingy sweater, black yoga pants and boots...and that sexy crooked smile.

I, on the other hand, must have looked terrible.

"You look terrible," Wanda said, sliding into the booth.

She said it with good-natured concern, but I had to bite my tongue and not say something nasty back to her. I don't know if Sylvia sensed it, but as she sat next to me, she gave me a reassuring smile and put her hand on my thigh. It did nothing to take the edge off.

I pushed the envelope containing my information across the table. Wanda's half-smile disappeared as she examined the contents.

"What is this?" she asked.

"My death warrant, apparently."

"Where'd you get it?"

"Long story. The Angel of Death I told you about? Slade? This is his briefcase. It's full of files on people he's killed and is planning to kill."

I turned to Sylvia.

"Your father was one of them."

Her grip tightened on my leg, but she stayed quiet. I looked back at Wanda.

"I need you to get all this to Detective Clements and see if she'll change Linsky's cause of death."

"I'll take care of it," Wanda said. "This could also give us more ammunition against Law & Order. Together with what Robert got for us, I think we can hit them pretty hard. I forgot to ask: were you able to find him?"

"Yeah. But I wasn't the only one. Knott's dead."

"No." Wanda put a hand to her mouth.

"And Gideon could be next. One of these files is his. You might want to give him a heads-up."

Wanda nodded, her mind still processing the news about Knott.

Sylvia put her hand over mine and whispered: "Will you tell me what's going on?" She tilted her head toward Wanda. "*She* won't tell me a thing. And now I'm really worried about you. This is all my fault, isn't it?"

"Pretty much," I said, meaning it to be a joke, but it didn't come out that way. "It doesn't matter. It's not just about you and your father now."

Sylvia looked completely lost. No wonder. She'd just heard me say a lot of scary things and didn't know how to process it. I turned to face her.

"If I'm still alive when this is over, I'll tell you everything. For now, I need you to sit there and let me talk to Wanda, OK?"

Her brow started to wrinkle, but then she nodded and sat back.

I turned to Wanda and said: "You may already know this from what was on Knott's flash drive, but the STG project—the thing Sylvia's father was working on—was all about implants and, somehow, mind control. I think they put one in me when I got jumped at my office. I'm pretty sure that's what's causing my headaches. And it's keeping me awake. It's been three days and even those heavy-duty sleeping pills can't touch it. If this is what Linsky went through, I can understand why he put himself out of his misery."

"We need to get you to a hospital," Sylvia interrupted, panic in her voice.

I shook my head.

"There's no time. Another day or two and I'll be a vegetable. Even if I could find a doctor who'd take me seriously, I don't think they'd know how to deal with it. I have no idea what it is, how it works or what removing it might do to me. My best hope is to find someone who worked with STG and knows what to do about it."

"Where is Slade?" Wanda asked, suddenly snapping out of her stupor.

"He was at the Big Surf Lodge, just up the PCH from here. But probably long gone now."

I handed Wanda the wallet and the passports from the briefcase.

"Here are his IDs."

She took them, but kept her eyes on me.

"I'll put all our resources on finding him," she said. "What's your plan? What else can I do to help?"

I pulled the other envelopes from the briefcase.

"I think there's one person still out there who might know what to do about my implant. And his information is in one of these files. I just need to find out which one. Were you able to get in touch with Clements?"

Wanda nodded and took out her cell phone.

"Yeah. I'm guessing there's a story with you two."

"Kind of. Not really."

Wanda punched in a number, then handed the phone to me. After a few rings, Detective Clements answered.

"Clements."

"It's Murphy," I said.

I half expected her to hang up, but she didn't. Maybe Wanda had done some positive P.R. work on my behalf. I thought about apologizing for interrupting her weekend, but it was probably best to get straight down to business.

"Any luck with those names Wanda gave you?" I asked.

"Lucky for you, maybe. Not for them. Samuel Q. Jones died two weeks ago, down in L.A. Speeder crash, just like the Davis woman up here."

"What about Greg Call?"

"Nothing. And I do mean nothing. I'm not sure he even exists."

"Bosworth Clark?"

"More than Call, but not much. No permanent address or contact info."

At least Clark wasn't dead, as far as the cops knew. And there was a lead to his whereabouts in his file. He was the one I'd try to track down first.

"Thanks for checking," I said. "Maybe I can return the favor. I have evidence that Jones was murdered, even though it was made to look like an accident. And he's not the only one. I'll send over what I found."

Clements didn't respond immediately. Maybe it sounded crazy to her. But having CAPRICORN involved gave it at least a little credibility.

"I'll take a look," she said.

I thanked her, then hung up and handed the phone back to Wanda. I nudged Sylvia and we all slid out from the booth.

"So…?" Wanda asked.

I pulled her aside and lowered my voice so Sylvia wouldn't hear.

"Have Clements look for an implant in Linsky's brain. I'm sure they'll find one if they look hard enough."

She nodded, then asked: "What about you?"

"Looks like I'm headed to the Land of Enchantment. From what Clements just told me, it may be my best lead."

I felt Sylvia's hand on my arm and turned around. Before I could do anything, she moved in and kissed my cheek, then whispered into my ear.

"Thank you, Tex. I'm so sorry about all this. I hope I get a chance to make it up to you. Please come back to me."

I took her by the shoulders and pushed her out to arms' length.

"If I'm still alive next weekend, I just might take you up on that."

33

The files in Slade's briefcase confirmed that he and whoever hired him were getting rid of everyone who'd worked on the STG project…with the exception of John Klaus; his standing in the Law & Order Party probably explained why he wasn't on the hit list.

I knew Klaus, Linsky, Davis and Morgan had been team members and, assuming Bosworth Clark, Samuel Q. Jones and Greg Call were as well, that accounted for seven of Linsky's eight 'chessmen'. It was possible that J. Saint Gideon was number eight, but he'd said he knew nothing about Overlord and I had no reason not to take him at his word.

So, just maybe, there were *three* people still alive who knew about the implants and could help me get mine out of my head: Clark, Call and a mystery person Slade had no info on. I had no idea who the mystery person might be either, so Call and Clark were my only options.

And Greg Call was a ghost. Other than being the CTO of Gideon Enterprises, there was almost no information in his file—not even a photograph. Robert Knott had said Call was the one person Law & Order was most worried about, and that made him the one I most wanted to find. But there was nothing to go on in the file. Even Detective Clements had come up empty.

So, it all came down to Bosworth Clark. The info in his file described an off-the-grid kind of guy, and his photograph looked like it. He had a beard flecked with grey, an unruly mop of salt-and-pepper hair and glasses that made his eyes look disturbingly large.

But if he was trying not to be found, he wasn't very good at it.

Whoever had gathered his information had picked up his trail in New Mexico. According to the file, he lived out of an RV and moved around every few weeks. Most recently, he'd been in Shiprock, NM.

I had all the information I needed, so I gave the briefcase and everything in it to Wanda, with the exception of the STG passcards. I wasn't sure if they would be of any use, but they were important enough for Slade to make a point of collecting them. You never know when you might need bargaining chips. I'd asked Wanda to bring Linsky's card and I added it to the others, along with the one Sonny had given me.

Wanda said she would follow up with Gideon—check to see if he was still alive and well and find out if he knew anything about the implants. I'd contact her later and come back if he could help me. If not, Bosworth Clark was very likely my last realistic hope.

*   *   *   *   *

It was a little over eight hundred miles as the Lotus flies from Santa Cruz to Shiprock, New Mexico. I made it there in just under four hours.

It was a tiny town on a Navajo reservation, not far from the Four Corners area where Utah, Arizona, Colorado and New Mexico all meet up. There was a huge rock formation nearby that looked, appropriately enough, like a ship sailing across the desert plain. It reminded me a little of Devil's Tower, from the Close Encounters movie, which made me wonder if Bosworth Clark could be a UFO nut, traveling around the country searching for evidence of aliens. Like that would ever pan out.

The sun was sinking into the western horizon as I searched for Clark's RV. I flew my speeder back and forth, like a boat using sonar to find sunken treasure, until I finally spotted an RV tucked into a small clump of rocks about ten miles from Shiprock. There was nothing else for miles around. It seemed like the kind of place you'd camp out if you didn't want to be found.

I landed my speeder and approached. There were no lights on inside the RV, no sign that anyone was in it. But when I pulled the door open, I realized I was wrong. Dead wrong.

An invisible wave hit my face and I staggered back, instantly nauseated. I'd never smelled anything like it—a putrid sweetness, like rotting meat sprinkled with perfume.

I stepped away and took a few deep breaths, waiting for my stomach to settle. The hot desert sun had turned the RV into the Easy-Bake Oven from hell. And I had no doubt Bosworth Clark was the one who'd been left to cook.

After taking a few moments to psyche myself up, I pinched my nose and stepped into the vehicle. The driver's and passenger seats were to my right. The middle section was a typical layout, galley-style, with a kitchenette against one wall. The other wall had been retrofitted with a long desk and storage bins. A sleeping area and bathroom were in the back.

A rolling office chair sat in the middle of the galley. A body was sprawled in the seat. In the low light, it looked almost like he'd pushed back from the desk to take a nap. Several tiny points of light from various items on the desk were flashing intermittently. That meant they were getting power. If they were running off the RV's battery, Clark couldn't have been dead that long.

I felt around the wall near the door and found a light switch. I flipped it and almost threw up again. Half of Bosworth Clark's head was gone.

Brain matter and blood was sprayed across the kitchenette and cabinets. More blood had pooled around the chair and there was a handgun on the floor, just below his dangling right arm.

I didn't have the time or inclination to preserve the crime scene for the cops. The space was too tight for me to work around the corpse, so I needed him out of the way. And I wasn't about to carry the body outside and get blood all over me.

I grabbed a dish towel and used it to get hold of the back of the chair. Then I rolled the chair toward the door and spun it so Clark was facing the opening. It felt wrong, but there was no way around it. I got a rolling start and shoved the chair with Clark in it out the door and quickly turned away. Outside, I heard a sickening crunch and thud.

With space to maneuver, I picked my way to the rear of the RV, grabbed the blanket and sheets off the bed and spread them out on the blood-soaked floor.

The desk was uncluttered, with just a pair of reading glasses, a set of speakers, two laptops—one with the Gideon Enterprises logo on it—and a keyboard. Not a computer keyboard, but the piano kind. If Slade had been here—and despite the illusion of a suicide, I was sure he had been—I wondered why he hadn't taken the laptops. Maybe his only concern was killing Clark.

The Gideon laptop was closed and shut down. I expected it to be as inaccessible as Linsky's was, but it had the STG passcard reader attached and I booted it up anyway. As I waited, I opened the second laptop; its screen lit up, flickering out of sleep mode.

I bent down and took a closer look. There were several icons on the screen, but one immediately jumped out at me: a symbol of a camera.

I double-clicked the icon. A small window appeared, and a video started playing. It showed a nervous-looking Bosworth Clark staring into the laptop's camera. He turned the laptop so it pointed toward the RV door, then moved off-screen.

As I watched the empty scene, I heard five musical notes. I recognized it immediately and had to smile, despite the circumstances; it was the sequence from the Close Encounters movie. When it finished, I heard a faint whirr and click, then a second whirr and click.

Seconds later, the RV door opened and Slade stepped up into view. He was wearing leather gloves and the same overcoat and black turtleneck he'd had on when I saw him.

Clark turned in his seat, as if he'd been taken by surprise. He was smart enough not to block the camera.

"Who are you?" he said, trying to sound angry, but I could hear the fear. "What do you want?"

"Hello, Bosworth."

Slade's tone was silky and menacing.

"My name is Slade. I'm here to play a game with you."

"A game?" Clark sputtered. "What are you talking about?"

"A game of chance."

I could hear the sadistic smile in Slade's voice. "And there are two ways we can play."

Clark stayed silent. I couldn't imagine how he felt, probably realizing that this man was here to kill him.

"One way is better," Slade said. "Fast...painless...easy-peasy, lemon squeezy. You even have a chance to win. The other way is, well, worse. Very slow...very painful. And you will lose in the most horrible way imaginable. I'll let you choose."

Clark still said nothing.

Slade pulled a .38 out, opened the cylinder and extended the gun toward Clark, handle first. Clark hesitated, but finally took it.

"There's a good boy," Slade said softly. "Now give the cylinder a spin. We'll see how lucky you are. You have one chance in six."

Clark's hands were shaking, but he followed the instructions.

"Now close it up."

Clark complied.

"You know what to do."

I knew how it was going to turn out, but I hoped Clark had at least made a move on Slade. I would have. But the guy didn't have it in him. I watched as he slowly raised the gun to the side of his head. I couldn't watch. I turned away just before the sound of the gunshot.

Thankfully, Clark's body had slumped out of view. Slade stood still for a long moment, admiring his handiwork, then moved closer to the camera. He bent down, his face almost filling the screen. He spent a few minutes staring at the screen and clicking on the keyboard.

He then straightened up and the screen went dark as he closed the laptop. A second later, the video recording ended.

Slade must not have noticed that he was being recorded or he would have either deleted the file or taken the laptop. If we didn't already have enough on him, this would seal the deal. But Slade was the least of my worries at the moment.

I turned my attention back to the Gideon laptop. If I could access what was on it, it might give me details on the STG project, maybe even give me some idea how to disable the thing that was killing me.

As with Linsky's laptop, there was a message asking for a passcard. I pulled the STG passcards out of my pocket. One of these had to work. Slade had collected them from all the other victims, so I didn't think he would have left here without Clark's. I kept trying until I found it. It was the one marked with an 'H'.

What came next was familiar from my attempts to access Linsky's laptop. A login dialog appeared with 'clark@stg.net' in the user name field and a blank password field.

Another stupid password.

I straightened up and looked around. No post-it notes in sight, so I took a moment to think back to what I'd seen in Linsky's attic. Linsky's STG passcard had been marked with an 'F' and his password had corresponded to his chess piece, the bishop. Maybe Clark's passcard and password were the same. 'H' was the eighth and final letter; that meant he was a rook.

I clicked in the password field and typed in ROOK, then hit enter. 'Invalid Password'.

So much for that. I sat back and tried to think. The password could be literally anything.

Unless…

I typed in CASTLE, said a little agnostic prayer, and hit Enter.

Bingo.

For some reason, Clark's account was still active, unlike Linsky's. I took a quick look through Clark's files. There was no mention of implants, mind control, or anything similar—nothing that could help me with my implant. Clark's area of expertise was satellite technology. I wasn't sure how it connected to the rest of the project, but it did me no good whatsoever.

Another dead end.

Bosworth Clark had seemed like my best bet, but I'd guessed wrong. Now it was down to Greg Call. Call. Or a mystery person I wasn't even sure existed. Maybe there was something here that could give me a lead to one of them.

My eyes drifted to the keyboard—the piano one—and I remembered hearing the 'Close Encounters' music on the video of Clark's murder. It now struck me as odd that Clark had decided to play his keyboard right before Slade showed up. Why would he do that?

The keyboard wasn't full-size, just 32 keys, less than three octaves. I found a power button and pressed it, then touched a key. It was working. I then experimented with the keys until I figured out the five-note sequence from Close Encounters.

Nothing happened.

Maybe I was playing in the wrong key. I've never been accused of having perfect pitch. I moved up one key and repeated the sequence. Then again. And again.

It wasn't until I started the sequence on the G key that it finally worked. G-A-F-F (an octave lower) –C. Then I heard the same whirr and click I'd heard on the recording. A small tray popped out from below the keyboard, like a DVD player, except this one was a storage compartment.

There was a cell phone inside it.

I picked it up, saw that it was turned off, and powered it up. The Home Screen appeared, which was a picture—ironically enough—of Devil's Tower. Overlaying the photo was a text message preview. It contained just two words: '*Rendezvous ASAP*'. There was also a symbol of a blue diamond. Since Clark hadn't opened the text yet, it must have come either just before or after he died.

I swiped my thumb over the screen and nine dots appeared. Another password required, of sorts. If the phone had used biometric security, I could have gotten into it, though the thought of what it would take to do that almost made me gag. But, with this nine-dot system, there was no way to know what pattern Clark would have chosen to unlock his phone.

I turned the display off, then on again—clearing the nine dots—then took another look at the text message. '*Rendezvous ASAP*', with a blue diamond symbol. The text had been sent by someone named 'Q'. The only person involved in all this with a Q name was Samuel Q. Jones, but Clements said he'd died two weeks ago. There was, however, another possibility.

The bulletin board in Linsky's attic had the STG members sequenced like chess pieces. Linsky was a bishop. John Klaus and Val Davis were knights. Rona Morgan and Bosworth Clark were rooks.

Maybe 'Q' referred to 'Queen'. The most powerful chess piece. I wondered if that could be Greg Call. Wishful thinking, probably, but maybe he'd sent this message to everyone on the STG team, asking them to meet up to see who was still alive and figure out how to stay that way. If I could crash the party, I might find someone who could help me.

But where was the rendezvous location?

Unless everyone had been told ahead of time where to meet up in case of emergency, the blue diamond symbol in the text message was the only possible answer. That symbol hadn't appeared anywhere else during my investigation and, as far as I knew, it didn't have any significance related to chess.

I used Clark's personal laptop to enter 'Blue Diamond' into the search engine. The first listings were for Blue Diamond Growers, the maker of delicious and nutritious snacks. After that was a bunch of links to information about literal diamonds. There was even a 'Blue Diamond' strain of marijuana.

Moving on to the second page of search results, I found something more promising: a listing for Blue Diamond, Nevada. It linked to a Wikipedia page, which described a tiny town of less than three hundred residents, west of Las Vegas. More searching revealed that this Blue Diamond was of interest to a particular group of conspiracy theorists. I found several articles describing 'subterranean tunnels' near Blue Diamond, which may or may not connect to abandoned military installations…and may even have held 'flying saucers' at one time.

It sounded like the kind of place that would be right up Bosworth Clark's alley. Remote town…tunnels…military bases…flying saucers. And it was only three hundred miles away—less than two hours by speeder—and more or less on the flight path back to San Francisco. If I was wrong, at least it wouldn't be a huge waste of time.

And time was precious.

I had one pain pill left and it was taking all my will power not to use it. The shock of finding Clark and the ensuing adrenaline rush had provided some temporary relief, but it was wearing off quickly. Every heartbeat felt like a sledgehammer to the forehead. My peripheral vision was starting to play tricks on me. I thought I might start hallucinating. And the lack of sleep felt like it was literally killing me. I wasn't sure how much longer I could keep it together.

I found a computer bag and stowed Clark's laptops and phone inside it. As I climbed out, I averted my eyes from the horrific scene I'd created and returned to my speeder. The footage of Slade could go a long way toward proving my case…provided I could stay alive long enough to show it to someone. Hopefully, someone in Blue Diamond could help me with that.

34

I was halfway to Blue Diamond, NV when it hit me that I should have taken the .38 from the RV. Slade had almost certainly left it there to sell the idea that Clark had shot himself, but I'd ruined that illusion. I'd thrown the sheet and blanket onto the floor, covering up the gun, and then promptly forgot it was there. I wasn't sure what sort of trouble lay ahead, and it would have been nice to have a weapon, but it was too late to go back now. It felt like I was on a countdown clock.

The lights of Las Vegas lit up the desert from almost a hundred miles away and were glowing on the eastern horizon when I arrived at Blue Diamond. Mountains separated the tiny town from Sin City, making it feel more remote than it actually was. A sign welcomed me, saying: 'Blue Diamond, NV – Population Low – Elevation High – Burros?', but that was the only welcoming thing. It looked like they'd rolled up the sidewalks a couple hours ago.

Blue Diamond had an Old West ghost town feel to it, especially at this hour. There was a touristy area that looked like a western movie set, and a handful of normal homes scattered around, but the town felt mostly abandoned. It took only a few minutes to do a thorough fly-over. There seemed to be only one place for visitors to stay in town. If this was the STG team's rendezvous point, they'd be staying in the Bonnie Ranch Motel.

The motel sat in a sea of sagebrush and was fronted by a large entry gate made of logs. Nearby was a corral, occupied by a few four-legged creatures I assumed were burros. I landed my speeder near the motel entrance and walked into the lobby.

I seemed to catch the desk clerk by surprise, but he was friendly enough. I said I was supposed to meet some friends and asked if there was anyone here from out of town. He said *everyone* staying there was from out of town, and only a couple guests were registered at the moment. And they had both gone out for the evening.

I asked if Greg Call was one of them. He wasn't, not that Call would have used his real name. The clerk was sorry he couldn't help, then said I might try the Area 51 Saloon. It was the closest place to get food and drink, just a few miles outside of town.

I returned to my speeder. The air here was bone-dry and fragrant with desert flora and burro droppings. I lifted off and followed the clerk's directions.

Five minutes later, I landed outside the Area 51 Saloon. It was pretty much what you'd expect—a large clapboard box with neon signs and a hitching post for your horse. If I'd just had a small bag of gold dust, I could get a cold beer, a warm bath and a hot date with one of the madam's girls of ill repute.

There were a dozen vehicles parked outside, half of them speeders, the other half old-fashioned cars. If any of the STG members were here, I was sure they would be using speeders. It was possible they'd flown in on a commercial airline to Las Vegas and rented a car, but all that would be traceable.

Most of the license plates were Nevada-issue. One speeder was from California. People came to Vegas from California all the time, but the Area 51 Saloon wasn't in Vegas…and wasn't exactly a hot destination spot. This speeder gave me a tiny bit of hope that Call might be inside.

And just in case he was, but then things went sideways for some reason, I decided this would be a good use of the tracking device I'd taken from Sonny Fletcher's room. I attached it to the underside of the speeder before heading into the bar.

The sound of slot machines and drunken laughter came spilling out the saloon door, along with an off-balance patron. I kept the man from falling and got him onto solid ground before stepping inside. The dark interior flickered with lights from behind a long bar, a few TVs mounted high in the corners and rows of one-armed bandits on two sides of the large room. There were several private booths along a third wall, plus a dozen tables in the center, but most of the customers were seated at the bar.

A few people turned to look as I sashayed in. I took a long, slow look around the room and saw a sudden movement in one of the booths. A small man had turned away and put a hand to the side of his head, blocking his face from my view.

This, of course, piqued my interest.

I crossed the room, straight to the man. There was an open laptop on the table, which lit him up, making him even more conspicuous. He peeked out from behind his hand and then turned his entire body away from me, like a doggie at bath time.

As I got closer, he seemed to be trying to shrink himself and disappear into the corner of the padded bench seat.

"Mind if I join you?" I asked.

The little man dropped his hand and turned to look up at me with a painfully forced smile. I recognized him. It was the baby Frankenstein mutant I'd caught watching me in the Rank & File, back in Freaktown.

"You can have this booth," the little man squeaked through bared teeth, his Adam's apple bobbing around his throat. "I was just leaving, actually."

"What are you drinking?" I asked.

"Uh…" he said, licking his lips nervously and glancing at his empty glass. "Lemonade?"

"Good choice. Refreshing. Especially in this dry desert climate. Harder to stay hydrated here than back in San Francisco."

The little man swallowed hard, like he was choking down a golf ball. He closed his laptop, picked it up and turned to slide out of the booth.

"I think you could use another lemonade," I said, blocking him.

He glanced toward the bar. For a moment, I thought he might yell for help.

"I'm not here to hurt you," I said. "I'm a friend of Jorge Valdez's. Of course, you already know that."

The man swallowed another, slightly smaller golf ball.

"How'd you find me?" he managed.

"It's a long story. Let's have a drink and I'll tell you all about it."

The little man thought for a minute, weighing his options, then said: "What if I don't want to talk?"

"Then I might have to hurt you."

"But you said you weren't here to hurt me."

"I wasn't," I said. "Now I'm reconsidering."

The guy looked like he might pee himself.

"Look," I continued, trying to be gentle, "I'm a private investigator. And, seeing as how you and I are both here in the middle of nowhere, I'm guessing we're mixed up in the same thing. I was hired to look into Carl Linsky's death. And then I found out about Rona Morgan. And Val Davis."

I might as well have slapped him as I said each name. The poor guy flinched as I said each one. Clearly, he was familiar with the list of victims. Maybe I'd gotten lucky.

"Are you Greg Call?" I asked.

Another figurative slap across the face.

"What? No!"

We locked eyes for a long moment. He wasn't lying. But he was familiar with the STG people. So maybe this was my mystery person.

"I need your help," I said.

After a brief pause, the man nodded and slid back into his seat. I moved to the other side and, as I started to sit, he made a move, trying to get out before I could stop him. He underestimated the length of my arms. Classic little guy mistake.

I caught him by the shirt collar and yanked him back into place. It didn't take much effort. He weighed maybe a hundred pounds, soaking wet. Or full of lemonade.

"Look, I've got trust issues, OK?" the mutant whined. "All things considered, I've got the right to be a little paranoid."

I felt a fresh, toxic wave of irrational anger swelling to the surface. I was in no mood to coddle this clown and the effects of my implant had me dangerously punch drunk—emphasis on *punch*. This guy was in no position to bargain. It was going to take every ounce of my will power not to just beat him into submission.

"What's your name?" I asked, as calmly as I could.

The little man adjusted his shirt and I noticed a large patch of scar tissue where his neck met his shoulder, like he'd had some huge growth removed—not uncommon for a mutant. I waited for him to answer, but he just sat there, silent, staring down at the table like a kid refusing to eat his creamed spinach.

"Tell me your name or I'll smash that laptop," I said. "With your face."

It was like I'd threatened to punch his baby. He picked up the laptop and literally cradled it against his chest.

"Larry. Larry Hammond," he whispered, defensively.

"OK, Larry. We need to talk, and we're going to. It'll save us both a lot of time if you just play along. I don't think either one of us wants things to get violent."

"You're the one who's being violent," he whined. "I couldn't hurt you if I tried."

"Well, I have sensitive knuckles," I explained.

The bartender appeared and asked if we wanted drinks, probably an excuse to make sure things were copasetic between me and the little mutant. I half expected Larry to say I was threatening to kill him, but he kept quiet. I ordered two shots of tequila and a lemonade.

"No ice," Larry added. "In the lemonade."

The bartender nodded and left. Larry glanced at me.

"Ice is a rip-off," he said. "If I buy a drink, I want it to be *all* drink."

"I'm buying," I said. "Get it with ice. Treat yourself."

"It's the principle of it."

The mutant set his laptop down and arranged it to be perfectly parallel with the edge of the table.

"Do you smoke?" he asked.

"No."

"You should. All the cool detectives smoke."

"I don't try to look cool," I lied. "Besides, I like not having cancer."

Larry started babbling. Some people do that when they're nervous.

"You don't have to worry about getting cancer," he said. "Big Pharma's trying to keep it under wraps, but a research group in Norway just came up with the holy grail of cures. Cancer's about to go the way of smallpox. It'll take a few years to get out to the public, but the Tobacco Industry will make sure it gets fast-tracked. In a few years, everyone'll be smoking again."

"No kidding. If it's a big secret, how do you know about it?"

"I know a lot of stuff."

"Well, that's good, because I've got a lot of questions. Let's start with the STG project. I'm assuming you worked on it."

Larry looked like I'd kicked him in the balls. A moment later, the bartender returned with our drinks.

"What do you know about STG?" Larry asked in a whisper, after the man left.

"I know I've got one of your implants in my head."

Larry's eyes went wide.

"Seriously?"

"Seriously. And it's gonna kill me if I don't get it out or turn it off or whatever the hell you do to make it quit working."

"You don't."

"What do you mean?" I said, before pounding the first tequila shot.

"The implant is designed to be virtually undetectable. It's a nanite—microscopic—and made of organic materials, so it won't show up on a normal brain scan. I guess you might be able to find it if you knew the chemical composition, but—"

Larry probably would have kept talking if I'd let him. Which I didn't.

"—How do you stop it?"

"I have no idea. You could try aluminum foil."

If he'd been a little closer, I would have slapped him on pure reflex. I was in no mood for jokes. But he wasn't joking.

He started thinking out loud: "Maybe if you got into a Faraday Cage. Or I don't know if they could make a helmet that works like a Faraday Cage. I'm pretty sure the implants are connected to a satellite system. I guess you might be able to block the signal or scramble it. What's it doing to you?"

I rubbed my temples. This guy's voice wasn't helping my headache.

"I haven't slept in days," I said. "I've taken some heavy-duty sleeping pills and it didn't do a thing."

Larry cocked his head and looked at me intently, curious, not sympathetic.

"Yeah," he said, "I'm guessing the implant probably can't do that much—just affect basic functions—sleep, hunger, vision, that kind of thing. It's not like it can control your actions. Not yet, at least."

What little patience I had left was running out.

"Look," I said, "maybe I'm not making myself clear, but I'm…going...to die…if I don't get some sleep. If you can't help me, who can?"

"Bosworth Clark, maybe. He works in satellite technologies, so he might know how to disrupt the signal. I'm hoping he'll show up here, then you can pick his brain."

"Yeah, well, his brain already got picked. It was splattered all over the inside of his RV down in New Mexico."

I threw back the second shot of tequila as Larry's frankenstein face went ghostly white.

"Not him, too," Larry whispered.

Apparently, Larry knew about the other deaths.

"That's why I'm here," I said. "I saw the text message about this rendezvous on Clark's phone. I'm assuming you got the same message."

Larry nodded.

"So why were you all meeting *here*?" I asked.

"Gideon Enterprises bought up a bunch of old military bases years ago. There's one not far from here. Everyone on the team—at least the ones who worked with Gideon before—would know what the Blue Diamond meant."

"Who else are you expecting?"

"I don't know. STG was a real mysterious operation. No one was supposed to know who else was working on it, or what anyone else was working on. I accidentally found out who else was on the project after Greg brought me in to do some UI coding. And, to be honest, I'm just making educated guesses about the implants."

"Tell me more about Greg."

The mutant looked away nervously.

"That would be Greg *Call*, right?" I prompted.

Larry realized there was no point in dancing around it.

"Yeah," he whispered. "I've known Greg for a long time. We were in Mutant League together. We met on the forum. I ended up doing some jobs for him. STG was just one of them."

"Have you heard of 'Overlord'?"

I'd seen every kind of reaction when I'd mentioned Overlord before, but Larry's was new. Very matter-of-fact.

"Sure," he said. "That was the codename of the STG project. All the projects had codenames. There was one really weird one: 'Prizrak'. That project had something to do with Whole Brain Emulation—"

"—So was Greg in charge of Overlord?"

"Hard to say. He had a lot on his plate, project-wise. I think the pressure started getting to him. He was always super private, but then he started getting real paranoid—almost as paranoid as me and I'm paranoid all the time. Right after I finished up my work on Overlord and Prizrak, Greg burned down the place where we'd been working, told me to go lay low, and then disappeared."

"Any idea where he went?"

"I'd heard him mention a place called Nexus. I think it might be up in

Oregon or Washington. But there's no way he'd leave a trail to follow."

"And you haven't heard from him since?" I asked.

"Not directly, other than the text for us to rendezvous here."

"What do you mean 'not directly'?"

Larry shifted, uncomfortably. Another thing he hadn't meant to say, apparently. He glanced at me and then shrugged, probably deciding there was no point in holding anything back.

"There was a message waiting here at the motel."

"From Call?"

"Yeah. He said whoever got the message needed to try and find all the STG passcards we'd been issued. He didn't say why, but he designed them, so I guess they're important. He said there were eight of them. He also said that he had gone to New San Francisco and, that if he didn't show up here in the next day or two, that we should contact the police there."

"And he hasn't shown up."

The mutant shook his head. I was sure he was telling the truth…and he was terrified. Of me, of everything. He'd probably hoped that Call would arrive with some brilliant plan to fix everything, but now something may have happened to him. And he was probably right. I just hoped he wasn't.

"So," I asked, "do you have one of the passcards?"

Larry nodded, then pulled it out of his pocket.

"Take it," he said. "Just holding onto this thing is giving me the hives."

"No, it's probably that polyester you're wearing."

"Really?"

The little mutant looked down at his petroleum-based, computer geek ensemble: wrinkle-resistant khakis, cheap plastic windbreaker and white cotton-poly (but mostly poly) dress shirt with built-in pocket protector.

"Any idea what Call wanted us to do with these?" I asked, holding up the passcard.

Larry's head shot back up.

"*Us*? Uh-uh. It's *your* problem now. I told you everything I know and I gave you my passcard. Now I'm gonna go somewhere and try not to get killed. Hasta la pasta, baby."

"You're not gonna wait for Greg?"

Larry thought for a second.

"Yeah. I guess I should."

He was a lousy liar. It didn't matter. With the tracking device on his speeder, I could find him later if I needed to. But I wasn't done with him yet.

I ordered us a fresh round of drinks. The alcohol was taking the edge off, enough to keep me focused, ironically. After two more shots, I asked Larry to tell me what he knew about Greg Call.

Call was a mutant—grossly disfigured, apparently—and had been J. Saint Gideon's right-hand man and Chief Technical Officer for years. Gideon had allowed Call to work in complete seclusion, with almost total anonymity. Call had done the same for Larry, which helped explain why Larry's name hadn't come up for me…or Slade.

It wasn't clear if or how Call was currently involved with Gideon Enterprises, now that Schimming had pushed Gideon out of his own company. Larry didn't know if Overlord had been Call's project or Schimming's—or what its ultimate purpose was—but he was adamant that Call wouldn't do anything to help the Law & Order Party.

"One last question," I said. "Are you the Poisoned Pawn?"

Judging by Larry's blank stare, he wasn't.

I'd probably gotten everything I could out of the little guy, so I let him go. He literally ran out of the bar.

All I could do now was wait and hope Greg Call showed up. He'd left the message for Hammond at the Bonnie Ranch Motel, so my plan was to fly back there and stake the place out.

As I paid the tab, I noticed a vid-payphone in the corner. It had been a while since I'd checked in with Detective Clements and Wanda Peck. It was almost midnight and Clements wouldn't be in her office at this hour, but Wanda had said I could call anytime, 24/7.

I dialed Wanda's number on the vidphone and she answered immediately, her face filling the screen. She was as beautiful as ever, but the cool façade was gone.

"Tex! Where are you?"

"Nevada. Why? What's—"

"How soon can you get here?" There was panic in her voice.

"I can't leave right now. I've got a lead on Greg Call. Why?"

"It's Sylvia."

Now it was my turn to panic.

"What about her?"

"I thought I could trust her and left her alone. Now she's gone."

My heart started racing.

"Did you check her father's house?"

"She's not there."

Wanda looked away, her expression equal parts frustration, guilt and concern, then she looked back at me. "But I know where she's going to be."

She ran a nervous tongue over her lips.

"We may have been wrong about Carl Linsky being the Poisoned Pawn. Whoever it is just sent another message. They have Sylvia. And they won't release her unless you meet with them. Alone…tonight. And they want the STG passcards. They said I should contact them as soon as I heard from you and then they'll tell me where you need to go."

"I can't," I said. "Greg Call might be the one person who can keep me alive. And I can't save Sylvia if I'm dead."

Wanda went quiet for a long moment, then said: "Detective Clements thinks they may have found Call's body."

It felt like a punch in the gut. I leaned against the wall and closed my eyes. If Call was dead, I was all out of options. It wasn't a matter of *if* I died, but *when*.

And *how*.

I stepped back up to the vidphone.

"I can be there in a couple hours."

35

As my Lotus sped through the darkness, my brain was on fire, my body quivering. For the first time, I let all the rage boil to the surface. I was angry about everything—Sylvia…the Poisoned Pawn…Slade…Law & Order…my implant…all of it.

It was looking like I wouldn't get out of this alive, but I wanted to go out on my own terms—not wait for the implant to do it. And I wanted my death to count for something, the way Sonny's had. He'd stayed alive just long enough to pass the torch to me. Now I needed to stay alive long enough to take that torch and go out in a blaze of glory.

I wanted to kill someone.

Slade came immediately to mind, but I had no clue where to look for him. And he was just a hired gun, anyway. There was a 'Man behind the Curtain' who had given him the orders to kill me and all the other innocent people. Maybe it was John Klaus or Frank Schimming or someone I hadn't heard of. Whoever it was, they were almost certainly connected to Law & Order, so my plan was to kamikaze the L&O Headquarters after it opened for business. There was at least a chance I'd take out the man responsible. Slade, too, if I was lucky. Worst case, I'd get a bunch of other neo-Nazi bastards.

I just had to stay alive for nine more hours.

In the meantime, I needed to deal with the Poisoned Pawn, who claimed to be holding Sylvia hostage. At this point, I had no idea who the Poisoned Pawn might be. A long flight would have been the perfect time to sort it out, but my brain was too fried to make sense of anything.

The only thing I knew for sure was this: depending on who it was and what they'd done to Sylvia, I might kill them, too. I had literally nothing to lose.

* * * * *

I pushed my Lotus as hard as it would go until I reached the outskirts of New San Francisco, then landed at a convenience store and used a vid-payphone to call Wanda.

She had arranged the meeting as instructed: 3 a.m., at the San Tomas Mission.

It was just after 2 a.m., so we had some time to talk. I didn't tell Wanda about my plan to go out in a blaze of glory, but I filled her in on everything else, including Bosworth Clark, Larry Hammond and Greg Call.

Wanda had tried repeatedly to contact J. Saint Gideon, without luck. She was worried that Slade had somehow gotten to him, but I found that hard to believe, given the fortress-like security Gideon surrounded himself with. But it was concerning, nonetheless. And disappointing. I'd really hoped that he'd fess up to knowing all about Overlord and how to disable my implant.

In the meantime, Wanda had been working with various law enforcement agencies to get search warrants for the Law & Order offices. Things were moving slowly because there were Law & Order Party members in both the New San Francisco Police Department and the F.B.I., and she didn't want tip them off. If they had a head start, they would get everything incriminating cleared out before a search could be conducted.

Wanda figured we had about twenty-four hours before all hell broke loose. I didn't tell her that all hell would be breaking loose long before then.

"Tell me about this last message from the Poisoned Pawn," I said. "It doesn't seem to fit with the others."

"No, it doesn't," Wanda said. "The first two were warnings about the STG project. Now he's taking action. Do you know why he'd be so desperate to get the STG passcards?"

"No, but Greg Call wanted Larry Hammond to find them. And Slade was collecting them from the victims—and I think they were more than just trophies. They must be important. I guess I'll find out soon enough."

It was time to go. Wanda mustered a smile.

"Be careful, Tex."

I hung up and took the last pain pill. I needed to be as clear-headed as possible from here on out. A week ago, I'd been a young, idealistic P.I. embarking on a career I'd always dreamed of. Now I was planning out the last day of my life.

*   *   *   *   *

The San Tomas Mission was an old Spanish-style church with a huge clock tower that had been converted into a variety of businesses over the decades, none lasting very long. Maybe it was haunted. It had been abandoned for years.

I showed up a half-hour early, on the off chance that I might catch the Poisoned Pawn off-guard. I parked my speeder some distance away and made a stealthy approach.

There was no sound or sign of anyone. As I entered the structure through a door-less opening, I half expected to be assaulted by a startled transient, but the place appeared to be empty. I looked around the ground floor, but there was nothing to find. If anyone was here, they were on the upper level.

I climbed a set of stairs and immediately caught sight of Sylvia. She'd been positioned in a swath of moonlight shining through a large, arched window. Her hands were tied and she looked to be asleep, her head lolled forward.

My instinct was to run to her, but I held back long enough to take a look around the room. In the center was a large contraption of cogs and wheels that controlled the tower clock, still functioning after all these years. I watched as a cog turned. Up above, the huge minute hand of a massive clock shuddered and ticked ahead.

The perimeter of the room had shadowy nooks and crannies everywhere. There might be a dozen people hidden here and I wouldn't see them. I could hide myself and hope to take the Poisoned Pawn by surprise, but I had to assume he was already here and watching my every move.

I crossed to Sylvia and knelt down in front of her. She stirred and slowly raised her head.

Her face was bruised and bloody. One eye was swollen. She had been crying, and mascara was smeared around her eyes. Her mouth was covered in duct tape and trickles of dried blood ran from her nostrils, over the tape and down her chin.

I wrapped my arms around, hugging her to my chest. Felt her choking sob against me. All my anger came roaring back. Whoever had done this to her was going to die.

"It's a shame to cover such a beautiful mouth, don't you think, Mr. Murphy?"

The voice came from behind me. Sylvia jumped at the sound of it. It was a voice I'd never heard before. I held Sylvia a moment longer and then released her, before standing up and turning to see who was speaking.

It was John Klaus.

He was very short, almost dwarfish, dressed all in black. He had a long, crooked nose and a fleshy face that curled up around a big, unpleasant smile full of discolored teeth. He was like something out of a fairy tale—an evil trickster come to steal your baby.

"It was necessary, of course," Klaus sneered. "I couldn't have Dulcinea warning off her knight errant from charging the windmill."

"I was wondering when you'd crawl out of your rats' nest," I said, taking a step toward him.

Klaus swung an arm out from behind his back. There was a gun in his hand. He pointed it up at me.

"*Au contraire*, Señor Quixote. It is *you* who are the rat."

He then leveled the gun at Sylvia.

"And you, my dear, the perfect piece..." he paused dramatically, "…of cheese."

Somehow, his fierce smile got even wider, like it would split his face in two.

"I assume you're in love with her," he said, turning the gun back at me. "She has that effect on men."

I didn't know if I was in love with her or not, but I wasn't going to give him any more leverage than he already had.

"She's just my client," I said. "I like keeping my clients alive. It's good for business."

Klaus scoffed.

"I've seen enough to know she's more than a client to you."

I must have looked confused.

"You think we haven't been keeping tabs on you?" he continued. "We've been watching Sylvia here since she moved back into her father's place. You, we weren't too worried about. I thought we might keep you out of all this, but then you went to see Gideon."

So Klaus had been onto me the whole time I was looking for him. That would explain why the killers had shown up at Knott's cabin right after I did. At least they were dead, too. Maybe that was the only reason Wanda Peck and Larry Hammond were still alive.

"And now, unfortunately, you don't have much time left," Klaus said with mock concern. "But I invited you here to offer a trade. Tell me what you've found out and I'll let the little missy free. Let's start with what you and Gideon talked about."

I didn't think Klaus would let Sylvia go no matter what I said, but I wanted to keep him talking and look for a chance to make a move on him.

"OK," I said. "Gideon told me he'd lost control of his company."

"Yes, yes. Frank Schimming is running things. Common knowledge. What else?"

"He said someone sent him a letter, warning him that Law & Order was trying to take over a secret project being developed by Gideon Enterprises. Whoever sent it called himself the Poisoned Pawn. Which I'm a little confused about. I don't think you would have sent that letter. So, are *you* the Poisoned Pawn?"

"Of course not. It was my dear friend Carl who sent it."

"And how do you know that?"

"Because he told me. We were very close at one time and I suppose he had no one else to confide in."

Klaus glanced at Sylvia when he said this. More salt in her wounds.

"I'd never heard of STG until Carl came to me," he continued. "He'd been tasked with the neurological aspects—how to affect specific brain functions via a microscopic implant. He consulted me about how such a device could be most effectively implanted. He also mentioned there was a possibility that the project was being funded by Gideon Enterprises. This, as you might imagine, was of great interest to me."

"And that's when you joined the STG project."

Klaus laughed. At my ignorance, apparently.

"That's when I went to another dear friend, Frank Schimming, and asked him about STG. He was completely unaware that his own company was involved, but soon got to the root of things. The project had been in the works for years, all very hush-hush. But, once he learned what was going on, he provided me with private access to it."

"And Linsky found out?"

"No one knows what Schimming and I have done. I think Carl began to have concerns about what his work would be used for. And then I may have pushed him too hard for details, aroused his suspicions. Which were well-founded; Schimming and I fully intend to take control of the project once it's completed."

"It's not completed now? The implants you put into me and Linsky seem to be working."

"Oh, they are. I won't bore you with the details but, eventually, they'll be controlled remotely. The test implants have been a little more crude; they were preset to have specific neurological effects. Yours was designed to disrupt your sleep patterns."

"I noticed."

"I must say, I'm very impressed with how you're holding up. You were supposed to be a good little detective and die."

"Just like your dear friend, Carl?" I asked.

Klaus's eyes went cold.

"He *was* my friend. But friendship has its limits."

"But why kill him?"

"He'd become a threat to our plans. When he told me he'd sent the Poisoned Pawn letter to Gideon, I gave him a choice: join me and Law & Order…or stay on the losing side. He chose poorly."

"With friends like you, who needs enemies?"

The evil dwarf smirked.

"I do what needs to be done. Now, for the sake of Miss Linsky here, tell me what else you've discovered."

"I know someone—you, probably—hired Slade to kill everyone on the STG project."

Klaus's eyebrows arched.

"I knew it was you who stole the briefcase. Mr. Slade was not happy about that. Not one bit."

"Glad to hear it."

Klaus reached into a pocket.

"What about these?"

He held up an STG passcard.

I wasn't about to tell him what I'd learned, but I had to say something.

"I know they were required to access the project from remote locations," I said. "You also need a reader and a special laptop."

"Yes, I'm aware. Schimming provided me with all the necessary hardware after he, shall we say, *replaced* one of the team members. But there's something unusual about these passcards. Do you know if there's anything else you can do with them?"

"No. But I can tell you what I'd like to do with them."

Klaus laughed out loud.

"I do admire your moxie."

He put the passcard back into his pocket.

"On the off chance the passcards do have some importance," he said, "I will need you to give me the ones you have. Where are they?"

"Beats me. Probably somewhere on the high Spanish plains with my trusted servant, Sancho."

Klaus slowly pivoted, turning the gun on Sylvia.

"They're in my speeder," I said.

"Excellent! Now, as a token of my appreciation for your cooperation…"

He waved me away from Sylvia. After I took a few steps back, he walked over to her and tore the duct tape off her mouth, then gestured grandly toward her.

"One last kiss."

As he moved off to a safe distance, Sylvia glared at him, then turned the glare toward me.

"You really think he's not gonna kill both of us?!" she cried out.

Klaus chortled.

"Well, I'm sorry, Mr. Murphy. It looks like she's not in the mood. For once!"

Klaus turned the gun toward his own face and scratched his chin theatrically with the tip.

"Well," he said. "I guess we'll just move on to the murder/suicide portion of the program."

"You said you'd let her go."

"Oh, Mr. Murphy, please. Don't compound your gullibility with stupidity. *She's* more of a danger to me than you are."

"What are you talking about?" I asked.

Sylvia rocked forward in her chair, quivering with anger.

"You're a liar! Don't listen to him, Tex!"

Klaus looked at her, mockingly.

"Shall we tell him?" he sneered. "Maybe just one or two names?"

"I had nothing to do with any of this!" Sylvia pleaded. "I swear it!"

"Well, I didn't say you were involved," Klaus said. "But you do have the capacity for treachery. For all I know, you may be as innocent as you claim to be. I'm just not a risk-taker."

He swiveled his head toward me and made an exaggerated frowny face.

"Oh, don't look so sad, Tex. At least you know that you were the last, hmm? I mean, perhaps she even cared for you—as much as she's capable."

He looked back and forth between me and Sylvia, gloating, then raised his arm and laid the gun over his shoulder.

"Well, down to business." Then, raising his voice, he called out: "Mr. Slade?"

A moment passed. Klaus's smile was frozen on his face. Another moment passed and Klaus called out again, this time louder:

"Mr. Slade?"

Klaus kept his eyes on us as a figure stepped silently out of the shadows behind him. Slade moved closer, staring straight at me, the ghost of a smile on his lips.

"I'll leave the necessary un-pleasantries in your capable hands," Klaus said.

Slade, who was a foot and a half taller than Klaus, put his hands on the smaller man's shoulders and, in his Australian accent, drawled:

"My pleasure, Mr. Klaus."

The sadistic dwarf was still smiling broadly when Slade's hands suddenly took hold of Klaus's head and, with a short, violent twist, broke the man's neck.

Slade plucked the gun from Klaus's hand as the body crumpled to the floor. The hit man never took his eyes off me.

My rage completely disappeared, replaced by complete shock. I glanced down at John Klaus's lifeless body, the evil clown smile still spread across his face. When I looked back up at Slade, there was almost a twinkle in his eye. Whatever he was up to, it couldn't be any worse than what Klaus had in mind. I glanced over at Sylvia, who looked up at me, hopefully.

"Whew!" I said, turning back to Slade. "That was close. I was beginning to wonder how we were going to get out of this."

He smiled and pointed Klaus's gun at me.

"Don't stop wondering on my account."

36

"See, the way I got it figured," Slade said, "between those passcards and everything Klaus just said, I'll bet I can get someone to pay top dollar. I'm just taking out the middle man."

Klaus had been a zealot—he reeked of it; Slade was just looking to make a buck. Greed is a motivation I can work with. I flashed my most charming smile.

"If you'll take a personal check, I'd be happy to put in my bid."

Slade nodded graciously.

"Well, I appreciate the offer but I don't think you're in the right tax bracket. I was thinking more along the lines of, say, J. Saint Gideon."

He flipped the gun around and pointed it at me.

"So, who wants to go first?"

My brain was scrambling, trying to figure a way out of this, and not coming up with anything. I needed to buy more time.

"Will you grant me one last request?" I asked, finally.

Slade shrugged.

"I suppose. As long as it's reasonable."

"Let me kiss Sylvia goodbye? At least that way I can die a happy man."

Slade half smiled, half sneered.

"Well, I wouldn't want you to die *un*happy. Go ahead. But don't do anything stupid."

I hadn't planned on doing anything stupid, not until he suggested it. As I turned to Sylvia, blocking Slade's view, I fished something out of my pocket. I kneeled down and slipped Sonny's lockpick set into her hands, then closed mine around hers. I wasn't sure if anything on it would be sharp enough, but it was the only thing I had that might work.

"We're going to get out of this, OK?" I whispered.

Sylvia nodded and then kissed me. I could taste the salt of her tears and blood on her lips. The anger started to build again.

"Oh, that was very touching," Slade said. "Now…let's get down to business."

Somehow, I had to get Slade away from Sylvia. And that couldn't happen while he had a gun pointed at me. I just needed to figure out how to get him to drop the gun.

Or maybe there was a better option. Maybe I could cut a deal with him.

"I saw what you did to Bosworth Clark," I said, standing and turning to face Slade.

He smiled.

"That poor man killed himself," he said in a mocking tone.

"No, I actually *watched* what you did. There was surveillance video."

The smile vanished.

"It was on Clark's laptop," I added. "Let us go and I'll give it to you."

Slade stared me down, thinking it over.

"I think you're bluffing," he finally said. "Even if you're not, it's too late. No deal."

It had been worth a shot. Back to the first plan.

"You're a coward," I said.

Slade raised his gun, his jaw tightening.

I kept going: "If you had any guts at all, you wouldn't need to hide behind that gun. How 'bout you man up? You think you're so tough. Let's settle this like real men—*mano a mano*."

Slade suddenly laughed.

"I'll give you one thing. You've got some crown jewels on you."

"You afraid I'm gonna kick your ass?"

He shook his head, still laughing.

"Wow. OK."

He dropped the gun onto Klaus's body and started taking off his overcoat.

"I'm really gonna enjoy this," he said.

I turned and ran.

Before Slade could recover, I'd gotten around the huge gear

contraption and slipped into the shadows.

Slade called out: "No honor among thieves, eh Murphy?"

I stayed quiet. As my eyes adjusted to the darkness, I looked around for something I could use as a weapon. There was nothing useful in sight.

"Come on out," the hit man said. "If you don't, I'll shoot your girlfriend."

I knew it was an empty threat, but I needed to get him away from Sylvia. Across the room, I saw a set of stairs leading up. But Slade would get a clear shot at me from where he was standing.

"You can't hide forever," Slade said. "I'll find you sooner or later. Sooner's better for me."

I searched my pockets. I still had Sonny's Zippo. Maybe this could get Slade to move. I pulled it out and then tossed it into a corner. It clattered loudly. Slade's footfalls headed in that direction.

I ran for the stairs.

As I hit them at full speed, Slade got a couple shots off. The bullets missed, splintering wood not far from my head.

I vaulted up the stairs to the room above. This area was smaller and offered no place to hide. There was no railing around the opening to the stairs, so maybe I could get a clean shot at Slade as he came up. But I wouldn't stand a chance in a fight; I needed something to hit him with.

I looked around frantically, searching for something—anything—I could use. The only thing of any use was a piece of 2x4, about three feet long. On the bright side, it had two nails sticking out on one end. I picked it up and crept back toward the stair opening.

A minute passed. Slade didn't come up the stairs. He was probably waiting below, deciding how to make his approach. He had to know I didn't have a gun. If I'd had one, I would have pulled it out before now. But he had to assume I'd try to jump him. The question was, would he be cautious or charge in?

I heard the stairs creak. He was coming up slowly. Once he got within hitting distance, he'd probably move fast. And then he'd have to guess which side of the stairs I was waiting on.

A moment later, he made his move. And guessed wrong.

He came up running, with the gun extended, facing to his left. I was on his right. I swung the piece of wood, aiming for his head, but he moved faster than I anticipated; I mistimed the swing and caught him in the shoulder. The nails sank into his arm and he cried out. I heard a thunk on the stairs as the gun he'd been holding dropped from his hand.

His momentum carried him to the top of the stairs, where he tumbled forward. He probably should have gone back for the gun, but now he was on tilt. Getting hurt hadn't been part of his plan. Now all he wanted was to get his hands on me. He ripped the piece of wood from his arm and tossed it aside, then moved toward me.

I mirrored his moves, keeping the stairway opening between us.

"Look, I'll give you the passcards," I said. "Just let me and Sylvia go."

Slade didn't bother to respond. He just kept moving, circling the stairway opening until we were facing each other across the narrower direction of the opening.

Then he leaped across. I wasn't ready for it and we went down in a jumbled heap. I managed to pull away, kicking violently, and get to my feet. I wanted to beat him back to the gun, but before I could get to the top of the stairs, he unleashed a leg kick that sent me sprawling.

As I struggled up from the floor, he came at me and then stopped. He started to turn away, but then jumped and spun around, catching me in the jaw with his boot.

I literally saw stars as I dropped like a bag of rocks.

After a few moments, my vision cleared enough to see Slade checking the damage done to his shoulder. His fingers came away bloody and he looked down at me.

"That wasn't very nice," he said, like I'd hurt his feelings.

I tried to shake away the cobwebs and pulled myself into a sitting position.

"Are you OK?" I asked.

"Yeah."

"That's too bad."

Slade reached down and pulled me up by the lapels. Now I knew what Larry Hammond had felt like. I was no match for Slade.

He slammed me against the wall and put his hand up under my chin, gripping me hard by the throat. At the same instant, I heard a grinding sound. Above us, the massive clock hands moved and a bell tolled.

Slade glanced up and then back into my eyes.

"Oh, look. Time to die."

His hand tightened on my windpipe. I clawed at his arm, but it was like steel.

The bell tolled again. Then again.

As the sound and vibration faded, I heard a soft, mechanical click. And then a voice.

"Let him go."

It was Sylvia.

Slade froze, but maintained his grip.

"Let him go…or I'll blow your goddamn head off."

"You're shaking," Slade said to Sylvia, not taking his eyes off me. "I can hear it. You wouldn't want to accidentally shoot your boyfriend."

"I won't," Sylvia said.

After a long pause, Slade released me.

"Now step away."

Slade raised his hands and backed off. Sylvia was at the top of the stairs, holding Klaus's gun with both hands. Slade had been right. She was shaking.

Slade spun around to face her. She took a reflexive step back and almost tripped.

"Hey, Slade," I said, coming up beside him. "This is for Sonny."

He turned and I punched him in the mouth as hard I could. He dropped to the floor, out cold. It felt like I'd broken my hand.

Totally worth it.

37

Standing over the unconscious body of a stone-cold killer, my gorgeous, rescued client holding a gun and sobbing against my chest, my body and brain bruised and beaten, was the single greatest moment of my life. This was what I'd always wanted, who I'd always wanted to be. Even if I ended up dying, I'd have this one perfect moment.

But I no longer intended on dying, at least not kamikaze-style. My busted-up hand, for some reason, seemed to help my mental state even more than the pain pills. And, after my chat with John Klaus, I had at least a glimmer of hope for saving myself.

Klaus had said that Frank Schimming gave him 'private access' to the STG project. I'd been searching for team members, in part so one of them could tell me how to disable my implant. But if I could find out where Klaus had access to the project, maybe the information I needed would be found there.

After tying Slade up, I searched John Klaus's body, hoping that he was carrying something that might lead me to his STG access location. Even better, maybe he'd have some little remote control device labeled 'Murphy's Implant Controller' with a big On/Off switch.

No such luck. But he did have a cell phone. It was locked, but had an Emergency Call button, which I used to call the cops.

I then went through Klaus's pockets and found a wallet, a set of keys, a small vial half-full of what I thought must be cocaine, a pair of pink panties—which I did not want to think about at all—and a high-security Law & Order ID badge.

There was also his STG passcard—this one marked with a 'G'. I still had no idea why the passcards might be important, but I now had seven of them. And I was willing to bet the last one belonged to Greg Call. Maybe the cops had found it with Call's body, but that was the least of my worries at the moment.

In Klaus's wallet, there was a business card and a home address listed on his driver's license. The set of keys probably included ones to both his clinic and residence. It seemed likely that Klaus's access to STG was either in his home, his clinic, or at Law & Order. I now had access to all three places. Since it was still the middle of the night, I decided to start at Law & Order Headquarters. If I didn't find what I was looking for there, I'd move on to the clinic and then his home.

Sylvia tried to talk to me the entire time I was searching Klaus's body. I didn't have the time or inclination to discuss her checkered past and how Klaus had unfairly portrayed her and that she had intense feelings for me and she was a changed woman and had deep regrets, but had tried to move on and make a new life and wanted so much to have a strong, trusting relationship with a good, honest man and that maybe I was that man and we had a real connection and it would be so unfair if I walked away from something that could be so amazing just because of something an evil lying bastard like Klaus might say.

Or something like that.

I told her to keep an eye—and the gun—on Slade until the cops showed up. I went down the stairs, took a minute to find Sonny's Zippo, and then left.

* * * * *

I flew over the sleeping city, headed downtown, feeling reckless and empowered. Sylvia was safe. Klaus was dead. Slade was about to be in police custody. I didn't want to die, but I no longer feared it. I felt so invincible, I double-parked my speeder outside the Law & Order building.

Flashing Klaus's badge on the card reader unlocked the main doors and I marched into the lobby. My old pal, Harry Rice, was gone—replaced by a guy with twice the eyes and twice the size.

I ignored him and walked straight to the security scanner. Waving the badge turned on the green light, giving me access without the required scan. I walked through to the other side.

In the security station, the big new security guard must have been alerted that I'd used Klaus's ID and was clearly not John Klaus. He jumped up and came out the backside to confront me. He was reaching for his gun when I hit his face as hard as I could. A fresh wave of agonizing, invigorating, mind-clearing pain shot up my right arm. The guy staggered back, but didn't go down. I came at him, this time with my left fist and hit him again. This dropped him to the floor. I jumped on him and kept punching until he quit moving.

I took the guy's gun and went off in search of John Klaus's office. I expected it to be in some subterranean stone-carved lair—the kind of place evil dwarves inhabit—but it turned out to be in the High Elven area, on the top floor. I waved his ID badge—which was starting to feel like a magical wizard's staff—and pushed his office door open.

I wouldn't have been surprised to find a torture chamber inside, but it was just your typical office. After twenty minutes, I'd searched the office from top to bottom. There was nothing that would give me access to the STG system—no console, no laptop with the Gideon Enterprises logo. He had a desktop computer, which could have contained what I was looking for, but it was password-protected and I didn't have a password. I could take it back to Wanda and see if her people could get into it, but that could take days. I was down to hours.

I went through Klaus's desk and file cabinet. There were items of interest, but none related to STG or Overlord. At one point, I came across a schematic, but it turned out to have nothing to do with the STG project. It was for a massive space station, code-named 'Incubus', which was apparently under construction.

There were also quite a few documents related to 'The Mutant Problem' and a 'Crusade for Genetic Purity', which sounded disturbingly similar to the Nazi's 'Final Solution'. It just reinforced the idea that Law & Order was a group of murderous Fascists. It gave me immense pleasure to know that they were about to go down in flames…and that I'd helped make it happen.

I decided to take the documents with me. They seemed like something Wanda Peck would find interesting.

After going through everything in the office, I checked the time. It was just after 4 a.m. The Bel Viso surgical clinic, where Klaus performed his surgeries, would probably be closed for business, so that would be my next stop.

I took one last look around the room, then stepped out into the hallway. Voices echoed down the corridor, from the direction of the elevator. In the other direction was an emergency exit door, leading to stairs, with a sign warning that opening the door would trigger an alarm.

I had three options, none of them good. If the voices belonged to Law & Order security, I had to assume they were coming for me. I could hide in Klaus's office, hope they didn't look there, and wait for them to move on. I could confront them. With the gun I'd taken from the guard in the lobby, I might be able to get past them. Or I could take the stairs. If it didn't set off an alarm, it would be the best option.

I turned around and ran for the emergency exit. I hit the door and the alarm went off.

Taking two or three steps at a time, I made my way down. Up above, I heard several sets of footfalls echoing off the concrete walls.

A minute later, I reached the ground level. There were two doors—one leading into the lobby and one to exit the building. Depending on how many security guards there were, they could have one waiting by my speeder, but I doubted they'd have one outside the door. I pulled out the gun, pushed the exterior door open and stepped through.

I was wrong. Someone was waiting outside. Just not anyone I was expecting.

It was a cop.

"Drop the gun!" he yelled.

Behind him, the dark street was lit up with flashing red and blue lights. It looked like law enforcement had made a pre-dawn raid. The Fall of the Law & Order Empire had begun.

I'd never been so happy to see the fuzz.

38

The happiness didn't last.

As usual, the cops had no interest in hearing my side of things and could not have cared less that I was literally dying and that every minute was vital. Instead of getting in to search John Klaus's clinic before business hours, I ended up getting cuffed, waiting in a squad speeder, eventually being escorted to police headquarters and almost getting booked before Detective Clements finally showed up and sorted things out.

In exchange, she wanted a full account of everything that had happened to me since we'd last spoken. So, as the sun rose, I found myself sitting in her office with a steaming hot cup of the N.S.F.P.D.'s house blend, commonly referred to as Camel Spit, and explaining how and why I was about to die.

When I finished, Clements settled back into her chair, her eyes moving around my face. It seemed like an eternity since I'd first walked into her office on my hands and knees, begging for scraps of information about Carl Linsky's suicide. The cop was looking at me differently now. It also helped that Wanda Peck—and, by extension, CAPRICORN—had vouched for me. If I somehow managed to survive this case, maybe I'd have at least one ally in the police department.

To my surprise, she got on the phone and made a few calls, arranging to have John Klaus's clinic and home searched immediately. If they found anything, they were to contact her directly.

She hung up and said she had something to show me.

Some*one*, to be more precise.

"We're still getting confirmation," she said, "but it looks like we've got Greg Call's body. We fished it out of the Bay yesterday."

"The Bay? As in the one here?"

"Yeah," Clements said. "About the same spot where we found Carl Linsky. Body's at the morgue. And you might want to see it."

She got up and I followed her through a maze of corridors and out to the parking lot. We climbed into her unmarked N.S.F.P.D. speeder.

"I got Linsky's cause of death changed to 'Undetermined'," Clements said, as we lifted off.

"Good. Thanks."

"They couldn't check for an implant. His body had already been cremated. You think there's one in Greg Call?"

"I don't know. I doubt it. It sounded like Slade and Klaus couldn't track him down. I'm not even sure why he was here. All he had to do was lie low."

Clements smirked.

"Speaking of Slade, he's trying to cut a deal as we speak. We already had a lot of dirt on Law & Order, but he'll be the final nail in their coffin."

She glanced over at me.

"I'm impressed you were able to take care of him."

I didn't tell her how unimpressively I'd managed it.

The Medical Examiner was just a few blocks away and we were back on the ground a minute later. Clements led the way into the building and flashed her badge at a series of bored-looking personnel until we reached the morgue.

As we entered, a bald, bearded, bespectacled man in a white lab coat was pulling a sheet over a body laid out on a gurney.

"Detective," he said to Clements.

"This is Murphy," she said, then gestured toward the covered corpse. "Is that Call?"

"Presumably. I'm expecting the DNA results any minute."

Clements turned to me.

"Call's DNA is on file with the Feds. Gideon Enterprises did some work with the NSA a few years back and they required genetic identification. Good thing, too. I'm not sure we could have identified him any other way. There's virtually no information about him anywhere."

The Medical Examiner had crossed the room to a sink and spoke up as he washed his hands.

"To be honest, I'm a little surprised the Feds let me do the autopsy," he said, "but it might be a good thing they did."

"Why's that?" I asked.

He dried his hands as he walked to his desk.

"For one, I found this."

He picked up a small metal and plastic object, no bigger than a postage stamp.

Clements stepped forward to take a closer look. "This was on the body?"

"*In* the body," the M.E. replied. "In the stomach, specifically. And it hadn't been there very long."

"And how did he die?" Clements asked.

"The cause of death was drowning. No question."

"So," I said, "you're saying he swallowed this object right before he drowned?"

"It would seem so."

Clements looked over at me. We were thinking the same thing. Whether Call himself swallowed the object, or someone else forced it down his throat, it was put there to be found. And only the police and coroner would find it.

"Can we take this?" I asked Clements, pointing to the object.

She looked at the doctor, who shrugged and said: "If the feds ask, you didn't get it from me."

I picked it up and examined it. It looked like it would fit into a USB drive. Maybe it was some kind of data storage device. But if Call's intent was to expose the STG project, there were easier ways than swallowing a device and drowning yourself. An email, for example. It didn't make any sense.

Whatever it was, I hoped the device could provide some information. All I needed was a USB slot. I thought about asking the doctor if I could plug it into his laptop, but for all I knew, it would blow this place up. Which I was willing to risk.

I was about to ask when a phone beeped on the desk. The M.E. answered the call and listened for a few minutes before thanking the caller and hanging up.

"DNA results are positive," he said. "It's definitely Greg Call."

I felt a stab of disappointment. I'd been hoping that this wouldn't be Call, that he was still alive. But maybe this device was a dying clue—a high-tech version of the note fragment left in a dead man's hand. There was only one way to find out.

"Is there a laptop here I could use?" I asked. "I'd like to see what this thing is."

"We can probably find one," the coroner said. "First though, there's something else you might want to see."

He moved to the covered body of Greg Call and pulled the sheet back.

Larry Hammond hadn't been exaggerating when he said Call was horribly disfigured. I'd never seen anything like it. His face looked like it had been run through a cheese grater. If I hadn't known better, I would have thought it was a prosthetic mask. But it wasn't the face that the doctor found strange.

"You may have heard of Werner Syndrome or Progeria," he said. "It's a condition that causes premature aging. I'm not an expert in mutation, so maybe there's an explanation for this that I'm unfamiliar with, but I've never heard of a condition that stops or reverses aging."

He looked up at me and raised an eyebrow.

"I would estimate the age of this person to be no older than eighteen years."

I took a closer look. He was right. Once you got past the mutation, you could see that this was the body of a teenager or young adult.

The doctor fixed his eyes on me.

"Greg Call's DNA sample was taken ten years ago."

My brain was running on fumes, but this was simple math. If this body was eighteen years old, Call would have been a child—eight years old, or younger—when his DNA was tested. While working for Gideon on a government contract.

Really? Eight years old? Maybe it was possible. I'd seen old Doogie Howser reruns. But it seemed highly unlikely.

Nothing about Greg Call was making any sense. But it didn't matter. All I cared about now was finding out why this device had been planted for the cops to find.

The coroner left us for a few minutes, then returned with a laptop. The device taken from Call's stomach seemed too small to be an explosive, but I didn't blame the doctor when he took us to an empty room and excused himself quickly. Even Clements took a few steps back after I booted up the laptop and finally plugged the device in.

Nothing happened for a few seconds. Then a red light lit up on the device and slowly blinked. Nothing appeared on the laptop screen. No message, no wizard, no application opening. Just the blinking light.

"Anything on the screen?" Clements asked from behind me.

"No."

I bent down and turned the laptop so Clements could see the screen. As I did, the blinking light changed from red to green and quit blinking.

The device seemed to have detected the movement. I picked up the laptop and moved it from left to right. Red…red…green…red. I moved it back until the light went back to green. I took a few steps forward. The light stayed green. Then I moved it back and forth. Same thing as before.

"Which direction am I facing?" I asked.

Clements looked around, getting her bearings.

"North, I think."

I thought back, once again, to what Larry Hammond had told me about Greg Call, that he may have relocated to a place called Nexus…somewhere in Oregon or Washington.

More or less due north of where we were standing.

This device definitely had some kind of GPS thing going on. A guidance system, or a beacon locator. Apparently, I just had to keep the light green on and this device would lead me somewhere.

And there was a USB slot in my speeder.

39

Larry Hammond had said that Call's message back in Blue Diamond told him—or whoever else showed up—to find the STG passcards, but also to contact the N.S.F.P.D. if Call hadn't joined them within a few days.

Maybe the reason for that was now plugged into my speeder's USB port. I had to hope it would lead me to his base of operations—Nexus—and that I'd finally find what I needed to save myself when I got there.

Clements took me to my speeder and dropped me off. I was a little surprised when she shook my hand; maybe she was thinking it might be the last time we'd see each other.

I fired up my Lotus and plugged in the device. A few minutes later, I was headed north. Keeping one eye on the airspace ahead and one on the green light kept me focused, at least for a while. I could feel I didn't have much time left. My brain was scrambled. My vision was blurring. The headache had returned with a vengeance and I was all out of pain pills. I started slapping myself in the face every few minutes, but it wasn't helping.

At one point, I realized I was nose-diving and had to jerk the steering wheel to avoid a crash. I'd never been blind drunk before, but this was how I imagined it would be.

* * * * *

I'd managed to hold on for another hour and a half when the green light switched to red. Mount Shasta had just come into view, so I hadn't yet reached the Oregon border.

I flew around until I determined that I was more or less at ground zero. Mount Shasta was miles to the east and the terrain below was remote, mountainous and thick with trees. The only sign that humans had ever been here was a railroad track snaking through the rugged landscape.

After landing my speeder, I grabbed a few things from the glove compartment, opened the door and climbed out. My legs buckled and I dropped to the ground. I turned onto my back and stared up at the sky. There was no way I could make it back to San Francisco. If I couldn't disable my implant here, this is where I would die. At least it was a nice spot for it.

After resting for a few minutes, I got back on my feet and surveyed the area. I wasn't sure what to look for. If there was an installation here, it was well-hidden, and this was a good place to hide something.

My eyes went to the train tracks. If there was a facility here, maybe the tracks had been laid specifically to deliver materials used to build and supply it. Maybe this was one of the old abandoned military facilities Gideon had bought years ago. I walked over to the tracks and took a look. The rails were rusted. It had been many years—decades, at least—since a train had come through here.

I followed the tracks. About fifty yards ahead, they passed close by a thick wall of trees fronting the steep face of a mountain spur. As I got closer, I thought I caught a glimpse of something through the trees.

With each step, I became more sure of it. With a trickle of fresh adrenaline, I picked up the pace and then veered off the tracks into a wall of Western Junipers. The trees were several rows deep, creating a thick and effective cover, but there was also a path through them that was only visible from a discrete angle.

It led to a metal door built into the rock.

The surface of the door had been made to match the surrounding rock, but the metal had rusted, making it stand out. There was no handle on the door, no visible means of opening it.

Fortunately, it had been left slightly ajar.

By Greg Call, I hoped. If someone else had forced Call to swallow the GPS device, I could be walking into a trap. Too late to worry about that now.

The door was several inches thick. It took what little strength I had left to pry it open enough so I could squeeze through. It was pitch-black on the other side, the air much cooler and damp. I hadn't thought to bring a flashlight and started walking into the darkness, taking short steps, with my arms extended.

Then I remembered Sonny's Zippo. I pulled it out and lit the flame. It didn't provide much light, but enough to see I was in a roughly carved-out tunnel.

As I headed down the passage, my headache felt like it was easing up and my vision seemed to get clearer. Maybe it was the darkness or the cool air. Or maybe, if my implant was linked to a satellite, the signal was being dampened.

I followed the tunnel around a curve and then it suddenly widened. The next instant, the area was flooded in white florescent light. I must have tripped a motion detector. I shielded my eyes until they got accustomed to the harsh light, then looked around. I was at the edge of a large cavern. There were dozens of crates of all different sizes, several large metal containers and other loose pieces of equipment strewn around.

On the far side was a small door. It, too, had been left ajar. I crossed the space and pulled the door open. Again, lights flickered on as I stepped through.

This space was different. It was much smaller and, clearly, the inner sanctum of Nexus. There were several work stations and the layout reminded me of the bridge of the Starship Enterprise, as if whoever had designed it was a Star Trek fan. If this was Greg Call's design choice, he'd been a man after my own heart.

I detected a faint hum. At the same moment, I felt something change inside my head, like a switch getting flipped. A wave passed through me, but this time it wasn't pain. Or rage.

My eyes suddenly couldn't stay open. I looked around for something to lie down on. There was a couch in a corner, across the room, which now seemed much too far away. My legs were turning to jelly, so I knelt down and then turned over, onto my back.

Sleep was washing over me like warm bath water. It was heavenly. Nothing had ever felt this good. I just needed a quick nap and then I'd—

Part IV:

Castles & Kings

40

"Sleep, oh gentle sleep…Nature's soft nurse," St. Germain says with a smile.

"There was nothing soft about it," I say, standing up and stretching. "Passed out on a rock-hard floor for who-knows-how-long? I woke up sore as hell. But it was nothing compared to the torture I'd been dealing with. I felt more or less back to normal."

St. Germain struggles to shift his massive girth, turning to watch me stretch.

"Clearly, the effects of your implant had been disrupted," he says. "Did you find out how?"

"No. I just figured there was something in the lab that scanned me and zapped it. This was Greg Call's base of operations and if anyone had the capability, it would be him. In fact, when I told this story to Chelsee, I *may* have implied that that's literally what happened."

"A little poetic license?"

I return to my chair and reach for the scotch.

"I didn't want her to worry," I say, "or—even worse—make me go see a doctor."

"Yes, women get men to do the most irrational things," St. Germain says, smiling.

"Don't I know it. But, from that point on, the insomnia, the headaches, the massive mood swings—they all went away and never returned."

St. Germain nods and reaches for his glass.

"It seems you were fortunate to survive. And, with that, can I assume your case was now finished? You'd convinced the police that Linsky's death was suspicious enough to change the cause of death; I presume that means Sylvia received her life insurance settlement and, by all appearances, your work was done."

"Yup. By all appearances."

The Count gives me a sly smile.

"Something tells me it wasn't."

"Why's that?"

"From what I know of you," he says, "I can't imagine that you would simply walk away. John Klaus, with the assistance of Slade, had used implants on you and others, and the STG project—Overlord—still existed. Other people, including Frank Schimming, were aware of the project and could continue to use it. I doubt you would rest easy knowing that."

"You're right. Especially after I heard everything Greg Call had to say."

The Count gives me a baffled look.

"You spoke to Greg Call?"

"No, he was dead."

St. Germain cocks his head to the side.

"Am I missing something?" he asks pleasantly.

"Yeah. Call recorded a video message before he went to New San Francisco. But first things first."

I take a sip of scotch before resuming the story.

"So I woke up on the floor, in the exact same position. My lack of movement must have caused the lights to turn off, so I was in total darkness and utter silence. Eventually, I raised my arm and waved it around, which triggered the lights. I rolled over and got onto my hands and knees. My lower back was in rigor mortis, so I took some time to stretch it out before standing up. When I finally got on my feet, I realized I had two pressing issues: an uncomfortably empty stomach and an agonizingly full bladder. Eventually, I found a bathroom and—"

St. Germain broke in.

"—If you'll fast forward to what Greg Call said, I'll double what I'm paying you—"

"—so," I said, smoothly switching gears, "Call's message was on a laptop that he'd placed conspicuously for me—or whoever—to find. There was a video file on the desktop. When I opened it, a face filled the screen.

The image and voice were both heavily distorted, but I recognized the distinctive skin mutation, like Call's face had been run through a cheese grater, shards of flesh hanging off.

"He started off by saying that his first plan must have failed, and that he was probably dead, so it would be up to whoever was watching to finish what he'd started. Then he talked about his long friendship with J. Saint Gideon, how they built Gideon Enterprises together. He said Gideon was a good man with honorable intentions, but that he disagreed with Gideon's ideologies. Especially with regard to Overlord."

"So Gideon knew about Overlord. He was lying when he told you he knew nothing about it."

"Yup."

"And Gideon was adamantly opposed to it, I presume."

"No. According to Call, Overlord was *Gideon's* baby."

St. Germain is stunned. After a moment, he shakes his head sadly.

"I'm disappointed to hear that. It's shocking, really, given what I know of the man."

I pull out a cigarette and pause to light it.

"I think Call had the same reaction," I say. "Gideon had pitched the concept as a way to counteract the growing violence in society, especially toward mutants like Call. But later on, Gideon revealed the true scope of his plan. It wouldn't be just about controlling violent behavior. He intended to target political figures, industry leaders, anyone with influence. In his mind, this would give him the power to achieve world peace."

The Count takes a deep breath.

"A benevolent dictatorship."

"Call described it as 'playing god'. He also gave details on some things I'd already learned, that the implants would initially control basic things: sleep, hunger, vision, hearing and so on. But there was the potential to do much more. Overlord could eventually turn people into junkies, doing whatever they were told to get their fix."

St. Germain nods, with a look of deep concern.

"A kind of Pavlovian remote control."

"That's one way to say it. I prefer 'zombie apocalypse'."

My host is silent for some time, then asks: "Did Call have anything else to say?"

"Just that whoever found his message needed to do what they could to stop Gideon before Overlord went online."

"So Klaus was right about the project not being completed yet."

"Yes, but it was close. And Call said that once it was ready, Gideon would become invulnerable."

"Invulnerable?"

"That's the word Call used. He didn't give an explanation, but I got the sense he felt responsible for it, somehow."

"And did Call say how Gideon might be stopped before that happened?"

I nod.

"He had a few suggestions. The first was a little impractical. He said the Overlord hub was almost certainly at Gideon's home and blowing the place up would destroy it."

"That does seem impractical."

"The next idea was to infiltrate Gideon's compound. But Wanda had said Gideon was *incommunicado*, so I couldn't contact him, try to play dumb and get invited in for another visit. The other option was to break in, which would require getting past the doming security, and Call had an idea how I might do that."

"Interesting. A chink in the armor?"

"A tiny one," I say. "He and Gideon had developed the doming security together and tested it out on Alcatraz Island, which Gideon had bought years earlier. Call said Gideon always insisted on running daily diagnostics on his security systems and reset them every twenty-four hours. This created a very small window of time when the doming security would be down."

"How small a window?"

"A few seconds. You'd have to already be moving—fast—and time it exactly right."

"And know the exact time it would happen," St. Germain adds. "Call couldn't know when that would be, could he?"

"No, but he knew the exact time when the diagnostics ran on Alcatraz; if it was the same time Gideon was using for his home security, getting through was theoretically possible."

"But if Gideon had set the diagnostics to run at a different time, which he likely had…"

"Yeah. I'd be flying into the world's biggest bug zapper. It was too big a risk to take."

"So, did Call have any viable suggestions?"

"He did," I say. "At least slightly more viable. When he'd first learned what Gideon's true intentions were, he'd secretly implemented an 'off switch' into Overlord."

St. Germain raises an eyebrow.

"An off switch?"

I nod and take a drag off my smoke.

"A fail-safe program he called *Stalemate*. And that's where the STG passcards came into play. Call had encoded them so anyone could use them to run the Stalemate program. There was just one problem."

"You were missing one of the passcards," St. Germain says.

"No, I'd been right about Call's passcard being the last one, and he'd left it at Nexus. So now I had all eight. The catch was, Call said I'd need direct access to Overlord to run the Stalemate program."

"Direct access? That puts you back to getting through Gideon's doming security, doesn't it?"

"No, Call said it could be done remotely, using one of the team member's hardware—the Gideon laptop, the STG passcard reader and the corresponding passcard—as long as they could still connect to the Overlord hub. Gideon had locked Call out of Overlord, so I'd need to find another team member's setup. I had Linsky's equipment, but his account had expired, which I think meant he'd been locked out like Call had."

St. Germain considers for a moment.

"What about Bosworth Clark's?"

"I tried that, right after watching Call's message, but Clark had been locked out, too, sometime after I took his laptop from the RV. And I'd put the GPS tracker on Larry Hammond's speeder, so I could try to find him, but that would take precious time. Plus, he'd said his work was already done, so I had to assume he was also locked out."

"It sounds like everyone had been locked out at this point," St. Germain says, watching me take a last drag.

"There was just one possibility. John Klaus."

"But, surely, Gideon would have blocked him."

"Yeah," I say, grinding my cigarette butt into the ashtray. "*If* he'd known about Klaus. Thing is, Klaus had said Schimming gave him *private* access—basically, a back door into the program. I'm not sure how they pulled that off, but Call seemed to have no clue Klaus was involved. So Gideon probably didn't either."

"You said the police were going to search Klaus's home and clinic for his STG equipment. Did they find it?"

"No. I checked with Clements and they'd come up empty. But there was one person who would know where I'd find what I needed."

I give St. Germain a minute to figure it out. He finally does.

"Frank Schimming."

"Exactly," I say. "And I had to work fast. I wasn't the only one who knew Schimming was working with Klaus; Slade did, too, and I figured that little tidbit would probably come up in his plea deal conversations with the cops. I needed to contact Schimming before anyone else did and try to blackmail him into helping me, in exchange for keeping quiet."

"A dangerous play."

"Well, I used an alias. I told him my name was Buck Wad."

"So you spoke with Schimming?"

"I did. I called Wanda Peck, who was able to find the number for Schimming's direct line. Apparently, CAPRICORN had dealt with him previously. Long story short, I called Schimming and convinced him that I had incriminating evidence of his dealings with Law & Order, but that I was willing to keep that to myself in exchange for info on John Klaus. I told him Klaus was dead and that we could pin everything on him; we just needed to know where to find Klaus's STG stash."

"And did he go for that?"

"I think he'd caught wind of the bust at Law & Order. He was in an accommodating mood. And you'll never guess where he sent me."

41

Alcatraz Island had been off-limits to the public for years. Officially, the island was 'structurally unsound', due to an earthquake or damage sustained during the 'nuclear incident'.

Of course, this made it like industrial-strength catnip for conspiracy theorists around the world. Several times a year, the Coast Guard would have to rescue someone who tried to fly, float or swim their way onto the island. According to some accounts, there was an invisible force field around Alcatraz, perhaps extraterrestrial in nature, which prevented anything from entering by sea or air.

As I'd recently discovered, Doming Security had been developed by Gideon Enterprises, tested on Alcatraz, and then left running to protect the island from intrepid urban explorers.

The total privacy provided by the doming security was the reason John Klaus had set up shop on Alcatraz, according to Frank Schimming. But Klaus had control over the doming security, so Schimming couldn't help me with that.

Schimming also claimed ignorance about what John Klaus might have been doing on Alcatraz—or what additional security might be there—which may or may not have been true. It didn't matter. All I cared about was finding Klaus's direct access to Overlord.

I found it ironic that John Klaus—who could very well have ended up taking control of Overlord—might be the key to destroying it. He and Greg Call may have been the only people capable of matching wits with Gideon and now they were both dead.

This was a chess match and, in the end, Gideon had outplayed everyone. Now we'd come to the endgame and, as outmatched as I might have been, I was going to do my best to play it out. A weapon this powerful—and there was no question that Overlord was a weapon—was too much to entrust to mere humans. Call knew that. Now it was up to me to finish the job. It felt like, now, *I* was the Poisoned Pawn.

* * * * *

At the stroke of midnight, Alcatraz was in my sights. As I circled around the island, I could see the same rippling effect I'd seen at Gideon's mansion. From what I knew about doming security, trying to fly through it would fry my speeder's electrical system, maybe even electrocute me, depending on how powerful the energy field was, and I had to assume Klaus had turned it up to 11.

There was only one way I'd get through. Back at Nexus, Call had described how he and Gideon had set up the system to run a diagnostic check at the same exact time each night. Starting at 12:12:12—twelve minutes and twelve seconds after midnight, the system would reset; while this happened, there would a brief period—no more than a few seconds—when the doming security would be vulnerable.

It seemed unlikely that anyone else knew about this little loophole and there was no reason for Gideon to change the time setting, so I was fairly confident I knew when my window of opportunity was.

I would have to try to fly through the perimeter of the dome within those few seconds. And I couldn't tell exactly how far the perimeter extended, but I had to assume it went out some distance into the water surrounding the island. Bottom line was, I'd need to be moving fast.

And that presented another problem: speeders don't stop on a dime. I had to hope I could slow down before I hit the dome when it rematerialized on the far side.

Alcatraz Island is much longer than it is wide, which made it easy to decide which angle to attack from; the long way would give me more room to slow down.

I made a few test runs to determine the timing, then guided my speeder into position and set it to hover. I was about a hundred yards off the island and maybe eighty feet above the water, which I figured to be the optimal height. The atomic clock on my dashboard read 12:09:49.

Two and a half minutes to go.

Out the driver side window, the Golden Gate Bridge glowed red against the night sky. My case, which had started with Carl Linsky jumping off that bridge, had brought me full circle. Alcatraz may have been the last thing Linsky saw.

12:10:32…

The island below looked decrepit and abandoned. No movement, no lights. For a moment, I wondered if I was taking this risk for nothing. Maybe Alcatraz would be the last thing I saw, too.

12:11:00…

On the other hand, I was playing with house money. Two days ago, I'd been making plans to kill myself. Now I was feeling more or less back to normal. If the implant was still working, there was no indication of it. But as long as Overlord was operational, I would never feel safe again. And it wasn't just me. No one would be safe.

But mostly it was about me.

12:11:40…

I checked my seat belt and pulled it tighter. It would take five seconds to reach the island from a dead stop. I waited.

The clock hit 12:11:56 and I put the pedal to the metal.

Acceleration seemed to take longer than in the test runs. It felt like the speeder was crawling. I found myself leaning forward, trying to push my Lotus ahead. I checked the speedometer—I was already going sixty miles per hour.

When I looked up, I was almost to the island. I braced myself for impact.

There was none.

But now I was headed straight toward a large, three-story building in the center of the island. I took my foot off the accelerator and pulled up, trying not to yank the steering wheel too hard—just enough to clear the building, but staying low enough to not hit the ceiling of the dome.

Through my windshield, I saw the doming security turn back on, the rippling effect refracting the city lights in the distance. I wrenched the steering wheel and banked hard to the left. My speeder must have come within inches of hitting the invisible barrier.

I continued banking, like I was skating on a roller derby track, until my speeder slowed to a crawl, then leveled out. I looked for a place to set down and spotted a large, flat spot at the base of the water tower that would do nicely.

After removing my seat belt, I checked the glove compartment to see if I had anything that might come in handy. A gun would have been handy. I had to settle for my flashlight and Sonny's lockpick set.

I had no reason to think there was anyone else on the island but, as I got out of the speeder, I half expected to see a patrol squad of uniformed minions—or, more likely, a swarm of armed drones—coming for me. But so far, so good.

There was no fog and the night sky was unusually clear. Even with all the light pollution—the bright city glow of New San Francisco to the south and Oakland to the east, with the Golden Gate Bridge to the west and a sprinkling of lights from Tiburon to the north—the stars in the night sky were clearly visible, shimmering like a mirage through the dome.

I decided to start my search in the three-story prison building that now towered over me. My footsteps crunched loudly as I walked up an old paved road, now cracked and rutted, looking for an entrance.

The only movement I could detect came from swaying tree branches. I was surprised by how many plants and trees were on the island, including rose bushes, succulents, apple and fig trees. A breeze was blowing in off the bay, thick and salty. The distant city sounds were muffled by the lapping of waves. Other than the wind and water, the island was eerily quiet.

As I got closer, I saw a section of the prison wall that was cracked and crumbling. At some point, a seismic shift had created several fissures that ran from the foundation to the roof. This had caused the stone around one of the barred windows on the ground floor to crack open and then erode over time. It looked like I might be able to move one of the bars.

I reached up and grabbed one. It felt loose. I started pushing and pulling on it. A minute later, it came out, like a rotten tooth.

Just then, I heard something moving inside. A split second later, a bright light flared like a camera flash and a small blast shook the wall.

Someone had fired a laser.

42

I dropped to the ground and lay still, my heart pounding. I strained to listen, expecting to hear footsteps approaching. But there was nothing. Total silence inside the building.

I wasn't sure what was happening. If there was an armed guard in there, I was pretty sure he would come after me. And then what would I do? I was unarmed and had nowhere to run. And the doming security had me trapped on the island for another twenty-four hours.

There weren't a lot of options, but I needed to know what I was dealing with. I got back to my feet and pulled myself up toward the window. A sickening smell drifted out from inside. Burnt hair.

I peeked up over the ledge, then ducked back down. No response. I straightened up again and took a longer look. Total silence. No movement. No indication of where the laser blast had come from.

Through the window I saw a small prison cell, about nine feet deep, five feet wide and seven feet tall. Other than a bunk against one wall, the cell was empty. Through the bars and across a wide expanse, I could see an identical set of cells on the opposite side, with more above.

Then I saw it. A drone.

It was on the far side of the room, drifting slowly through the air. I wondered if the blast had come from that. It was small, no bigger than a toaster, but apparently equipped with a laser that could toast the living hell out of me. I waited for it to pass out of my line of sight, then pulled myself up onto the window ledge.

A washbasin and toilet were directly under the window. Next to them was the source of the sickening smell: the smoldering remains of a huge bat. Apparently, the drone was motion-activated and had fired at the flying bat.

I looked up. Before I could move, another drone came into view, also on the far side of the interior, following the same flight path as the other.

For some reason, it didn't fire at me. Maybe the drones—and there were at least two, maybe more—scanned in only one direction, probably to avoid detecting each other.

A few seconds later, I heard a faint hum. I scrambled back out through the window and dropped down, out of sight. The humming came closer, moving steadily, then passed by and kept going. I stayed where I was and started counting. About thirty seconds later, another drone went past.

I waited for it to drift out of earshot and then climbed back through the window. I dropped to the floor, then squeezed under the bed and slid back against the wall.

As I waited for the next drone to approach, I heard a light scratching sound. Trying to keep perfectly still, my eyes moved around the cell until I saw the source of the scratching: a massive rat. It was staring at me from just outside the bars.

It wriggled through the bars and started scurrying toward me.

Then it burst into a ball of flame.

I took a deep breath and froze, then counted to ten before taking another breath. My heart felt like it would pound out of my chest.

I stayed under the bed for several more minutes, listening to the movement of the drones. About every thirty seconds or so, one would pass just outside the cell, so they were following a set path. Given the size of the building, I guessed that there were four drones patrolling this area.

Once I'd calculated the timing, I slid out from under the bed. With only a few moments to look around, my first move was to check the cell door. It was locked. The lock itself was rusted, so I could probably kick it open, but doing so would draw fire from any drone facing my direction.

I hurried back under the bed before the next drone scanned the cell. There was only one way I could imagine getting past the drones. And it was probably a terrible idea. But a bad plan is better than no plan at all.

In the next thirty-second window, I exited the cell the way I'd come in, through the window, and started looking around for something I could use. An apple tree provided a long branch and an apple. I also found a tangle of barbed wire. They weren't ideal components, but they'd have to do.

A few minutes later, I was back in the cell and under the bed. After the next drone passed, I slid out and got into position, standing near the bars at the front of the cell, my back against the wall. In my left hand, I held what looked like the least-intimidating medieval weapon imaginable; the apple was in my right hand.

I hadn't been able to see the drones passing by the cell, so I didn't know how far off the floor they were…or how close they were to the bars; I had to hope it was no more than six feet away or I was about to be chicken-fried Tex.

The humming sound of the next drone grew closer.

I made sure my medieval contraption was in position. I had to time this just right, but it would be better to move too soon than too late. The sound of the approaching drone got closer; I waited until the last second, then tossed the apple through the bars to my right.

From my left, a laser beam blasted the apple. Based on the angle of the laser, it looked like the drone was about six feet off the floor.

I stuck my jury-rigged contraption through the bars; I'd attached the nest of barbed wire to the end of the tree branch, creating something like a butterfly net.

A blast went harmlessly through the barbed wire, and then the drone floated straight into the tangled nest. As I gave the branch a hard twist, there was a bright flash and sparks showered the cell door. I pulled the branch closer as another blast hit the wall behind me, then stuck my right hand between the bars and into the barbed wire nest. It shredded the skin on my fingers, but I managed to get a solid grip on the drone. Then I dropped the tree branch and stuck my left hand in.

Now with both hands holding the drone, I turned it to face away from me and, like an old airplane machine gunner, directed the laser fire at the three other drones.

One by one, my drone detected their movement and shot them down. I waited for several minutes to make sure I'd gotten them all and that there were no reinforcements coming. When I was sure the coast was clear, I lowered the live drone to the floor—still holding it through the bars—then maneuvered my leg out and stomped on it.

I felt like a stone-cold killer. High on adrenaline, I stepped back and unleashed a ninja kick on the rusty cell door.

43

I stepped out onto the walkway and took my first full look around the inside of the Alcatraz Penitentiary. It looked pretty much like in the movies, only creepier. I've never believed in ghosts, but if any place could be haunted, it would be this one.

It was possible that Klaus had equipped every building on the island with killer drones, but I doubted it. The only thing that would need protection would be whatever Klaus had been doing here. And that meant what I was looking for had to be somewhere close.

My footsteps echoed as I walked around. I explored a warden's office, a visitation room, a library and a barber shop, all long-abandoned and decrepit. No sign of Klaus.

The only areas left to search were the four cell blocks, marked A through D, and it was in the A block that I found what I was looking for: fresh footprints—tiny, evil dwarf-size—leading to an old, rusted door.

I opened it; ancient stone steps led down into darkness.

I pulled out my flashlight and switched it on. The stairs were covered in thick dust, except where Klaus's footprints had left a trail. It looked like Klaus was the only one who'd been here. Even so, I descended the stairs slowly and as quietly as possible, not knowing what—or who—might lie ahead.

As I made my way down, something about the stone and the stairs triggered a memory. I'd read that Alcatraz had originally been home to a fortress built in the 1800s and used by the military to protect San Francisco Bay. The prison had been built over the top of it. The subterranean area was known as the 'Spanish Dungeon' and had rarely been used.

At the bottom of the stairs, I followed the trail of footprints past several very old cells that had been carved out of the rock. The place felt like an ancient crypt.

At the end of the passage was a large, relatively new metal door. Behind it, I could hear a humming sound; probably a generator. Unlike the door above, this one was locked.

I fished Sonny Fletcher's lockpick set out of my pocket and went to work. Eventually, I heard the lock click.

The door was thick and heavy, but opened effortlessly, revealing a large room bathed in bright, florescent light. It looked like a morgue. Or a cross between a morgue and a dungeon. The walls were rough stone, but the contents of the room included several stainless-steel tables and the type of equipment you'd see in a hospital operating room.

This was what I'd expected Klaus's room at Law & Order to look like. Bad things had happened here, I had no doubt. Klaus was a surgeon; I could imagine him cutting into bodies—live or dead—maybe experimenting with the placement of implants. Fortunately, there were no corpses left behind, but there were bloodstains on the floor and the room smelled of chemicals and rusty iron.

As I'd suspected, the humming sound was coming from a generator in the corner. Several power cords lay on the floor, extending out like tentacles from the generator to various pieces of equipment. One cord ran to an old, dust-covered computer terminal. I wondered if this could be what controlled the doming security.

Another cord extended to a small workstation: a chair and a desk with a laptop and several other items on it. Even from across the room, I could see the flaming sword logo of Gideon Enterprises on the laptop.

I'd found my access to Overlord.

I sat down at the workstation. In addition to an STG passcard reader, there was a virtual reality headset attached to the laptop. When the laptop finished booting up, the STG passcard reader lit up. On the monitor, a message appeared: 'Insert Passcard'.

I found the 'G' passcard—the one I'd taken off Klaus's body—and swiped it.

As with the other laptops, a login dialog appeared with a filled user name field and a blank password field. Thinking back to the placement of Klaus's photo on Linsky's bulletin board, I hoped the password would be

KNIGHT. I was right.

The screen flickered, then the Gideon Enterprises logo appeared.

So far, so good. Now what?

I watched the screen, waiting for something to happen. After a minute, I decided there were no instructions forthcoming.

Not knowing what else to do, I took the first passcard off the top of the deck—it was the 'B' card—and inserted it. The Gideon logo disappeared, replaced with a single word onscreen:

SINGER

I stared for a moment. I had no clue what this meant, or what I was supposed to do. After a few seconds, the word disappeared and the Gideon logo reappeared.

I tried a different passcard, this one marked with a 'C'. A new set of letters appeared, but this one wasn't a word.

TCAHCMEKE

As I stared at the letters, something tickled my brain. I kept staring at them until they disappeared. Suddenly, a thought struck me.

I ran the same card again and, once TCAHCMEKE was displayed, I pressed the 'C' key on the keyboard. Doing this highlighted one of the C's onscreen.

Now I was onto something. I then pressed the 'H' key. The H highlighted. Feeling a tingle, I pressed 'E', then the other 'C', followed by 'K', 'M', 'A', 'T' and, finally, 'E'.

CHECKMATE

The highlighted letters flashed once and then disappeared. The screen went black and a command prompt appeared with a flashing cursor. I could barely program a remote, but this seemed to indicate that I was supposed to enter some kind of command. I typed in CHECKMATE.

'Invalid Command'

It returned to the command prompt and flashing cursor. I thought for a minute, then entered OVERLORD.

'Invalid Command'

Call hadn't said anything about this, just that the eight passcards would be needed to run the fail-safe program. Then I remembered.

I typed in STALEMATE.

After a pause, which I figured was either a good sign or a really bad sign, a message appeared: 'STALEMATE PROTOCOL INITIATED'.

My heart started pounding.

The Stalemate message disappeared and was replaced by an image of eight blocks, alternating white and black, displayed across the top half of the screen. On the third square from the left, a black bishop icon appeared.

Just like the bulletin board in Linsky's attic. Eight spaces for eight chess pieces. And eight STG passcards.

Below the image of the eight blocks, another message: 'Insert Passcard'.

I swiped the 'B' card again.

SINGER

I now realized that this must be an anagram, but I wasn't sure what it was an anagram for. I set that passcard aside and tried the 'A' passcard. This one brought up the following letters:

KORO

If this had been the first anagram, I probably wouldn't have figured it out, but with only four letters, it was pretty simple. I pressed the 'R' key, followed by 'O' twice, and then 'K'.

A black rook appeared on the white block at the far left.

I swiped the 'H' passcard.

LESCAT

This one took a minute, mostly because I couldn't get the image of a cat named Les out of my head. Then I got it.

CASTLE

A white rook appeared on the far right square.

I was reaching for the next passcard when I suddenly heard a voice:

"Stop what you're doing! Exit this program immediately!"

44

The voice sounded thin and distant, but there was no mistaking whose voice it was.

J. Saint Gideon's.

"Exit the program!"

It was coming from the headset on the desk. I ignored him and swiped the 'F' passcard—Carl Linsky's card.

HIPSOB

Hip S.O.B., I thought. *Funny*. I'd already figured out Linsky's password; I typed in BISHOP. A white bishop appeared in the third block from the right.

"Whoever you are, you don't understand what you're doing," Gideon said through the headset.

I paused.

Gideon was right. I didn't understand what I was doing. And suddenly, I was wondering if maybe I had this all wrong. When Call said Overlord had to be destroyed, I hadn't questioned it. But I knew almost nothing about Greg Call. At least I'd met Gideon face-to-face. I'd felt his sincerity, believed that he was a good man. And Wanda Peck did too. That carried weight with me.

Maybe I needed to give Gideon a chance to tell his side of things. I had no reason to trust Call over Gideon. And if Gideon had an easy way to stop me from running the Stalemate program, he probably would have done it already. I could hear him out and then decide what to do.

I picked up the VR headset and put it on.

I suddenly found myself in a giant arena, overlooking a huge chessboard. Staring back at me from the opposite side was Gideon, or at least a virtual version of him. He was dressed in black and standing—no wheelchair, just the way I'd seen him with Jorge Valdez at the Rank & File. And my headset must have projected a similar virtual version of me.

"There you are," he said with a smile. "Mr. Tex Murphy."

"Mr. Gideon."

"Not at all who I was expecting. This is Greg Call's doing, I presume. Are you in Nexus?"

"No. I'm in a little hideout that Frank Schimming set up for John Klaus."

There was a long pause while Gideon connected the dots.

"Alcatraz," Gideon said.

"But Call is the one who sent me here. He thinks you've created a little bit of a monster," I said. "I'm inclined to agree."

"I am not the enemy."

"But Overlord is."

"Then you do not understand its purpose."

"I know what it's capable of. It almost killed me."

Gideon nodded, his expression turning grim.

"I am sorry for that. That was never my intent."

"No, it was Law & Order's intent. Do you know how close they came to taking control of your system?"

"A calculated risk, my friend."

Gideon's attitude seemed awfully cavalier, given the circumstances.

"A lot of innocent people have been killed because of your calculated risk," I said, some anger creeping into my voice. "I'm just trying to make sure there are no more victims."

"It is better that some die rather than allow the entire planet to degenerate into total chaos."

"And you get to decide that? No one's got the right to play god."

"I agree! It's unconscionable. But the fact is, it's done every day and, moreover, by people who aspire to nothing more than avarice and domination."

"And how are you any different?"

Gideon made a fist and pumped it for emphasis.

"Overlord is the hope, Mr. Murphy! With it, I can influence events in the global political arena for good."

"Good for you, maybe."

Gideon smiled and spread his arms wide.

"Good for all those who respect mercy and justice."

Call had been right about Gideon. I didn't doubt that he had the best of intentions, but no one should be allowed to wield this kind of power. It was time to pull the plug.

I adjusted my headset so I could focus on the laptop in front of me.

"You've lost control of your creations before," I said, inserting the 'G' passcard.

THKING

"Schimming took control of your company and he and Klaus were taking control of Overlord," I continued, as I typed in K-N-I-G-H-T. "Eventually someone's going to manage to do it."

I swapped out passcards, replacing the 'G' card with the 'E' card.

GINK

There was only one other word to make from these letters: KING. I typed it in.

"You're wrong," Gideon said. "Overlord and I will soon become one and the same, and safely locked away inside a castle that no key can open. I assure you; no one will be able to take control from me or Overlord again."

There were two squares left to fill. The 'D' passcard brought up 'MIGTAB'. This card corresponded to the Queen position—Greg Call's piece—so I'd been expecting an anagram for QUEEN. No surprise that he'd have a different, trickier password. I stared at the screen, mentally rearranging the letters.

"You're sure about that?" I said, just trying to buy more time. "I managed to get in here. And I'm no genius."

I heard Gideon chuckle.

"Alcatraz is not the castle."

"Call wanted to blow up your compound," I said, still working on figuring out MIGTAB. "No one is totally invulnerable."

"The castle is not a place," Gideon said.

I finally got the anagram.

GAMBIT

Just one passcard to go: 'B', the one I'd started with. The word SINGER appeared again.

"It was Greg Call's crowning achievement," Gideon said. "Thanks to him, Overlord will live forever."

The SINGER anagram had to be a chess term of some kind. Then it hit me.

RESIGN

"I don't think so," I said. "This little nightmare of yours has got to be destroyed."

With one final stroke of the 'N' key, the screen went black. I readjusted the headset and found myself back in the arena.

As Gideon looked on in stunned silence, the massive chess board began to fill in with pieces. The chessmen appeared in seemingly random locations, as if in mid-match. Judging by their positions, Gideon was playing black. And he was hopelessly outnumbered.

But now what?

Was I supposed to make a move? Even with an obvious advantage, I barely knew how to play chess. Gideon was a grandmaster.

Then I saw the white bishop move. It slid on the diagonal to a space occupied by a black pawn, which then disappeared.

Gideon pointed to the board and waved his hand; a black knight took the white bishop.

Immediately, a white knight took a black rook.

Gideon gestured again; his black knight took a white rook.

The moves continued, almost too quickly to follow. One piece after another disappearing from the board. It was a valiant effort from Gideon, but he was doomed. The entire sequence lasted less than a minute.

Then, with one final move, the White King advanced, trapping Gideon's Black King. Even I knew what that meant.

"Checkmate, Mr. Gideon."

45

Gideon's avatar stood silent; head down, utterly defeated.

I could picture the flesh-and-bones Gideon sitting in the rickety old wheelchair, somewhere inside his vast, empty fortress, slowly coming to grips with the fact that it was over. His vision of a better world…long years of planning and execution…his life's work…all gone in an instant.

I wasn't sure how I should feel. Part of me was elated. I'd just taken down Overlord, the source of torture I'd been subjected to and barely survived. And even though Gideon wasn't the one who'd tried to kill me, he and his creation were ultimately responsible.

Still, I'd destroyed the man's dream. A good man, I believed, with good intentions. Another part of me felt horrible about it.

"I'm sorry, Mr. Gideon," I said, "but this had to happen."

After a long pause, Gideon nodded slowly, still not looking up.

In the space between us, the few remaining pieces on the massive chessboard began to fade. I watched and waited for Gideon to say something, but he stayed silent. I was about to remove my headset when, at last, he spoke up:

"He finally did it."

Gideon slowly raised his head. To my surprise, he was smiling.

"After all these years."

He inhaled deeply and straightened up, composing himself.

"Greg is an excellent player," he said. "A bit too aggressive, perhaps, which has often worked against him in our matches. We've played to a draw on many occasions, but he's never beaten me. Not until today."

The pieces had all disappeared from the chessboard. Now the board itself was fading.

"I'm no expert," I said, "but it did look like he had a pretty unfair advantage."

Gideon nodded.

"Yes, well, the outcome was a foregone conclusion once you gained access. There was no recourse, apart from convincing you to take my side rather than Greg's. But I suspect you and he are cut from similar cloth."

"I wouldn't know," I said. "Other than agreeing that Overlord was a bad idea."

Gideon lowered his gaze to the chessboard, now turning to virtual stardust.

"Greg was…is…very dear to me, but we disagreed about many things. I was aware of his abhorrence of Overlord. And not just Overlord. In recent years, he'd come to despise the effects of modern technology on society and regret much of what we'd created together. But I never saw this gambit coming. It seems I underestimated him…and you. A mistake I've made all too often."

Gideon went quiet, lost in thought. After a minute, he turned away and reached for something I couldn't see.

"I intended to have one final drink to celebrate the culmination of my work," he said, turning back to face me. "Now, I suppose, we must drink to *your* success."

I'd never had alcohol at the time I met Gideon, but I would have gladly shared a drink with him now. I wasn't sure how I'd handle all this had I been in his place. Probably not well. But Gideon was resigning with an admirable amount of grace and dignity. It made me feel even more guilty. He probably didn't care to hear it, but I wanted to rationalize what I'd done.

"I think I understand what you hoped to accomplish with Overlord," I said, "but I'm not sure you can force the world to be a better place."

Gideon smiled sadly.

"Hope is a fragile luxury, Mr. Murphy. As the years pass, we are all hurt…damaged. We become covered with scars—some physical, many more emotional. It's all too easy to forget what it was like before the scars, when we had vast reserves of optimism and the open road stretched out ahead of us, full of endless possibilities."

He brought his hands together, cradling something between them.

"That time is long past for me," he said, "and there's no going back. It will be up to you and others like you to carry on."

The chessboard had disappeared, leaving an immense, dark void between us.

"Hold onto your hope as long as you can," Gideon said. "Don't let life beat it out of you."

"I'll do my best."

"I know you will." Gideon smiled. "I'd come to believe that there was no good left in the world, no heroes anymore—"

"—only villains of varying degrees," I said. "I remember."

Gideon nodded.

"Perhaps I was wrong about that."

The virtual space was slowly getting darker. It was like Gideon was sinking into the void.

"What will you do now?" I asked.

Gideon shook his head and looked away.

"The only thing I *can* do: take the leap into the abyss and discover what awaits: immortality…damnation…or nothingness."

Gideon looked like a ghost now, fading away.

"Say goodbye to Greg for me, will you?"

I didn't have the heart to tell him Call was dead.

"I will," I said.

With one last smile, Gideon raised his hand toward me, holding an invisible glass.

And then he was gone.

Part V:

Checkmate

46

St. Germain is quiet for some time.

"There is a great deal to process," he says at last. "I daresay this makes clear why Gideon took his own life. Like the rest of the world, I could make no sense of it at the time."

I'll never forget the day I heard they'd found Gideon's body. It was months later. But he'd been dead a long time. Probably since right after we last spoke. It wasn't something I liked to think about.

"A tragic end for a tortured soul," St. Germain says.

I just nod and raise my glass.

Rest in peace, Mr. Gideon.

St. Germain watches me drink.

"But you were certainly in the right," he says, pointedly. "I hope you don't blame yourself for his death. We are all responsible for our own choices."

I shrug and dig out a cigarette.

"I've known a lot of people who ended up dead. You learn how to live with it."

St. Germain gives me a look.

"Do you? Really?"

I ignore the question and light my smoke.

The Count waves his hand, dismissing the subject, and then extracts a fat cigar from the inner pocket of his suit coat.

"Enough of that," he says. "What about Overlord? Are you certain it was destroyed?"

"I have no reason to think it wasn't. I followed Call's instructions and it all went the way he said it would."

My host nods, thoughtfully, as he snips off the end his cigar.

"I suppose, on behalf of the free world, I should thank you."

"Don't mention it."

St. Germain produces a small matchbox and takes out a wooden match.

"As I said, since the moment we met, I've sensed that something significant was in store for you. But it seems Fate found you long before I did."

I watch as he strikes the match, then holds it to the tip of the cigar and takes a series of puffs.

"I'm not sure how much I believe in fate," I say. "More like dumb luck. Of all the heads on all the PI's in all the towns in all the world, they had to stick an implant into mine."

"But honestly," he says through the smoke, "so many things had to happen exactly as they did—not only for you to become involved, but to survive and then, against virtually impossible odds, succeed. Do you think many other people could have accomplished what you did?"

I shrug—modestly—and take a drink.

"Considering you're my client, I'll go ahead and say 'no'."

The Count chuckles and leans back. After a delicate sip and a moment of reflection, he changes the subject away from my cosmic significance.

"So, tell me what happened after your confrontation with Gideon."

47

I removed the VR headset and leaned back in the chair.

I guess that's it, I thought.

For the first time in what felt like weeks—though it had been only a few days—I had no leads to track down…no mysteries to solve…no ticking clock in my head.

My case was finished and it felt like I should be in the mood to celebrate, but I wasn't. I was just exhausted.

I shut everything down, including the generator, which I expected would disable the doming security. Then I gathered up all the hardware from the workstation and carried it out to my speeder.

The starry night sky was crystal clear—no dome overhead. I loaded the equipment, got behind the wheel and lifted off. At this hour, the city was fast asleep and I was ready to join it, but I had to make one stop. Or more like a pause.

I flew out to the middle of the Bay and set my Lotus to hover. I opened the door and tossed the Gideon laptop out, then the passcard reader, then the STG passcards. One by one, I watched them flutter down into the black, sparkling water.

I kept the VR headset. It was probably worth a few bucks.

Then I turned for home.

*　*　*　*　*

I was out cold before my head hit the pillow on the cot in the back of my office. When I finally woke up, I staggered out to the main room and saw that it was still dark outside the big window. I checked the time and realized I'd lost an entire day. I wasn't going to miss it.

I *had* missed about six meals, though, and the tootsie pops in my ashtray weren't going to cut it, so I got freshened up and went out to forage. At an all-night diner in the Mission District, I ordered enough breakfast to feed a family of bears, then got a newspaper and read it over plates of bacon, hash browns covered with melty swiss cheese, over easy eggs and wheat toast with raspberry jam. And coffee. Lots and lots of coffee.

The frontpage headline in the early morning edition was the bust at Law & Order. There was a lot of speculation concerning the whereabouts of Robert Knott, but no mention of Klaus, Slade or Schimming, or anyone else I'd come across during my case.

Nothing about Wanda Peck, either, though there were references to CAPRICORN. And no mention of the small-time private investigator who'd infiltrated Knott's office to get the incriminating evidence on Law & Order. No surprise, though a little disappointing. It was a feeling I'd eventually get accustomed to.

After pounding my prodigious hunger into submission, I read the Sports section, then finished the Jumble puzzle and half the crossword. I left a celebratory tip and headed out.

On the sidewalk outside, I spotted a penny. Cash was becoming as obsolete as floppy discs, and they'd quit minting coins almost a decade ago; I couldn't remember the last time I'd seen one. It made me think of my dad. Anytime he found a penny, he'd say: "Find a penny, pick it up….all the day, you'll have good luck." Typically, I'd leave the penny where it was, but it seemed like a good omen. Plus, I'd used up a lot of luck in the past few days.

Not that I was planning on doing anything risky. My to-do list consisted of checking in with Wanda and Detective Clements. Maybe another nap.

And then there was Sylvia. There might be some riskiness with that. We needed to settle up my tab, but that wasn't the risky part.

I'd done my best to obey the P.I. Rule of not falling for a client. Not very successfully. I could try to blame our *hookup interruptus* back in Freaktown on the STG implant, but it was more than that. I knew she was trouble, but I'd also seen her softer, more vulnerable side. It made me want to protect her, take good care of her. And she was the most gorgeous thing I'd ever laid eyes, hands and mouth on.

Unfortunately, the last time I saw her, she was holding a gun on Slade, her face sticky with blood and duct tape residue, trying to convince me she wasn't as bad as everyone seemed to think she was. We'd almost gotten killed that night and it was because of me and my investigation. Maybe she'd hate me for putting her in danger, or feel humiliated by what Klaus had said about her, or be angry that I left her to deal with Slade and the cops and then went days without contacting her.

On the other hand, I'd solved her case, and she'd get her million-dollar payout. I had absolutely no idea what to expect when I saw her next.

Somehow, she still managed to surprise me.

* * * * *

"So, Tex Murphy, Private Investigator, are you ready to take the dive?" Sylvia handed me a flute full of champagne.

"Depends. What's in it for me?"

"Well," she said, "let me give you a little taste."

She stepped in close, put her arm around my waist and pulled me up against her body. She was all soft and warm. Then her lips were on mine. This time, it was a long, slow, wet kiss.

She stepped back and flashed a wide smile.

"Keep talking," I said.

Sylvia was wearing a long, white silk dress that hugged every curve from stem to stern, with spaghetti straps and a low-cut neckline that showed off her perfect neck, shoulders, arms and other stuff. Her blonde hair was slicked back; she looked like a cover model.

The room we were in was only slightly less impressive. The palette was rich, dark gold and linen, with a few splashes of crimson. A crystal chandelier hung from an ornate, recessed ceiling high above us. Thick, embroidered drapes were pulled back from floor-to-ceiling windows, offering a majestic view of the city. Two large Persian rugs lay on the gleaming parquet floor, one under a King-size bed, the other in a sitting area with two matching chairs, a gold-and-glass coffee table and a pillow-laden divan.

The Savoy Hotel's honeymoon suite was unquestionably the swankiest place I'd ever been.

Yeah. The honeymoon suite.

The past few days had been a total blur…even blurrier than the days I'd been on the case. As it turned out, Sylvia hadn't been upset with me. The exact opposite, in fact. After way too many celebratory cocktails, she'd proposed to me…and I took the first truly impulsive and irrational leap of my entire life.

"I'm thinking something tropical," Sylvia said. "Romantic nights in the Caribbean. Or maybe Rio. How about skiing at St. Moritz?"

"I don't ski."

Sylvia took a sip of champagne, then gave me a seductive look.

"I'll teach you how to ski…among other things."

"That sounds pretty good. But, just so you know, I'm a 'white picket fence/kids/dog' kind of guy."

Sylvia stepped toward me and adjusted my bow tie.

"We can talk about that later. Right now, we have the whole world to explore."

"Which is great," I said, "but I've been thinking. A million dollars isn't what it used to be. How would you feel about getting a financial advisor?"

"Well, $850,000. Which reminds me—"

She drained her glass and turned away.

"—You're gonna love this. Hold on."

She knelt down by the bed and pulled out two lavishly-wrapped gift boxes from underneath. I was busy doing some mental math.

"You already spent a hundred and fifty thousand dollars?!"

"Shush," she said, then carried the boxes to the coffee table.

"Go ahead. Open them."

I'm not sure I'd ever seen anyone look happier and I didn't want to spoil things. We could talk about the money later. I sat down and started to unwrap the first gift. It was about the size of a toaster oven. I didn't think it was a toaster oven, but I kind of hoped it was. It would be perfect for my office.

"You didn't have to get me anything," I said.

"This is in celebration of solving your first case."

A plain white box was under the wrapping paper. I opened it up. It was a hat.

"Wow," I said. "It's a hat."

"All great detectives wear hats. I thought you should have a fedora."

I pulled it out and put it on. Incredibly, it fit my oversized head.

"It looks good," Sylvia said, her eyes sparkling. "Just like Humphrey Bogart. But a lot handsomer."

"I hope you didn't pay too much for it."

"I paid way too much for it."

We'd definitely need to talk about the money later. I shrugged and moved on to the second gift.

Sylvia refilled her champagne glass as I unwrapped. This one was bigger—about the size of the Pizza Palace's Meat Mountain Pie. Which I hoped…but, nah.

There was another white box inside, like the kind your dry cleaning comes back in, or so they tell me. I lifted the top part off. Inside was some kind of tan-colored coat, folded up.

I pulled it out and unfolded it. It was an old, worn trench coat.

"What's this?" I asked, a little confused.

"It belonged to Humphrey Bogart."

"Seriously?! You know, he's why I became a detective. I saw The Maltese Falcon when I was a kid and that was all she wrote."

"I had a feeling," Sylvia said with a big smile.

I stood up.

"Here, help me try it on."

I stuck an arm into one of the sleeves, all the way to the end…and beyond. My arm was about a foot too long. I guess Bogart looked a lot taller on the big screen.

Sylvia giggled.

"Maybe we can put it in a frame or something," I said.

She helped me pull the tiny trench coat off and put it back in the box.

"That was very thoughtful," I said. "I don't know what to say."

Sylvia picked up her cigarette case from the coffee table.

"Say 'thank you, Sylvia'."

"Thank you, Sylvia."

She opened the case and extended it toward me.

"Would you like one?"

I'd never had a cigarette. Never planned to have one. But I was doing a whole lot of things I'd never done before.

"Sure, doll," I said, feeling downright Bogarty. "Why not?"

Part VI:

Endgame

48

"Your 'Paradise Lost'," St. Germain says with a half-smile.

"Like I said, it was a nutty few days."

I haven't thought about Sylvia in a long time. Not in that way, at least. The good times hadn't lasted long. But there were good times. I still wore the fedora she'd bought for me.

St. Germain nods, watching me with a sympathetic expression, then takes a moment to refresh his glass. Leaving me with my thoughts, I suppose. Always the gentleman. We sit in silence for a spell, smoking and drinking.

"OK," I say, "moving on. That was end of my case."

My host sets his glass down and shifts in his seat.

"And your career? Where did it go from there?"

"Into the toilet, pretty much. Like everything else."

St. Germain raises an eyebrow and inspects the end of his cigar.

"That's unfortunate. And somewhat surprising."

"Tell me about it," I say, flicking the ash off the end of my cigarette. "I thought Detective Clements and Wanda Peck had been impressed by my work. I figured one or both might throw me some bones, but they never did. And Wanda convinced me that it would be in everyone's best interest—including my own—not to advertise the details of my case."

"Why was that?"

"She said we couldn't be absolutely certain Overlord didn't still exist. And if it was just hibernating, we couldn't be sure someone wouldn't be able to wake it up in the future. It was best if no one else knew about it. She was also concerned that Schimming was still out there, along with a lot of other powerful people with ties to Law & Order. She wanted to keep a lid on everything until CAPRICORN could finish rooting them all out."

"Did she ask for your assistance with that?"

I shake my head.

"No. And I'm not sure why. I didn't work with CAPRICORN again until years later."

"December, 2042?"

"Thereabouts."

St. Germain leans forward and taps his cigar on the edge of the ashtray.

"That's something I'm eager to discuss, but first, let's go over the aftermath of your first case. What happened to Slade?"

"According to Detective Clements, he took a plea deal that kept him off death row. She wasn't happy about that, but she said the decision came from way above her pay grade."

"Hm," the Count says. "A plea deal would keep his name—and details of his crimes—out of the news."

He mulls this over, then continues: "So, Carl Linsky's cause of death was changed to 'undetermined', which gave Sylvia the life insurance payout, but no other details emerged. The other deaths—at least those that were discovered—were all left as suicides or accidents. The disappearance of Robert Knott remained unsolved. No mention of Overlord anywhere. And the fall of the Law & Order Party provided a huge distraction to divert the attention of the media and the public. No apparent loose ends. All very tidy."

I crush my cigarette into the ashtray.

"You think someone did a little housekeeping?"

"Undoubtedly. CAPRICORN had its reasons for doing so, but their influence only extended so far. There had to be more powerful forces at work. I believe this is where our adversary made his first moves."

St. Germain picks up his glass and swirls it.

"When I researched your background," he continues, "I could find nothing of note between this point and when you went to the Martian Colonies, almost two years later. What were you doing in the interim?"

"Not much. I got a few jobs…nothing very interesting. I picked up some new hobbies: smoking, drinking, and trying to keep Sylvia from blowing through all her money. I got pretty good at the first two; failed miserably on that last one."

"Let's jump ahead, then. How did your Martian case come about?"

"I got a call and ended up meeting Marshall Alexander."

St. Germain is impressed.

"The founder of the Terraform Corporation."

"Yup. Made a fortune mining on Mars," I say. "His daughter had gone missing—presumed kidnapped—and he needed someone to make the trip to Mars to find her and bring her back."

"Did Alexander say how he found you?"

"No, and I didn't bother to ask. I was just excited to get a job. Especially a job working for a trillionaire."

"And why do you think a trillionaire would choose *you*? Especially considering you had no apparent track record of success."

"I assumed he couldn't find anyone else willing to make the trip without having to pay them a mint. It was an 18-month commitment and I was happy to do it for a bargain price. I needed a break from Sylvia and I figured getting 92 million miles away ought to do it."

St. Germain takes a long, thoughtful sip.

"Why?" I ask. "You think there was some other reason he hired me?"

"From what I gather, your efforts on Mars were successful," he says, disregarding my question.

"Very."

"And?"

I shrug.

"I found Alexander's daughter, we had a few laughs and came home."

"And the Oracle Stone?"

Oracle Stone?

Once again, I wonder how St. Germain catches wind of these things. I'd found out about the Oracle Stone during my time on Mars, but it hadn't been especially important to my case and I hadn't given it any thought in the years since.

"What about the Oracle Stone?" I ask.

"Tell me what you know about it."

I reach for the Lagavulin.

"I know it made some people do some crazy things," I say, refreshing my glass. "Depending on who you ask, it was a religious artifact, or a relic left by an ancient Martian civilization. I wasn't that impressed."

"You should have been. I suspect the Oracle Stone may have been the primary reason for your going to Mars."

"Well, no offense, but that's ridiculous."

"I believe you may have brought it—or at least a piece of the same material—back with you."

"Well, I didn't."

"Not that you remember."

"Pretty sure I'd remember that."

St. Germain waves his cigar hand, leaving a trail of smoke.

"Regardless," he says, "the story of the Oracle Stone didn't end on Mars. And I think you'll agree that where it reappeared is extremely interesting."

He sets his cigar in the ashtray, then opens his briefcase and takes out a tiny object. I've seen it before. Or one exactly like it. Pound for pound, probably the most destructive thing ever created. I'd seen it turn a moon-sized space station into scrap metal.

"Is that—?"

"Yes," St. Germain says solemnly. "A Winter Chip."

"But, how—?"

"It took considerable resources to procure this, as you might imagine. CAPRICORN created three of them. This is the only one remaining."

He hands the Winter Chip to me. As I look it over, he continues:

"It seems a piece of the Oracle Stone was used to create this."

St. Germain waits for me to react. I'm just confused.

"I don't know what to tell you," I say. "I never heard anything more about the Oracle Stone after I left Mars, and microchip technology isn't exactly in my wheelhouse."

"Nor mine. But I was able to find some information on research done with the Oracle Stone. It's quite fascinating."

He reaches back into his briefcase and pulls out a sheet of paper.

"'The [Oracle Stone],'" he reads, "'had heretofore unknown properties, most notable of which was its capacity for signal transference. When the substance was used in lieu of silicon for conductive purposes within an integrated circuit, it could receive information *before it was sent.* On its own this was considered a low value goal; the same effect can be replicated with photonic light. However, when a compressed, artificially intelligent super-virus was installed onto a chip lined with the substance, the result defied explanation. This 'Winter Chip' annihilated our best AIs in any given scenario, adapting and counter-attacking through what was, by all indications, *foreknowledge*.'"

St. Germain looks up from the paper.

"You understand what this means? The Winter Chip could anticipate what the anti-virus software would do *before* it did it."

"That doesn't seem possible."

St. Germain raises an eyebrow.

"Some people believed the Oracle Stone could give one the power of prophecy."

I set the Winter Chip down and grab another cigarette.

"Some people will believe anything."

"Be that as it may," St. Germain says, returning the paper to the briefcase, "this information on the Oracle Stone came from a joint project between CAPRICORN and Gideon Enterprises. This links at least three of your cases: the first one, the one on Mars...and the big one."

"Ah, yes. The Case of the Murdered Girl with the Big...Hands."

I may have had too much to drink. St. Germain is starting to get impatient. I light my smoke and resolve to try and take this all more seriously.

"I'm referring, of course, to the tragedy on the Moon Child," my host says, drily. "The Titanic of this generation: the largest, most advanced space station ever constructed—so advanced that some conspiracy theorists claimed it was built using alien technology. And on New Year's Eve, 2042—during its maiden voyage, so to speak—it experienced a catastrophic systems failure. An unknown number of people on board, likely in the tens of thousands, died in the disaster."

"I wouldn't call it a disaster...but potato, potahto."

Damn scotch.

"As I've said all along," St. Germain says, "there was precious little information to be found regarding you or your cases. Almost as if your tracks had been intentionally covered. Details on what happened to the Moon Child were especially scant. Not only were they never made public, they were kept confidential by every security agency and organization. I was fortunate to learn that you—again, of all people—were the only survivor. I'd very much like to know how you managed that."

I let loose a long stream of smoke.

"What is it you're trying to figure out, exactly?" I ask. "I could tell you that whole story, but what's the point?"

"I want to know how you alone survived."

"Trust me, no one saved me. I did it all on my own. And I almost didn't make it out."

"There was an entire city of people on the Moon Child. And you were the only one to get away safely? I believe that you must have had help. And this is where something from your first case comes into play."

St. Germain leans forward and locks eyes with me.

"Do you recall the name of the other project Larry Hammond told you about?"

"Uh, lemme think…"

Throughout the evening, St. Germain had used his relaxation techniques to help me recall specifics, especially of my more important conversations. It was uncanny how much I could remember under hypnosis, but now it was like trying to recall a fading dream.

"It was Prizrak," the Count says.

"Right. Good memory."

"My memory is excellent, but that's not why I can recall it so easily. I was struck by it when you mentioned it, but I wanted to see if it came up later. And I believe it did."

"When was that?"

"During your final confrontation with Gideon. As I recall, he said that he would soon be locked into a castle, which you interpreted to mean his compound. Gideon laughed at this, if you'll remember, and said that the castle was not a place."

"OK…"

"He also said that it was, I believe the exact words were: 'Greg Call's crowning achievement'."

"Sorry I didn't make the connection. I was a little busy at the time. So what do you think he was talking about?"

"The key is the word 'Prizrak'. It's Russian. It means 'ghost'."

Ghost?

St. Germain is watching me, wondering if I'll catch up. I've got too much scotch in me for that.

"So…what?" I ask. "Are we talking something paranormal? Dying?"

"No, nothing paranormal."

I take another drag.

"I could use another hint."

"Larry Hammond also said the Prizrak project involved 'Whole Brain Emulation'."

"Sorry," I say, shaking my head. I'm not using my whole brain at the moment."

"Whole Brain Emulation refers to the as-yet-theoretical process of uploading human consciousness into digital form."

"Like A.I.?"

"The opposite of Artificial Intelligence. Literal human consciousness."

St. Germain leans closer.

"I suspect that Prizrak—Greg Call's crowning achievement—may have been executing the first successful upload of a human consciousness."

As I take a moment to snuff out my smoke, I suddenly get what he's saying.

"A ghost…you're talking about a Ghost in the Machine."

49

"Precisely," St. Germain says. "A Ghost in the Machine. Not an advanced artificial intelligence, but the mind of a human being, containing all its thought processes, emotions, memories and, perhaps most importantly, *motivations*. And now housed within circuitry, rather than a mortal body."

"But didn't you just say it's all theoretical?"

"Yes, until it isn't. Based on your account of what Gideon said—that he and Overlord would be one and the same, that he would lock himself into a castle that no key could open, and that it was on account of Greg Call's crowning achievement—together with the project name, Prizrak, I'm prepared to entertain the possibility."

"So, if there really is a Ghost in the Machine, it must be Gideon."

"He's a prime candidate," St. Germain says. "At the very least, we must reconsider who the adversary could be. Being alive is no longer one of the criteria."

"OK, so I have two issues. First, do you have any evidence there actually is a Ghost in the Machine? 'Cause I don't."

St. Germain smiles.

"I assume you're familiar with the 'curious incident of the dog that didn't bark'?"

"Of course," I say. "The Sherlock Holmes story. He identifies a thief because a dog that should have barked during the robbery didn't."

The Count nods, pleased.

"In a similar vein, it's the *absence* of another explanation that makes me believe the Ghost exists. The fact that you have been guided from one event to another, seemingly randomly and not by an identifiable, living source. Also, the dearth of online information, which is simple data that a Ghost in the Machine might easily gain access to and manipulate or delete. And, as I said earlier, I believe you needed help to escape the Moon Child—the kind of help a Ghost in the Machine would facilitate. There are other, more subtle indications, as well."

I mull this over.

"OK, assuming it's possible," I say, "that leads to my second issue. Even if Gideon got his consciousness uploaded into Overlord, running the Stalemate program would have destroyed it."

"Or, perhaps, Stalemate simply *disabled* Overlord. If it wasn't destroyed, the Ghost in the Machine could have survived. Or, Greg Call could also have uploaded the consciousness to a different network. And we know Gideon Enterprises had access to CAPRICORN's network. It's a reasonable assumption that data could move between the two and, wherever the Ghost originated from, this could have provided an avenue for him to migrate and expand."

"And then it could have gone beyond CAPRICORN," I say, starting to warm up to the idea. "Gideon was partnered up with a bunch of governments and big corporations."

St. Germain nods.

"Yes. It may have taken time for the Ghost to gain access and learn how to navigate the framework, but it's a viable explanation for how he eventually spun his global web. This is exactly the kind of thing I hoped to discover."

"And that was your reason for the Faraday Cage and ditching my Smart Alex. You think the Ghost could track us."

"Almost certainly. Possibly even eavesdrop on us."

I think this over. We're talking about a worst-case scenario, but it all seems plausible. Except for one thing.

"You said you think this Ghost was involved in what happened on the Moon Child," I say. "I don't see how it could. Their plans required cutting all ties with Earth, so the Moon Child's networks, its security, everything, was internal. That's why the Winter Chip had to be smuggled onboard: there was no way to introduce it externally."

St. Germain raises steepled hands to his pursed lips and gives it some thought before replying:

"CAPRICORN was developing the Winter Chip for years. The Ghost may have already known about it and what CAPRICORN intended to do with it when he was still alive, but could also have learned about it after accessing their network. Either way, I believe he arranged for them to get some of the Oracle Stone to improve their odds of success. Clearly, the Ghost did not want the Moon Child to serve its intended purpose."

"I get that," I say, "but you seem to think the Ghost ended up *on* the Moon Child."

"If CAPRICORN's development of the Winter Chip was on their network, the Ghost could have wormed its way into that."

"You mean literally?" I ask. "As in, the Ghost was on the chip?"

"It seems possible. It's only data."

"And why would the Ghost want to be on the chip? Knowing what it was going to be used for, it would have been basically committing suicide."

"Perhaps only a portion of its consciousness went onto the chip," St. Germain says, "or it replicated itself. Copying data is a simple thing."

"Fair enough. But that's just *how* the Ghost might have gotten on the chip, not *why*."

"Perhaps he felt he could help to ensure that the Winter Chip would destroy the Moon Child. But I believe he had another purpose."

"And what would that be?"

"You."

"Me?"

"If the Ghost had been monitoring your activities, he could have known that you were likely to end up on the Moon Child."

"No way," I say. "Even *I* didn't know I'd be on the Moon Child until the last minute. I was never part of the plan. And the Winter Chip had already been created. The Ghost couldn't have known unless he could see the future."

St. Germain raises his eyebrows expectantly.

"Maybe he did. The Oracle Stone?"

"That's a stretch."

The Count waves his hand.

"Immaterial. Perhaps it was fate…a fortunate coincidence. But if the Ghost was introduced into the Moon Child's network, he would have had access to all systems—security, cameras, alarms, doors…everything. He would have known you were on board and, with access to all the systems, could greatly facilitate your escape, which I believe he had a vested interest in doing."

I think back to what had happened in those final minutes on the Moon Child. I can't recall anything inexplicable happening. But I guess it was possible. Things had worked out almost perfectly for me to get out alive.

"OK. Let's say everything you're assuming actually happened," I say. "You still haven't made a case for why it was *me* the Ghost had a vested interest in."

"That is the simplest part of the equation, as I see it. For one, existing in a virtual space has its limitations, especially when interacting with the physical world. For example, the Ghost would be capable of purchasing a weapon remotely and having it shipped to an address—"

St. Germain watches me make the connection.

"—but it couldn't get the weapon and pull the trigger," I say.

"He could, however, cause lethal malfunctions in a variety of ways: air traffic control, hospital equipment, security systems, of course. Even manipulating a heating system to release high levels of undetected carbon monoxide…as happened this evening at the Ritz Hotel."

St. Germain pauses, as I absorb this.

"But let's get back to the question of 'why you'," he continues. "And this is why I suspect that Overlord was not destroyed. I should think it would be obvious."

He taps the side of his head.

"The implant?" I ask. "But it was deactivated."

"Who else had one?"

St. Germain has a point. As far as I know, everyone else who got an implant died from it. But I was sure mine had been short-circuited, so it didn't matter.

Before I can answer, St. Germain speaks:

"I believe you may have been the only person in the world the Ghost would have any control over."

50

"Think about it," St. Germain says. "You and the STG team members were the only implant recipients, and everyone but you died. As did anyone who could have administered other implants—Klaus, Call and Gideon."

"Or they *virtually* died. But I get your point. I may have been the only person left alive with one of the implants."

St. Germain nods.

"But I told you I never had any more of the symptoms," I say. "There is zero evidence that the implant has had any effect on me since I left Nexus."

The Count leans forward, pointing his cigar for emphasis.

"According to your own account, multiple sources said the Overlord implants would influence only basic physiological functions…*initially*, but the plan was to eventually implement more sophisticated effects to influence behavior. I don't know what would be involved, of course, but the Ghost had years to continue development. And I would venture to say that affecting brain functions such as memory would have been possible."

"You think the Ghost could make me forget things."

"It would explain your returning from Mars with a piece of the Oracle Stone and having no memory of it."

"And how would he get me to bring the Oracle Stone?"

"I don't pretend to know all the answers," St. Germain says. "Planting a suggestion in your mind seems extraordinarily complex, but perhaps he communicated with you directly. Or maybe he sent a message that appeared to come from Marshall Alexander. There are several reasonable possibilities. And then he could erase your memory of the communication."

"I don't buy it," I say.

I grab my glass and drain it.

"But you see that only a person with an implant could be controlled," St. Germain says, gently.

I shrug and reach for the bottle.

"And you have that implant in you," he adds.

St. Germain watches me refill my drink, his face sympathetic.

"It's possible I'm wrong about all this," he says. "But if I'm right—"

"—If you're right," I say, cutting in, angry, "why would he try to kill me? If I'm his only Manchurian Candidate?"

St. Germain pulls back, startled. He thinks for a moment before answering.

"You must be a potential threat to his plans. You may know something: a name, a place, a password—something that might seem unimportant to you, or maybe that you have no conscious memory of. Or...he may fear that you could lead someone to him."

"Which is exactly what's happening right now."

St. Germain nods.

"Yes, I have to assume he knows about me. You and I may represent the greatest danger to him."

We're both quiet for a long moment.

"Are you ready for this to end?" St. Germain finally asks. "I want to help you. We can help each other."

I take a drink and a minute to think. I'm still not sure I believe any of this. But if St. Germain is right—and there's some way to fight back—I'm all in. Being controlled is something I've fought against my whole life. The possibility of having been manipulated all these years is making my blood boil.

"I'm ready," I say. "But how are we supposed to kill a ghost?"

The Count takes a deep breath and rubs his hands together.

"There's only one place I can think of where we might find answers after all these years. Greg Call's lab. That's where the effects of your implant changed, where Call completed his Prizrak project. If the Ghost has a weakness or left a trail that we can follow, it must be found there. What are the odds that it's just as you—and Call—last left it?"

"Who knows? Pretty good, I expect. It was in the middle of nowhere and no one else knew about it."

"Can you find it?"

"Sure," I say. "Eventually."

"We don't know if or how the Ghost can utilize your implant or track you. To be safe, we should get you a new speeder and outfit it with the same Faraday Cage technology we've been using in this room. I can get that taken care of and have you ready to leave in a few hours."

I'm about take another drink when St. Germain reaches out a hand.

"You'll want to have your wits about you," he says.

I pause and nod, then set my glass down.

"You're safe here," he adds. "You should try to get some sleep."

"Fat chance of that."

St. Germain smiles and pulls himself out of his chair.

"If things go our way, perhaps we'll both sleep better after tomorrow."

"How's that?"

He locks his briefcase and picks it up.

"Greg Call worked on both Overlord and Prizrak. His lab might even be the source of both. He did name it 'Nexus', after all. It could be the center of the Ghost's web."

St. Germain points to the Winter Chip on the table in front of me.

"This was designed to take down a vast network with the most advanced security system imaginable. My hope is that it will do what it did to the Moon Child…and destroy the Ghost with it."

51

St. Germain doesn't make the trip to Nexus with me. He doesn't say it explicitly, but he doesn't have to: if anything bad happens to me, he wants to live to fight another day. I'm valuable, but expendable.

He makes a pretense of letting me choose to do it, saying I'm free to take the money and run. But if he's right about the implant, I may not have long to spend the cash. My going back to Nexus is a foregone conclusion.

But I do take the money.

Technically, I won't be alone. St. Germain gives me a tiny Remote Viewing Drone. It has a camera, microphone and holographic projector built in, so he can tag along with me, virtually, while sipping scotch and smoking a cigar from the comfort of some sumptuous hotel room.

Not that I'm complaining. If this is my last road trip, at least I'm going in style. The speeder St. Germain hooks me up with is a beauty: a pearl white Lexus with tan leather seats and an engine that thrills the ears and tickles the buttocks. And the vehicle title is in the glove compartment; it's mine for life…however long that might be. I'm not sure how the signal-blocking—the Faraday Cage—is installed, but he assures me it will get me to Nexus without being detected.

* * * * *

I lift off from the parking lot of my old office building and head north. The sun is just peeking over the eastern horizon; almost bedtime for everyone else.

The Lexus is the nicest speeder I've ever piloted. Exhilarating. Almost enjoyable enough to cancel out my lingering hangover. Fortunately, the speeder has tint control for the windows and I dial it up to the max setting.

The trip goes considerably faster than it would have in my old Lotus. It's about 250 miles to Mount Shasta and I get there in the time it takes to play Led Zeppelin II from start to finish. I generally prefer jazz, but I need a little boost. The Lexus also has a stellar sound system.

As Mount Shasta comes into view, I dial down the opacity on the windows and start looking for the old railroad tracks that led me to Nexus the first time around. The Lexus dips and banks effortlessly as I canvass the surrounding area.

It takes longer than expected. Thirteen years of verdant growth has almost completely covered the tracks. Which is good. It means the tracks haven't been used and the entrance to Nexus would be even harder to find.

I finally catch sight of a section of track and, with a few detours, eventually identify the spot where I'd found the door years before. I land the speeder, nestling it into a small clearing, then grab a backpack off the passenger seat and climb out.

"We're here," I say.

On the dashboard, the RV drone—which hadn't done anything during the flight—beeps and then flies up and out of the speeder. St. Germain had said the Lexus was outfitted with Faraday Cage technology, which I assumed would block the signal to the drone, but maybe it only works when the speeder is running. Or, maybe St. Germain set it up so his drone somehow still worked and just watched where we were going without saying anything. He probably hit the mute button when I started blasting Whole Lotta Love.

"Beautiful, isn't it?" St. Germain says through the drone.

It's still early and the sun hasn't risen above the tree line. The air is humid and cool, almost crisp. I take a few deep breaths. You have to pay for this much oxygen back in the city. I sling the backpack over my shoulder and head for the tracks.

The drone hovers beside me, like a pesky dragonfly, as I follow the tracks. Again, with the added layers of vegetation, it takes a while to locate the old door.

"There's the entrance," I say, when I finally spot it.

The drone zips away toward the door, which I can see is slightly ajar—exactly how I left it. A good sign. A locked door would make it significantly harder to get inside, though St. Germain had provided equipment to deal with that eventuality. A closed door would suggest someone else had been here. A wide-open door might mean a big, nasty critter had gotten inside.

Not that I believe in Sasquatch.

"Let's hope we don't lose the signal inside," St. Germain says, as I reach the door. "If we do, and it happens suddenly, it may temporarily disable the drone. You'll need to move the drone back to the last point where we had reception."

"Will do."

"I'll go in and do some reconnaissance."

The drone emits a beam of light and then disappears through the gap.

The door has rusted, making it harder to move, but I finally manage to pry it open wide enough to squeeze through. I get a flashlight from the backpack and turn it on.

I follow the gently curving passage that leads to the large cavern. The RV drone is still getting a signal; I can see the refracted glow of its headlight as it moves around.

The last time I was here, a motion detector had automatically lit up the cavern. Not this time. The space remains dark as I enter. I wonder if that means the generator—or whatever had powered Call's lab—is no longer functioning. And, without power, there'll be no way to access Overlord, or do anything at all.

The drone is hovering near a large, metal container, its headlight moving slowly around.

"Was all this equipment here before?" St. Germain's voice echoes.

"I think so," I say. "I didn't pay any attention to it. I went straight to that door over there."

"Fascinating."

"Not really. I have a gift for being oblivious."

"I'm referring to the equipment. From what I can see, most of it doesn't fit at all with what we know about Greg Call's projects."

I point my flashlight around. I'm not sure what St. Germain is finding so fascinating. Dozens of crates of all different sizes. A few large metal containers similar to the one the drone is focused on.

When I take a closer look, the only interesting thing is that some of the crates are stamped with symbols and letters that look Russian. I'm guessing that St. Germain speaks the language; you don't find words like 'Prizrak' in a Russian For Tourists guidebook.

"What is all this stuff?" I ask.

"I can't be certain, but this container…I believe it might be an Amniotic Tank."

"Huh," I say, with no idea what that means.

"I'd like to take a look inside this. We should examine the contents of these crates as well. There must be a tool somewhere in here that you can use to open them."

As St. Germain says this, I get a creepy feeling. I'm his live body, doing the heavy lifting. The same role I may have been playing for the Ghost in the Machine. It makes me feel like not cooperating.

"I'll see what I can find," I say. "First, I want to check out the other room."

The drone spins around and floats toward me.

"Yes," St. Germain says, "this can wait. Let's hope that what we're looking for is beyond this door."

As I cross the large space toward the door, the drone flies ahead. The door is barely cracked, with no gap to pass through. The drone hovers inches away, like a puppy excited to go on walkies.

I get to the door and pull it open. As the drone and I enter the room, I detect the same faint hum I remember from before…and then the space lights up like a carnival ride.

In the same instant, the drone drops to the floor with a clatter.

I stop cold.

Apparently, something in here cut off St. Germain's signal. Maybe the same thing that disrupted my implant thirteen years ago. And, obviously, this area is getting power. That's good. I think.

All around me, electronics are coming to life. The room is just as I remembered it. There are several work stations and a bank of servers along one wall. In the center of the room is what I can only describe as a Captain's chair. Again, I'm reminded of the bridge on the Starship Enterprise. The Captain's chair is surrounded on three sides by huge monitors and user interfaces, like the dream setup for a video gamer or an 80's rock band keyboardist who plays with both hands and one foot.

I look down at the comatose drone on the floor. For a moment, I debate whether or not to follow St. Germain's instructions and move it back outside the door to try and reestablish the connection. Maybe I should take a quick look around first—

"Welcome back, Tex," a voice says.

52

I don't recognize the voice. It isn't St. Germain's and isn't coming from the drone; it's emanating from a speaker somewhere in the console by the captain's chair.

"Oh, hi," I say.

"Why are you here?" the voice asks, the tone vaguely artificial.

To destroy you, if you're who I think you are.

"We need to talk," I say.

"About?"

I'm still trying to get my head around this. For all I know, there could be cameras and microphones here, and this is a real, live person monitoring me from another location. But I doubt it. No one's been here in years. Only a few other people—and maybe no one still alive—knew about this place. I have to assume St. Germain was right, that this is the Ghost in the Machine.

"I have a lot of questions," I say. "First of all, are you Gideon?"

"It doesn't matter who I was, only what I have become."

Definitely Gideon, I think to myself. *With that attitude.*

"What should I call you, then?" I ask. "Prizrak?"

A brief pause. Confirmation.

"You've been busy, haven't you?" the voice says.

"You tell me."

Another pause.

"How did you find out?" the voice asks.

"I'm a detective, remember? I just finally put some pieces together."

The voice chuckles. With its artificial edge, it sounds creepy.

"You are a clever man," it says. "Tremendously unappreciated. You have surprised me many times, but never more so than now. I'll ask again: why are you here?"

"I want answers. Who you are...what you've been up to the past thirteen years...how I've been involved. I assume it all started with the implant. Has it been active this whole time? Have you been screwing with my memory? I could go on all day."

"You feel violated."

"I feel stupid," I say. "I thought my implant had been zapped the last time I was here. Now I find out you've been playing me this whole time."

"I did save your life. Turning off the initial effects of your implant was one of the first and only things I could do after entering the framework."

He has a point.

"OK. I'll give you that."

"Nevertheless, I'm sorry for putting you through this," the voice says. "I would have preferred to communicate with you openly, but you've always resisted."

"What do you mean 'I've always resisted'? You're saying we've had this conversation before?"

"Yes."

"So you can control my memories."

"Control? No. Selectively delete."

"Like a Trance Inducer?" I ask. "I assume you know all about my experience with that."

"Your implant works very differently. One of the upgrades I made gave me access to a region in your medial temporal lobe—the hippocampus, where your short-term memories are stored. Before they are encoded into long-term memories—which are stored in the form of circuits throughout the nervous system—it's relatively simple to, in essence, erase them."

"OK, so you've erased some of my short-term memories. Why?"

"I've always wanted you to be a willing ally, Tex. You are intelligent and resourceful. You have uncanny intuition and luck—uniquely human attributes that I no longer possess. But you are also stubborn and willful. And easy to read. Each time we communicated, regardless of what you said, I was certain you would go to any length to free yourself from your perceived enslavement. I couldn't risk that. You had become indispensable to me."

"And what, exactly, have I done for you?"

"Nothing you wouldn't have done yourself, had you been in my place. Ending the Crusade for Genetic Purity, for example, and all that entailed. Most recently, preventing the deployment of the Immortal Coil."

"So we're just a couple of pals saving the world. If that's all it is, why do you need the implant?"

A pause.

"There have been other tasks," the voice says.

"No kidding."

"I couldn't expect you to see the larger picture...the greater good."

"Then why not use someone who does?" I ask.

"I had no other choice. I wasn't responsible for your implant. But you were the only surviving recipient, so I was forced to use you. There was little I could do on my own in the beginning. Having a human partner was essential. And, all things considered, you have been close to ideal."

"But then you tried to kill me."

"On the contrary. I've been intent on keeping you alive. You've made it fairly difficult at times, I might add."

"So, to be clear, you *don't* want to kill me."

"If I did, you wouldn't be here. That is not a threat, just a fact. As I said, I have long wished for a willing partnership. We have much more in common than you might think. We are both willing to risk our very existence to fight discrimination and tyranny. We both believe that man has become a slave to technology and its toxic effects. We both yearn for a simpler time. And that dream will soon become a reality. You, of all people, understand why the world must change. Join me and we will welcome the future together."

Here we go.

"OK," I say, "I've heard this kind of talk before and we'll get back to that, but let's rewind to the part about not wanting me dead. *Someone* tried to kill me yesterday."

"I'm aware of what happened. But I don't believe the motive was to kill you."

"Then what was it?"

"Do you recall the meaning of the poisoned pawn?"

"What does that have to do with anything?"

"You were the poisoned pawn this time. The bait in a trap...set for me. Your true enemy suspected that you and I were connected. His plan—which he seems to have achieved—was to put your life in danger and, by doing so, motivate you to help him learn about our connection."

"Hold on. Are you talking about *St. Germain*?"

"How was it that he happened to show up on Chandler Avenue within minutes of the paramedics and police?"

I'm trying to think, but my mind is still processing.

"What did he say when he picked you up?" the voice asks. "That you were in danger?"

"Yeah."

"How would he know that?"

I don't know what to say. Now that I hear it, it's obvious.

The voice goes on: "A speeder registered to him appeared on a security camera feed near the Ritz Hotel several hours before and then immediately after the 911 call was made."

He could be lying, but something tells me he isn't. I just can't believe St. Germain would allow innocent people to die.

"You may not want to believe me," the voice says, "but you need to know what kind of person you are dealing with. Unlike me, he would sacrifice you without a second thought if it served his purposes. And this is something I can't let you forget. Take a seat, if you would."

I don't think about why he wants me to sit. My brain is still numb. But, as I slide into the Captain's chair, I suddenly realize that something is probably about to hurt.

I'm right.

Searing pain rips through my skull. I grab my head with both hands. After a minute, the pain subsides, then gradually fades completely away.

"Consider this a gesture of good faith," the voice says. "Your implant has been destroyed."

"Along with half my brain," I say, rubbing my temples.

"There will be no permanent damage. Now, can you tell me what St. Germain knows…or believes he knows?"

"Look, I appreciate the, uh, good faith gesture, but I'm not sure whose side I'm on here. Right now, I'm thinking I might just take the Count's money and find a nice spot to retire."

"You are free to do as you wish."

There's a long pause as I wait for the qualifier.

"But—?" I ask.

"I expect that St. Germain sent you here in hopes of destroying me," the voice says. "He may believe that I am vulnerable in this place. I am not."

"Vulnerable? Or here?"

"I am everywhere. There is nothing St. Germain—or you, or anyone else—can do to harm me. But be warned. St. Germain may try to destroy this place regardless of what you say or do. As with the innocent people at the Ritz Hotel, to him you are disposable."

I already knew that, but it's different now. I'm wondering who St. Germain really is and what his intentions are.

"You must decide where your allegiance lies," the voice continues. "I no longer have any control over you. I sincerely hope you will decide to join me and achieve what I believe is a common goal, but the choice is yours."

"Just so I understand my options, who is St. Germain? What are his intentions?"

"That is for you to decide. He is about to reestablish contact with you. Good luck, Tex. I will be waiting, when and if you want to find me."

The room goes silent. Only then do I realize the humming sound has disappeared.

"…ello? Mr. Mur…? Are…there?"

St. Germain's voice is coming through the drone, but it's faint and distorted. The drone is still on the floor. Maybe it was damaged when it dropped or the signal is too weak for it to fly.

In just a few minutes, my view of the Count has changed significantly. I'm sure now that he's lied to me about what happened at the Ritz. Who knows what else he's lied about.

"Yeah," I say, trying not to let my inner thoughts creep into my voice.

"What's…ppening? Do…have access…verlord?"

I take out the Winter Chip and look down at the console in front of me.

"I don't know. Maybe."

A few minutes ago, I was ready to unleash hell on this place. Maybe I should anyway. St. Germain could be doing bad things for good reasons. He was right about the Ghost in the Machine having big plans. I'm not sure why the Ghost thinks I'd be on board with whatever those plans are but, in my experience, changing the world and welcoming a new future is never as rosy as it sounds.

The Ghost said no one could stop him, but what else was he going to say? This might be my only chance to do something.

It's now or never.

"If there is…possibility you do…must use…ter Chip!" St. Germain says, desperation in his voice.

The Ghost had warned me that St. Germain might blow this place up, no matter what I said or did. For all I know, he has his finger on a big red button right now and he'll press it if I don't do what he says.

"Mr….phy? …hear me? …may be…best and only... Do it!"

"OK," I say. "Wish me luck."

I take out the Winter Chip, hold it up, then find a slot for it on the console.

Decision made.

I jump out of the Captain's chair and start running. The drone crunches under my foot as I sprint through the doorway, across the cavern and down the tunnel.

I don't stop running until I get back to the speeder.

Then I slip the Winter Chip into my pocket and climb in the speeder.

Printed in Great Britain
by Amazon

64722826R00149